HIGH PRAISE FOR
EPITAPHS
AND THE "NAMELESS DETECTIVE"
SERIES

"THE CLASSIC PRIVATE EYE NOVEL."
—*The Purloined Letter*

"Thoroughly absorbing . . . with unerring plotting and an unabashedly retro narrative style." —*Publishers Weekly*

"A practitioner of the private eye form for more than twenty years, Pronzini has done much to redefine the genre that was shaped by Chandler, Hammett and Ross Macdonald."
—*Orlando Sentinel*

"Pronzini has a wonderful ability to set a mood in his writing. His descriptions are so vivid that you can taste 'Nameless''s fear, experience his horror, and rejoice in his simple pleasures. The series gets better and better. May 'Nameless' never retire." —*As Crime Goes By*

"Bill Pronzini is probably the best writer of all the current specialists in fictional private-eyeing, and his 'Nameless Detective' is one of the most vividly portrayed."
—*The Virginian-Pilot* (Norfolk)

"Pronzini is a magnificent entertainer of the first rank. His 'Nameless Detective' series . . . is now one of the three or four most important series being written—wry, melodramatic, colorful, contemporary." —*Gazette* (Cedar Rapids)

"Nameless Detective" Mysteries

by **BILL PRONZINI**

EPITAPHS

A "Nameless Detective" Mystery

BILL PRONZINI

A DELL BOOK

Published by
Dell Publishing
a division of
Bantam Doubleday Dell Publishing Group, Inc.
1540 Broadway
New York, New York 10036

The trademark Dell® is registered in the U.S. Patent and
Trademark Office.

ISBN: 0-440-21117-4

Reprinted by arrangement with Delacorte Press

Printed in the United States of America

Published simultaneously in Canada

January 1994

10 9 8 7 6 5 4 3 2 1

OPM

For Kit, Tiffany, and Arthur Knight

*In honor of the Petaluma
connection, the happy rhino,
and "standing alone, famous,
next to the cheap wine"*

Let's talk of graves, of worms, and epitaphs;
Make dust our paper, and with rainy eyes
Write sorrow on the bosom of the earth.

—SHAKESPEARE
Richard II

Poorly lived
And poorly died
Poorly buried
And no one cried

—EPITAPH IN AN
ENGLISH CEMETERY

Chapter 1

I LIKE SUNDAYS. Most Sundays, anyway.

Day of rest, day of relaxation. Stay-in-bed-and-read-or-watch-old-movies day. Putter day. Go-out-and-play day. Do-nothing-at-all day. Good old Sunday.

This one, in late June, had clear skies and warm breezes off the ocean and the bay—a pair of surprises, since too many June days in San Francisco are fog-shrouded and cold. Nature's air-conditioning, the locals like to say with pride; keeps the city nice and cool while surrounding communities swelter under the hot summer sun. Wouldn't have it any other way, they tell outsiders, lying through their teeth. If they really meant it, they would not take part, as plenty of them do, in the mass weekend exodus to those sweltering neighborhood communities. It is only on rare June days like this one that these none-too-true-blue San Franciscans stay put and take advantage of what they refer to as the city's "good-weather attractions."

So what was I going to do on this fine June Sunday? If Kerry were available, there were lots of possibilities, beginning with a couple of hours of lovemaking and proceeding to a picnic somewhere or maybe to the Gi- ants-Cubs game at Candlestick. But Kerry wasn't avail- able. One reason was that she had her mother to con- tend with, though maybe not for much longer. Cybil had been sharing Kerry's Diamond Heights apartment for nearly seven months now, the result of her inability to cope with the death of her husband, Ivan, and what remained of her life without him. Difficult and painful situation, made even worse by the fact that Cybil had taken an irrational dislike to me: I couldn't visit without provoking a crisis and could call only when I was certain Kerry was home. This had severely curtailed our love life, added an edge of tension to what had formerly been a pretty stress-free relationship. Recently, though, with the aid of a counseling group called Children of Grieving Parents, Kerry had succeeded in convincing her mother to move into a Marin County seniors com- plex. Cybil had agreed to make the move by the end of the month. But would she change her mind at the last minute? The whole thing was a tale well-calculated to keep you in suspense, right up to the last act.

The other reason Kerry wasn't available today was that she had work to do on one of her ad agency's major accounts. Kerry Wade, Bates and Carpenter's new Cre- ative Director. The title had been bestowed on her just last week; and along with it and a $5000 annual increase in salary went "greater responsibility," which translated to longer hours and an increased workload. Not such an ideal promotion, if you asked me. But nobody had, and I was not about to volunteer anything that might dampen her euphoria. The one time we'd made love since had been terrific.

So. My options for the day were limited. Under normal circumstances I could have called Eberhardt and suggested that we go watch the Giants get it on with the Cubs. But things were not normal between Eb and me, hadn't been for the past two months—since Bobbie Jean had called off their planned wedding, for good reason thanks to him, and the fight he and I had had as a result. That damned fight. Schoolboy stuff: I'd lost my head, stupidly, and punched him. He still hadn't forgiven me; it worried me that maybe he never would. We barely spoke in the office, and then only when business made it necessary. The few times I'd tried to talk him into having a beer together after work, he'd flatly refused.

No Kerry, no Eberhardt. Going to the ballgame by myself didn't appeal to me; neither did taking a drive or visiting one of those "good-weather attractions" alone. Barney Rivera? On impulse I called his number, and got his answering machine. Out getting his ashes hauled somewhere, probably. Barney Rivera, God's gift to women who liked little fat guys with soulful eyes and a line of sugar-coated BS. Mentally I ran down the list of my other friends . . . and a pretty short list it was. Devote your life to your profession, turn yourself into a workaholic, and this is what happens to you: short-listed as you approach sixty. The few others were married, had families. Had lives. Get a life, why didn't I?

Too old. Besides, I liked the one I had—most of the time.

Staying home was out. Too nice a day for that, and already I felt restless. Open air was what I needed, sunshine on my shoulder, people around me, maybe some familiar faces. No blue Sunday for me. . . .

Aquatic Park, I thought.

Sure, that was the ticket. I hadn't been down there in a while, and I always enjoyed myself when I went. What better way to spend a quiet Sunday than getting back in touch with your ethnic heritage?

I went and picked up the car and drove to Aquatic Park, to watch the old men play bocce.

IN SAN FRANCISCO, in the last decade of the twentieth century, bocce is a dying sport.

Most of the city's older Italians, to whom bocce was more a religion than a sport, have died off. The once large and close-knit North Beach Italian community has been steadily losing its identity since the fifties—families moving to the suburbs, the expansion of Chinatown and the gobbling up of North Beach real estate by wealthy Chinese—and even though there has been a small, new wave of immigrants from Italy in recent years, they're mostly young and upscale. Young, upscale Italians don't play bocce much, if at all; their interests lie in soccer, in the American sports where money and fame and power have replaced a love of the game itself. The Di Massimo bocce courts at the North Beach Playground are mostly closed these days; so are the handful of other public courts left in the city, including the one in the Outer Mission, where I'd been raised. The Potrero district's Monte Cristo Club is still open on a regular basis, but it's private. About the only public courts where you can find a game every Saturday and Sunday are the ones at Aquatic Park.

Time was, all six of the Aquatic Park courts were packed from early morning to dusk and there were spectators and waiting players lined two and three deep at courtside and up along the fence on Van Ness. No more. Seldom, now, is more than one of the courts used. And the players get older, and sadder, and fewer each year.

There were maybe fifteen players and watchers on this Sunday, almost all of them older than my fifty-eight, loosely grouped around the two courts nearest the street. Those two are covered by a high pillar-supported roof so that contests can be held even in wet weather. Up until a year ago, the roof was so badly weather-worn that it was in danger of collapse. Just when it looked as though the courts would have to be shut down, the Italian Consul General stepped in and hosted a benefit soccer match that raised enough money for the necessary repairs. *Viva il console.*

Under the roof are wooden benches; I parked myself on one of these, midway along. The only other seated spectator was Pietro Lombardi, in a patch of sunlight at the far end, and this surprised me. Even though Pietro was in his seventies, he was one of the best and spriest of the regulars, and also one of the most social. To see him sitting alone, shoulders slumped and head bowed, was puzzling.

Pining away for the old days, maybe, I thought—as I had just been doing. And a phrase popped into my head, a line from Dante that one of my uncles had been fond of quoting when I was a kid: *Nessun maggior dolore che ricordarsi del tempo felice nella miseria.* The bitterest of woes is to remember old happy days.

Pietro and his woes didn't occupy my attention for long. The game in progress was animated and voluble, as only a game of bocce played by elderly 'paesanos can be, and I was soon caught up in the spirit of it.

Bocce is simple—deceptively simple. You play it on a long, narrow packed-earth pit with low wooden sides. A wooden marker ball the size of a walnut is rolled to one end; the players stand at the opposite end and in turn roll eight larger, heavier balls, grapefruit-size, in the direction of the marker, the object being to see who can put his bocce ball closest to it. One of the required skills is slow-rolling the ball, usually in a curving trajectory, so that it kisses the marker and then lies up against it—the perfect shot—or else stops an inch or two away. The other required skill is knocking an opponent's ball away from any such close lie without disturbing the marker. The best players, like Pietro Lombardi, can do this two out of three times on the fly—no mean feat from a distance of fifty feet. They can also do it by caroming the ball off the pit walls with topspin or reverse spin, after the fashion of pool shooters.

Nobody paid much attention to me until after the game in progress had been decided. Then I was acknowledged with hand gestures and a few words—the tolerant acceptance accorded to known spectators and occasional players. Unknowns got no greeting at all.

These men still clung to the old ways, and one of the old ways was clannishness.

Only one of the group, Dominick Marra, came over to where I was sitting. And that was because he had something on his mind. He was in his mid-seventies, white-haired, white-mustached; a bantamweight in baggy trousers held up by galluses. He and Pietro Lombardi had been close friends for most of their lives. Born in the same town—Agropoli, a village on the Gulf of Salerno not far from Naples; moved to San Francisco with their families a year apart, in the late twenties; married cousins, raised large families, were widowed at almost the same time a few years ago. The kind of friendship that is virtually a blood tie. Dominick had been a baker; Pietro had owned a North Beach trattoria that now belonged to one of his daughters.

What Dominick had on his mind was Pietro. "You see how he's sit over there, hah? He's got trouble—*la miseria.*"

"What kind of trouble?"

"His granddaughter, Gianna Fornessi."

"Something happen to her?"

"She's maybe go to jail," Dominick said.

"What for?"

"Stealing money."

"I'm sorry to hear it. How much money?"

"Two thousand dollars."

"Who did she steal it from?"

"*Che?*"

"Whose money did she steal?"

Dominick gave me a disgusted look. "She don't steal it. Why you think Pietro, he's got *la miseria,* hah?"

I knew what was coming, now; I should have known it the instant Dominick started confiding in me about Pietro's problem. I said, "You want me to help him and his granddaughter."

"Sure. You're a detective."

"A busy detective."

"You got no time for old man and young girl? *Compaesani?*"

I sighed, but not so he could hear me do it. "All right, I'll talk to Pietro. See if he wants my help, if there's anything I can do."

"Sure he wants your help," Dominick said. "He just don't know it yet."

We went to where Pietro sat alone in the sun. He was taller than Dominick, heavier, balder. And he had a fondness for Toscanas, those little twisted black Italian cigars; one protruded now from a corner of his mouth. He didn't want to talk at first, but Dominick launched into a monologue in Italian that changed his mind and put a glimmer of hope in his sad eyes. Even though I've lost a lot of the language over the years, I can understand enough to follow most conversations. The gist of Dominick's monologue was that I was not just a detective but a miracle worker, a cross between Sherlock Holmes and the messiah. Italians are given to hyperbole in times of excitement or stress, and there isn't much you can do to counteract it—especially when you're a *'paesano* yourself.

"My Gianna, she's good girl," Pietro said. "Never

give trouble, even when she's little girl. *La bellezza delle bellezze,* you understand?"

The beauty of beauties. His favorite grandchild, no doubt. I said, "I understand."

"She's grown up now, not so close to her goombah—I don't know her so good like before. But *una ladra?* My Gianna? No, no."

"Tell me what happened, Pietro."

"I don't hear from her for a while," he said, "four, five weeks, so I call her up Thursday night. Right away she's start to cry. She don't want to tell me what's the trouble, but I get it out of her."

"She said she didn't steal the money?"

"Sure that's what she say. It's all big lie."

"Did the police arrest her?"

"They got no proof to arrest her."

"But somebody filed charges?"

"Charges," Pietro said. "Bah," he said, and spat.

"Who made the complaint?"

Dominick said, "Ferry," as if the name were an obscenity.

"Who's Ferry?"

He tapped his skull. *"Testa di cacca,* this man."

"That doesn't answer my question."

"He live where she live. Same building."

"And he says Gianna stole two thousand dollars from him."

"Liar," Pietro said. "He lies."

"Stole it how? Broke in or what?"

"She don't break in nowhere, not my Gianna. This Ferry, he says she take the money when she's come to pay her rent and he's talk on the telephone. But how she knows where he keeps his money? Hah? How she knows he have two thousand dollars in his desk?"

"Maybe he told her."

"That's what he says to police," Dominick said. "Maybe he told her, he says. He don't tell her nothing."

Pietro threw down what was left of his Toscana, ground it into the dirt with his shoe—a gesture of anger and frustration. "She don't steal that money," he said. "What she need to steal money for? She's got good job, she live good, she don't have to steal."

"What kind of job does she have?"

"She sells drapes, curtains. In . . . what you call that business, Dominick?"

"Interior decorating business," Dominick said.

"*Sì.* In interior decorating business."

"Where does she live?" I asked.

"Chestnut Street."

"Where on Chestnut Street? What number?"

"I never been there," he said sadly. "Gianna, she don't invite me. But I got address in my wallet." He dredged up a piece of paper and gave me the number: 250.

"You make that Ferry tell the truth, hah?" Dominick said to me. "You fix it up for Gianna and her goombah?"

"I'll do what I can."

"*Va bene.*"

"Pietro, I'll need your address and telephone number—"

There was a sharp whacking sound as one of the

bocce balls caromed off the side wall near us, then a softer clicking of ball meeting ball, and a shout went up from the players at the far end: another game won and lost. When I looked back at Dominick and Pietro, they were both on their feet. Dominick said, "You find Pietro okay, good detective like you," and Pietro said, *"Grazie, mi amico,"* and before I could say anything else the two of them were off arm in arm to join the others.

Now *I* was the one sitting alone in the sun, holding up a burden. Primed and ready to do a job I didn't want to do, probably couldn't do to anybody's satisfaction, and would not be paid adequately for, if I was paid at all. Some quiet Sunday outing. No bocce after all; no loafing in the warm breezes, listening to the sounds of kids along the beachfront, of old men at play. What was I going to do on this fine June Sabbath? Why, just what I did most other days of the week, good weather and bad. I was going to work.

This man Ferry was not the only one who had *testa di cacca*—shit for brains . . .

Chapter 2

THE BUILDING AT 250 Chestnut Street was an old three-storied, brown-shingled job, set high in the shadow of Coit Tower and across from the retaining wall where Telegraph Hill falls off steeply toward the Embarcadero. From each of the apartments, especially the ones on the third floor, you'd have quite a view of the bay, the East Bay cities, both bridges, and most of the waterfront from below the Ferry Building to Fisherman's Wharf. Prime North Beach address, this. The rent would be well in excess of two thousand a month.

Pietro and Dominick had a good point: If Gianna Fornessi could afford to live here, why would she steal a sum of money that was not even enough to pay a single month's rent?

There were plenty of parking places along the retaining wall. I drove down to where Chestnut jogged right into a dead-end, made a U-turn, came back and claimed a space behind a white Nissan directly opposite 250.

A man in a tan safari jacket was coming out of the building as I crossed to the front stoop. I called out to him to hold the door for me—it's easier to get apartment dwellers to talk to you once you're inside their building—but either he didn't hear me or he chose to ignore me. He came hurrying down without a glance my way as he passed. City-bred paranoia, I thought. It was everywhere these days, rich and poor neighborhoods both, like a nasty strain of social disease.

Bumper sticker for the nineties: FEAR LIVES.

In the vestibule was a bank of six mailboxes, each with Dymo-Label stickers identifying the tenants. Gianna Fornessi's name was under box number four, along with a second name: *Ashley Hansen*. It figured that she'd have a roommate; salespersons working in the interior design trade are well but not extravagantly paid. Box number one bore the name *George Ferry* and that was the bell I pushed. He was the one I wanted to talk to first.

A minute died away while I listened to the wind— sharper up here than it had been down at Aquatic Park —savaging the trees on the hillside below. Out on the bay hundreds of sailboats formed a shifting mosaic of white on blue. Sailboating . . . something I'd always intended to try but had never gotten around to. Too busy working on weekends like this one. Well, what the hell. It was probably a good thing I hadn't tried the athletic art of sailing. As clumsy as I was, I would no doubt have been clobbered by a jib or boom or whatever the first time out and been knocked overboard and drowned.

Get a life? Hell no. Just hang on to the one I had.

The intercom crackled finally and a male voice said "Who is it?" in wary tones.

"George Ferry?"

"Yes?"

I gave him my name. "I'd like to ask you a few questions about your complaint against Gianna Fornessi."

"Oh, Christ." There was a pause, and then he said, "I called you people on Friday, I told Inspector Cullen I was dropping the charges. Isn't that enough?"

He thought I was a cop. I could have told him I wasn't; I could have let the whole thing drop right there, since what he'd just said was a perfect escape clause from my commitment to Pietro Lombardi. But I have too much professional curiosity to let go of something, once I've got a piece of it, without knowing the particulars. So I said, "I won't keep you long, Mr. Ferry. Just a few questions."

Another pause. "Is it really necessary?"

"I think it is, yes."

An even longer pause. But then he didn't argue, didn't say anything else—just buzzed me in.

His apartment was on the left, beyond a carpeted staircase. He opened the door as I approached it. Mid-forties, short, rotund, with a nose like a blob of putty and a Friar Tuck fringe of carrot-colored hair. And a bruise on his left cheekbone, a cut along the right corner of his mouth. The marks weren't fresh, but then they weren't very old either. Less than forty-eight hours.

He didn't ask to see a police ID; if he had I would have told him immediately that I was a private detective, because nothing can lose you a California investigator's license faster than willfully impersonating a police officer. On the other hand, you can't be held accountable for somebody's false assumption. Ferry gave me a nervous once-over, holding his head tilted downward as if that would keep me from seeing his bruise and cut, then stood aside to let me come in.

The front room was neat, furnished in a self-consciously masculine fashion: dark polished woods, leather, expensive sporting prints of the British steeplechase variety. It reeked of leather, dust, and his lime-scented cologne.

As soon as he shut the door Ferry went straight to a liquor cabinet and poured himself three fingers of Jack Daniel's, no water or mix, no ice. Just holding the drink seemed to give him courage. He said, "So. What is it you want to know?"

"Why you dropped your complaint against Ms. Fornessi."

"I explained to Inspector Cullen . . ."

"Explain to me, if you don't mind."

He had some of the sour mash. "Well, it was all a mistake . . . just a silly mistake. She didn't take the money after all."

"You know who did take it, then?"

"Nobody took it. I . . . misplaced it."

"Misplaced it. Uh-huh."

"I thought it was in my desk," Ferry said. "That's where I usually keep the cash I bring home. But I'd put it in my safe-deposit box along with some other papers, without realizing it. It was in an envelope, you see, and the envelope got mixed up with the other papers."

"Two thousand dollars is a lot of cash to keep at home. You make a habit of that sort of thing?"

"In my business . . ." The rest of the sentence seemed to hang up in his throat; he oiled the route with what was left of his drink. "In my business I need to keep a certain amount of cash on hand, both here and at my office. The amount I keep here isn't normally as large as two thousand, but I—"

"What business is that, Mr. Ferry?"

"Excuse me?"

"What business are you in?"

"I run a temp employment agency for domestics."

"Temp?"

"Short for temporary," he said. "I supply domestics for part-time work in offices and private homes. A lot of them are poor, don't have checking accounts, so they prefer to be paid in cash. Most come to the office, but a few—"

"Why did you think Gianna Fornessi had stolen the two thousand dollars?"

". . . What?"

"Why Ms. Fornessi? Why not somebody else?"

"She's the only one who was here. Before I thought the money was missing, I mean. I'd had no other visitors for two days and there wasn't any evidence of a break-in."

"You and she are good friends, then?"

"Well . . . no, not really. She's quite a bit younger. . . ."

"Then why was she here?"

"The rent," Ferry said. "She was paying her rent for the month. I'm the building manager, I collect for the owner. Before I could write out a receipt I had a call, I was on the phone for several minutes and she . . . I didn't pay any attention to her and I thought she must have . . . you see how I could have made the mistake?"

I was silent.

He met my gaze for maybe three seconds, looked down at his empty glass, licked his lips, and went to commune with Jack Daniel's again.

While he was pouring I asked him, "What happened to your face, Mr. Ferry?"

His hand twitched enough to clink bottle against glass. He had himself another taste before he turned back to me. "Clumsy," he said, "I'm clumsy as hell. I fell down the stairs, the front stairs, yesterday morning." He tried a laugh that didn't come off. "Fog makes the steps slippery. I just wasn't watching where I was going."

"Looks to me like somebody hit you."

"Hit me? No, I told you. . . . I fell down the stairs."

"You sure about that?"

"Of course I'm sure. Why would I lie about it?"

That was a good question. Why would he lie about that, and about all the rest of it too? There was as much truth in what he'd told me as there is value in a chunk of fool's gold.

THE YOUNG WOMAN who opened the door of apartment four was not Gianna Fornessi. She was platinum blond, with the kind of fresh-faced Nordic features you see on models for Norwegian skiwear. Tall and slender in a pair of green silk lounging pajamas designed to show off the lines of her body; arms decorated with hammered gold bracelets, ears with dangly gold triangles. Judging from the expression in her pale eyes, there wasn't much going on behind them. But then, with her physical attributes, not many men would care if her entire brain had been surgically removed. I wasn't one of them, but I'm an old fart with a one-woman fixation and the antiquated idea that intellect is just as stimulating as bare flesh. Silly me.

"Well . . . hello," the blonde said, and favored me with a radiant smile.

"Ashley Hansen?"

"That's me. Who're you?"

When I told her my name she bobbed her head up and down in a delighted way, as if I'd said something amusing or clever. Or maybe she just liked the sound of all those vowels.

"I knew right away you were Italian," she said. "You're a friend of Jack's, right?"

"Jack?"

"Jack Bisconte." The smile dulled a little. "You are, aren't you?"

"No," I said, "I'm a friend of Pietro Lombardi's."

"Who?"

"Your roommate's grandfather."

"Gianna? Oh," she said.

"I'd like to talk to her, if she's home."

Ashley Hansen's smile was gone now; her whole demeanor had changed, become less spritely and self-assured. She nibbled at a corner of her lower lip, ran a hand through her hair, fiddled with one of her bracelets. Finally she said, "Gianna isn't here."

"When will she be back?"

"She went away for the weekend."

"Uh-huh. Due back when? Tonight?"

". . . I guess so."

"Where did she go?"

"I'm not sure. What'd you want to talk to her about?"

"The complaint George Ferry filed against her."

"Oh, *that,*" she said. "That's been taken care of."

"I know. I just talked to Ferry."

"He's a creepy little prick, isn't he?"

"That's one way of putting it."

"Gianna didn't take his money. He was just trying to hassle her, that's all."

"Why would he do that?"

"Well, why do you think?"

I shrugged. "Suppose you tell me."

"He wanted her to do . . . well, stuff."

"You mean go to bed with him?"

"Stuff," she said. "Kinky stuff, *real* kinky."

"And she wouldn't have anything to do with him."

"No way, José. What a creep."

"So he made up the story about the stolen money to get back at her, is that it?"

"That's it."

"What made him change his mind, drop the charges?"

"He didn't tell you?"

"No."

"Who knows?" She laughed. "Maybe he got religion."

"Or a couple of smacks in the face."

"Huh?"

"Somebody worked him over yesterday," I said. "Bruised his cheek and cut his mouth. You have any idea who?"

"Not me, mister. How come you're so interested, anyway?"

"I told you, I'm a friend of Gianna's grandfather's."

"Yeah, well."

"Gianna have a boyfriend, does she?"

". . . How come you want to know that?"

"Does she?"

"Uh, no. Not right now."

"So Jack Bisconte is yours."

"My what? My *boy*friend? No, he's just somebody I know." She nibbled at her lip again, did some more fiddling with her bracelets. "Look, I've got to go. You want me to tell Gianna you were here?"

"Yes." I handed over one of my business cards. "Give her this and ask her to call me. At home tonight, if it's not too late when she gets in."

Ashley Hansen looked at the card; blinked at it and then blinked at me. "You . . . you're a detective?"

"That's right."

"My God," she said, and backed off, and shut the door in my face.

I stood there for a few seconds, remembering her

eyes—the sudden fear in them when she'd realized she had been talking to a detective.

What the hell?

NORTH BEACH IS not a beach. Nor is there a beach within miles of its boundaries, hasn't been one in well over a hundred years. Back in the 1860s and 1870s, before the city began filling in the land along this part of the bay, there had been a popular bayside resort here that went by the name of North Beach. Even before the resort and beach vanished, the narrow district tucked between and along the slopes of Telegraph and Russian hills inherited the name.

Italians were the first to settle North Beach—fishermen, mostly, who immigrated alone, worked hard, saved their money, bought their own boats or small businesses, and then paid for their families to join them from the old country. They picked the Beach because rents were cheap, it was close to the waterfront, and for the nostalgic reason that San Francisco Bay resembles the Bay of Naples. When the burgeoning Italian community began to outnumber all the other nationalities in the area, the name "Little Italy" was applied to it and still adheres to this day, even though it really isn't a Little Italy anymore.

When I was a kid—hell, when I was a not-so-young adult—North Beach was the place you went when you wanted *pasta fina,* the best espresso and biscotti, conversation about *la patria d'Italia.* That, too, is no longer the case. There are still plenty of Italians in the Beach, and you can still get the good food and some of the good conversation; still get a sense, here and there, of what it was like in the old days. But most of the landmarks are gone—Vanessi's, the original Enrico's, the Boccie Ball, where you could hear mustachioed waiters in gondolier costumes singing arias from Verdi and Puccini—and so is most of the old-world flavor.

The Italian community and the Italian influence shrinks a little more with each passing year. There are more Chinese in North Beach now than Sons of Italy, by a good margin. Plus a proliferation of motorcycle toughs, aging hippies, homeless people, coke and crack dealers, and pimps and small-time hustlers who work the flesh palaces along Columbus and lower Broadway. On the upscale side, there are fancy new cosmopolitan restaurants and cafés, and the snobbish influence of the city's literati, who live and congregate in the area around Washington Square Park. A scattershot melting pot, that's North Beach these days. Me, I preferred it when it really was Little Italy.

Parking in the Beach is the worst in the city. On weekends you can drive around its hilly streets for hours without finding a legal space. So today, in the perverse way of things, I found a spot waiting for me when I came down Stockton.

In a public telephone booth near Washington Square I encountered a second minor miracle: a city directory that had yet to be either stolen or mutilated. The only Bisconte listed was Bisconte Florist Shop, with an address on upper Grant a few blocks away. I took myself off in that direction, through the usual good-weather

Sunday crowds of locals and gawking sightseers and drifting homeless.

Upper Grant, like the rest of the Beach, has changed drastically over the past few decades. Once the center of Little Italy, it is now an odd ethnic mixed bag: Italian markets, trattorias, pizza parlors, bakeries cheek by jowl with Chinese sewing-machine sweatshops, food and herb vendors, and fortune-cookie companies. The Bisconte Florist Shop was a narrow storefront near Filbert, sandwiched between an Italian saloon and the Sip Hing Herb Company. It was open for business, not surprisingly on a Sunday in this neighborhood. Tourists buy flowers, too, given the opportunity.

The front part of the shop was cramped and jungly with cut flowers, ferns, plants in pots and hanging baskets. A small glass-fronted cooler contained a variety of roses and orchids. There was nobody in sight, but a bell had gone off when I entered and a male voice from beyond a rear doorway called, "Be right with you." I shut the door, went up near the counter. Some people like florist shops; I don't. All of them have the same damp, cloyingly sweet smell that reminds me of funeral parlors; of my mother in her casket at the Figlia Brothers Mortuary in Daly City nearly forty years ago. That day, with all its smells, all its painful images, is as clear to me now as if it were yesterday.

I had been waiting about a minute when the voice's owner came out of the back room. He wasn't anybody's preconceived notion of a florist, but then how many of us actually look like what we are? Late thirties, dark-complected, on the beefy side; hair so thick on his arms and curling up out of his shirt collar that it was like a matting of fur. Wearing a floral-pattern shirt, a pair of beige doeskin slacks, and a professional smile.

We had a good look at each other before he said, "Sorry to keep you waiting—I was putting up an arrangement. What can I do for you?"

"Mr. Bisconte? Jack Bisconte?"

"That's me. Something for the wife, maybe?"

"I'm not here for flowers. I'd like to ask you a few questions."

The smile didn't waver. "Oh? What about?"

"Gianna Fornessi."

"Who?"

"Gianna Fornessi. You don't know her?"

"Name's not familiar, no."

"She lives up on Chestnut with Ashley Hansen."

"Hansen, Ashley Hansen . . . I don't know that name either."

"She knows you. Young, blond, looks Norwegian."

"Well, I know a lot of young blondes," Bisconte said. He winked at me. "I'm a bachelor and I get around pretty good, you know?"

"Uh-huh."

"Lot of bars and clubs in North Beach, lot of women to pick and choose from." He shrugged, took a package of Kools from his shirt pocket and fired one with a gold lighter. "So how come you're asking about these two?"

"Not both of them. Just Gianna Fornessi."

"That so? You a friend of hers?"

"Of her grandfather's. She's had a little trouble."

"What kind of trouble?"

"Manager of her building accused her of stealing some money. But somebody convinced him to drop the charges."

"That so?" Bisconte said again, but not as if he cared.

"Leaned on him to do it. Scared hell out of him."

"You don't think it was me?"

"Was it?"

"Nope. Like I said, I don't know anybody named Gianna."

"That's right, like you said."

"What's the big deal anyway? I mean, if the guy dropped the charges, then this Gianna is off the hook. Right?"

"Right."

"Then why all the questions?"

"Curiosity," I said.

Another shrug. "I'd like to help you, pal, but I can't do it if I don't know the lady. Sorry."

"Sure."

"Come back anytime you need flowers," Bisconte said. He gave me a little salute with his cigarette, waited for me to turn and then did the same himself. He was hidden away again in the back room when I let myself out.

Today was my day for liars. Liars and puzzles.

He hadn't asked me who I was or what I did for a living; that was because he already knew. And the way he knew, I thought, was that Ashley Hansen had gotten on the horn after I left and told him about me. He knew

Gianna Fornessi pretty well, too, and exactly where the two women lived.

He was the man in the tan safari jacket I'd seen earlier, the one who'd been leaving 250 Chestnut.

Chapter **3**

I TREATED MYSELF to a plate of linguine and fresh clams at a ristorante off Washington Square and then drove back over to Aquatic Park. Now, in mid-afternoon, fog was seeping in through the Gate and the temperature had dropped sharply. So much for the warm-and-clear aspect of this June Sunday. Those loyal, fog-loving San Franciscans would already be quitting the good-weather attractions in droves, grumbling and muttering, the heat turned up in their cars.

Even the number of bocce players and kibitzers had thinned by a third. Pietro Lombardi was still there, though; so was Dominick Marra. Bocce may be dying slow in the city, but not in men like them. They cling to it and to the other old ways as tenaciously as they cling to life itself.

I told Pietro—and Dominick, who wasn't about to let us talk in private—what I'd learned so far. He was relieved that Ferry had dropped his complaint, but was just as puzzled and curious as I was about the Jack Bisconte connection.

"Do you know Bisconte?" I asked him.

"No. I see his shop but I never been inside."

"Know anything about him?"

"Nothing."

"How about you, Dominick?"

He shook his head. "He's too old for Gianna, hah? Almost forty, you say—that's too old for girl twenty-three."

"If that's their relationship," I said.

"Men almost forty, they go after young woman," Dominick said, "they only got one reason. *Fatto 'na bella chiavata.* You remember, eh, Pietro?"

"Pazzo! You think I forget *'na bella chiavata?"*

I asked Pietro, "What do you know about Gianna's roommate, Ashley Hansen?"

"Nothing," he said. "I never meet her."

"How long have they been sharing the apartment?"

"Long time. Eight months, maybe."

"They know each other long before they moved in together?"

He shrugged. "Gianna and me, we don't talk much no more. Young people now, they got no time for *la famiglia.*" Another shrug, a sigh. *"Ognuno pensa per sè,"* he said. Everybody thinks only of himself.

Dominick gripped his shoulder. Then he said to me, "You find out what's happen with Bisconte and Ferry and those girls. Then you see they don't bother them no more. Hah?"

"If I can, Dominick. If I can."

The fog was coming in thick now and the other players were making noises about ending the day's tournament. Dominick got into an argument with one of them;

he wanted to play another game or two. He was out-voted, but still pleading his case when I left. Their Sunday was almost over. And so was mine.

I drove to Pacific Heights and my cold, cold flat. I hadn't put the heat on this morning because of the nice weather; and with the fog had come the wind, and when the wind blows across the Heights there isn't a building up there, no matter how well constructed and well insulated, that can retain warmth for more than an hour. I worked the thermostat up to sixty-five, checked my answering machine—no calls—and went straight to the bathroom, where I ran the tub full of hot water. My tub, or rather the landlord's, is one of those big old-fashioned claw-foot jobs, deep and wide and long enough for a man six feet tall to stretch out full length. Bathtubs nowadays are built for midgets and contortionists.

A good long soak not only warmed me up, it made me sleepy. I drowsed for a time, finally went under all the way . . .

. . . *and again I am lying belly down across the lip of that bare brown hill, the wind howling around me, the steep slope below and the pit yawning like an open wound below that . . . and I feel the strain on my arms from the two-handed grip on his arm and shoulder, the weight of his spread-eagled body . . . I see his face just inches from mine, that evil stranger's face, and in it there is an arrogance born of the certainty that I will pull him up to safety because I am not like him, I am not cold-blooded casual death . . . and I think of the victims, Kerry and how close she came to being one of them, Kerry with his hands on her, hurting her . . . and then I see the arro-*

gance fade, slowly transform into raw terror as he stares into my face, sees the truth in my face . . . and I let go of him, I just open my fingers and let go . . . and he falls away, that evil face grows smaller and smaller and I hear the voice of his terror as he slides and tumbles into the pit, hear it rising until it is louder than the wind, hear him screaming all the way down . . .

. . . but then the screaming changed, modulated into something else, and I came jarringly awake with my heart banging and a metallic taste in my mouth. Telephone—damn telephone. In automatic reflex I hauled myself out of the tub: big white hairy walrus heaving himself out of a puddle. I was still disoriented from the dream and I slipped on the floor tile, barked my knee on the tub; lurched, bruised my other knee on the toilet seat before I could regain my balance. The pain woke me up all the way. Cussing, I hobbled into the bedroom, all too aware of my nakedness, thankful that most times there was nobody around to see me when I was at my most ridiculous, and yanked up the receiver and growled a hello.

"You don't have to bite my head off," Kerry said.

"Sorry, babe. I, uh, I was doing something."

"Anything important?"

"No. Glad you called."

"Want some company tonight?"

"Sure. But I thought you had work to do."

"It's finished. I had an inspired day."

"I wish I could say the same."

"It's not over yet," she said. "I'll be there in twenty minutes." We rang off and I sat on the bed and massaged my knees. The left one had a welt and a little cut that trickled blood. Fine, let it bleed, the hell with it.

Vestiges of the dream still drifted like toxic smoke in the corners of my mind. Too soon since it happened, the images of that April afternoon still too sharp in my mental storehouse. You can blank hateful memories out of your conscious mind with enough effort of will, but the subconscious retains them, devils you with them when you let your defenses down in sleep. Not endlessly, though—I could take a measure of comfort in that. In six months to a year, if my psychological patterns held true to form, I wouldn't be having this particular ugly dream much at all anymore. I hadn't had the shackled-in-the-cabin nightmare in almost a year now, had I?

Back in the bathroom, I gave myself a fast rubdown and then took a look at my face in the mirror. Some face. Full of hollows and crags and little fissures, like a bas-relief map of a gray wasteland. What did Kerry see in a face like that? The eyes weren't too bad, if a little on the hound-dog side; maybe it was the eyes. Or maybe she was just nuts. Batty as an Arizona cave under that rational exterior of hers.

I hope she never gets sane, I thought.

I ran a knuckle over my cheek, decided I could use another shave. Mistake: I cut myself twice and couldn't find my styptic pencil and couldn't seem to make one of the cuts stop bleeding. When the doorbell rang I went to answer it wearing slacks and a sport shirt and two pieces of bloody toilet paper stuck on the gray wasteland. Kerry didn't seem to notice. She gave me a tender smile and a tender kiss to go with it.

I held her for a while, tighter than I would have normally, because enough of the dream was still with me to dredge up other nightmare images of that bad time in April: the night I'd found Kerry unconscious on the floor of my closet, blood on her face . . . almost a victim because of me. The images made me ache all over again. Losing her would be intolerable. Just the thought of losing her . . .

"Enough with the bear hug," she said against my chest. "You're squeezing the breath out of me."

I let go of her, reluctantly. "Sorry about that. I like the way you feel."

"It's mutual. Just don't get carried away."

I like the way she looks, too, in and out of clothing, any day, anytime. Tonight she was wearing tan suede pants and a white sweater, both of which hugged her body more tightly than I'd just been doing, and her auburn hair was tied up with a green scarf. I let her walk ahead of me into the kitchen so I could watch the play of her hips. Fifty-eight years old and horny as a teenager every time I'm near her. Like the old joke about the octogenarian who married the beauty queen sixty years his junior and dropped dead of a heart attack on their wedding night: it took the morticians three days to close his coffin. Take them a *week* to close mine if I dropped dead on a wedding night with Kerry.

We got drinks and sat on the couch, Kerry with her shoes off and her legs tucked under her. Tall and slender, my lady, with nice legs and beautiful feet. Most people's feet leave a great deal to be desired; mine are as ugly as sin. But hers are small, perfectly formed, with a high-arched instep—beautiful. Sometimes, like tonight, just contemplating them gives me erotic ideas. I reached over and fondled the nearest one. Definite erotic ideas.

"Hey, that tickles!"

"It does, huh?"

"What do you think you're doing?"

"Playing."

"Well, don't. I want to relax for a while."

"A foot massage is relaxing."

"Not the way you do it."

"Your toes inflame me," I said. "I want to nibble them."

"My God, you're a closet foot fetishist!" She smacked my hand and yanked her foot away. "Sit over there and behave yourself."

"For how long?"

"Go on, move."

I scooted back from her, not too far.

"Now," she said. "Cybil."

"What about Cybil?"

"We had a talk this afternoon, an old-fashioned mother-daughter talk."

"Is that good or bad?"

"Good. Very good."

"She's still going to Marin?"

"Sooner than expected. Saturday morning, nine o'clock."

"That's a nice surprise. It's definite, huh?"

"Definite. She notified the seniors complex yesterday, and called the storage company in L.A. and arranged for her furniture and other things to be shipped." Kerry drank some of her wine. "There is one thing she's asking for before she goes."

"Uh-oh."

"Don't worry, I think it's positive."

"You think? What is it?"

"Well, my guess is some fence-mending."

"Fence-mending?"

"With you. She wants to see you."

Another surprise. Cybil and I hadn't laid eyes on each other in six months. Hadn't exchanged more than a dozen words in all that time. On the few occasions I'd called and Cybil had answered the phone, she'd hung up as soon as she knew who she was talking to.

"This was her idea?" I asked.

"All hers."

"But she wouldn't tell you exactly why she wanted to see me?"

"Not exactly, no."

"So maybe she doesn't want to mend fences. Maybe she wants to tell me to my face what a bum she thinks I am. Hell, maybe she wants to spit in my eye."

"I doubt that."

"Then again, you don't know for sure."

"No, but I know my mother well enough. She's coming out of her shell. The Cybil I talked to today is the old Cybil, the one I grew up with."

"Mm. So when does she want to meet?"

"Whenever you're free. Tomorrow night?"

"Better make it Tuesday night. Tomorrow's pretty full."

"Seven o'clock okay?"

"Fine."

". . . You don't mind, do you? Talking to her?"

"Mind? Good God, no. If it'll make things better between the three of us, I'll talk to her all night. I'll do anything she wants, short of leaving you and doing away with myself. I'll even let her spit in my eye."

Kerry reached over and patted my cheek. "I love you, you know that?" she said. "Sometimes I think too much."

"Makes two of us. Can I move back over there?"

"Come ahead."

I came ahead. Cybil was no longer uppermost in my mind; what was perched there now, leering suggestively, was *'na bella chiavata.* "I am about to stop behaving myself," I said. "I am about to start playing again."

"With my feet?"

"For openers."

"In that case . . ." She leaned back, extended one leg, and wiggled her toes at me. "The game's afoot, Watson," she said.

Chapter **4**

I SPENT ALL DAY Monday in the East Bay, testifying at a felony extortion trial in Oakland in the morning and then chasing down information on a possibly fraudulent insurance claim that took me out to Orinda and Lafayette. I didn't get out of Lafayette until after five, and the commute traffic on the Bay Bridge was so snarled that it was almost seven before I got home. I was in bed and asleep by ten. Two good nights' sleep in a row, for a change, though I much preferred the postcoital variety I'd had on Sunday.

On Tuesday morning I opened the office at a quarter to nine. All I had on the docket for this day, aside from my promised follow-up on the Gianna Fornessi matter, was a routine skip-trace and a routine personal-injury investigation, neither of which I could begin working on until various city, state, and private business offices opened. So I got on the horn to the Hall of Justice and asked for Inspector Cullen on the Robbery Detail. He was in, and willing enough to talk about George Ferry's complaint, but he didn't have much to tell me.

Ferry had filed the complaint last Thursday morning.

Cullen had gone to Chestnut Street to investigate, talked to the two principals, and determined that there was not enough evidence to take Ms. Fornessi into custody. Thirty-two hours later Ferry had called in and withdrawn the charges, giving the same flimsy reason he'd handed me. As far as Cullen and the department were concerned, it was all very minor and ordinary.

I asked him if he'd run Gianna Fornessi's name through R&I to find out if she had a previous arrest record in the city. He had and she hadn't. He had not run Ferry's name, he said, because he hadn't seen any need for it. I didn't know Cullen well enough to ask him for a favor; but I did know a couple of Eberhardt's department cronies well enough. So I had Cullen switch me over to General Works, got Jack Logan on the line, and asked him to run a check on Ferry, and on Jack Bisconte and Ashley Hansen. Might as well touch all the bases.

Gianna Fornessi's name wasn't listed in the telephone directory, but the Hansen girl's was. No address, just the number. I tapped it out, waited through eight rings, and was about to hang up when a sleepy female voice answered.

"Ms. Hansen?"

"Yum. Who's this? You woke me up."

I identified myself, thinking that whatever she did for a living, it was not a job that required her to be up early and out battling the morning commute traffic. This time my name got a different reaction out of her: It woke her all the way up, seemed to put her on her guard.

"What do *you* want?" she said.

"Talk to your roommate. Is she there?"

". . . No."

"Left for work already?"

"Uh, no."

Something in her voice made me ask, "She did come home from her weekend, didn't she? Sunday night?"

"No, she didn't. She's still not back."

"How come?"

"I don't know. How should I know?"

"Didn't she call you?"

"No."

"Doesn't it worry you? Her not coming home when she's supposed to, not calling?"

"Why should it? Gianna's a big girl."

"She do that sort of thing often?"

"What sort of thing?"

"Go away for extra-long weekends."

"Sometimes."

"With her boyfriend, I guess. Or did you tell me she doesn't have a boyfriend right now?"

"You're sure nosy," Ashley Hansen said. "Ask Gianna, why don't you."

"I'll do that. Where does she work?"

No response.

"Maybe she'll go straight to work this morning," I said. "I need to talk to her, Ms. Hansen."

More of the same.

"Ms. Hansen? I'd appreciate—"

"Bye, now," she said, and hung up on me.

I considered calling Pietro Lombardi for the name of Gianna's employer, but there were other ways to get it, a little later on, and I didn't want to get into a dialogue with him until I had something to report. I drank coffee and did paperwork until ten o'clock, then called TRW and requested credit checks and background information on Gianna, Ashley Hansen, Bisconte, and Ferry. The rep said she'd have them for me by noon.

I was putting in telephone time on the skip-trace when Eberhardt clumped in at ten-thirty—the first I'd seen of him since Friday. He wore a blue suit that wouldn't have looked good on a corpse, a tie that deserved a citation for visual pollution, and had one of his smelly briars clenched at a Popeye angle between his teeth. Mr. Elegant. I resisted an impulse to needle him about his appearance; that kind of banter was no longer acceptable between us. Instead I settled for a simple good morning. He grunted something, shrugged out of his overcoat, went to the hot plate, poured himself a cup of coffee, took the cup to his desk, banged the briar into an ashtray, and made slurping noises as he drank. Then he pulled a face and muttered, "Lousy goddamn coffee."

"You could always come in early and make it yourself," I said. Mildly.

"Yeah."

"So how was your weekend?"

"Fair."

"Spend it with Bobbie Jean?"

"Yeah."

"Do anything interesting?"

"No."

"You know," I said, not so mildly, "trying to talk to

you is like trying to talk to a teenager. 'Where did you go?' 'Out.' 'What did you do?' 'Nothing.' Monosyllables, that's all I get."

"So?"

"So. See what I mean?"

He looked at me for the first time since he'd come in. "Bull—" he said, and paused, and then said, "—shit."

"Uh-huh, I get it." A bristling annoyance was building in me. Hold your temper, I warned myself. Not holding it is how the rift got opened up in the first place. "How much longer is this going to go on, Eb?"

"What?"

"The silent treatment, the big grudge. It's been more than two months now and I don't think I can take much more of it."

"So don't," he said.

"Now what does that mean?"

Some heavy silence. Then, abruptly, "All right, maybe it's time. Call it quits, get it over with."

"What're you talking about?"

"Us, the business—that's what I'm talking about."

". . . Bust up our partnership?"

"You got it."

I stared at him. "You're not serious."

"Dead serious. I been thinking about it for weeks."

"Eb, we've been together a long time—"

"Five years. That's not a long time."

"We been friends a hell of a lot longer than that."

"You think we're still friends? I don't."

"Come on, you don't mean that."

Flat, cold stare. He meant it.

Shaken, I said, "I apologized for what happened in April. How many times you want me to say I'm sorry?"

"Sorry doesn't cut it. I needed a friend when Bobbie Jean called off the wedding and what'd I get? I got a self-righteous know-it-all who tells me I'm at fault, calls me seven different kinds of schmuck, and then punches me in the gut."

"I lost my head. . . ."

"Yeah. And I could've lost my spleen."

"Oh for Christ's sake, I didn't hit you that hard."

"No? I puked up blood afterward."

"The hell you did."

"The hell I didn't. You calling me a liar?"

"No, I'm just . . . goddamn it, Eb, it's history. What's the sense in all this scratching at scabs? Why can't you just let it heal, let us get on with our lives?"

"Right. I get on with mine, you get on with yours."

"I meant—"

"I know what you meant."

"Okay. Okay, then. What've you got in your head? Quit me and get a job with some other agency?"

"Maybe."

"Or what, hang out your own shingle?"

"Maybe that too. None of your business what I do if I decide to walk."

His telephone rang; he picked up before I could say anything else, mostly listened for the thirty-second duration of the call. I sat watching him, thinking: It's the grudge talking. He won't walk. After thirty-five years of friendship? He's giving me a hard time, that's all. Jerking my chain.

Eberhardt put the receiver down. Went and shrugged back into his overcoat and then headed for the door, all without looking my way.

I said, "Where you going?"

He said, "Out," and banged the door behind him.

THE TRW REP called back at eleven-fifteen. I was still brooding at my desk; I hadn't done much of anything else since Eberhardt's departure. I took down the credit and background information I'd requested, stared at it for a couple of minutes until the phone rang again. Jack Logan this time, with the R&I report. More notes, more half-blank staring. I couldn't seem to get my head into the work. It was as if I were trying to make sense out of words written in a foreign language.

I got up, paced around, stood at the back-wall window and stared down toward Civic Center. No sun today; gray again, high foggy overcast that only added to my bleak mood. I went back to the desk, willed myself to concentrate on my notes.

Jack Bisconte. Good credit rating. Owner and sole operator, Bisconte Florist Shop, since 1978. Home address: a rented apartment on upper Greenwich Street, last three years. No listing of previous jobs held or previous local addresses. No felony or misdemeanor convictions or arrests.

George Ferry. Excellent credit rating. Owner and principal operator, Ferry Temporary Employment Agency, 510 Fremont Street, since 1972. Resident of 250 Chestnut since 1980. No felony convictions or arrests; one DUI arrest and conviction following a minor traffic accident in May of 1981, sentenced to ninety days in jail (suspended), driver's license revoked for six months.

Gianna Fornessi. Fair to good credit rating, established less than a year ago. Applied in March, three months ago, for dealer financing on a new Nissan Sentra; application approved thanks to a cash down payment of five thousand dollars. Employed by Home Draperies, Showplace Square, as a sales representative since 1989. Resident of 250 Chestnut for eight months. Addresses prior to that: two in Daly City, the most recent for a period of one year, the other her parents' home.

Ashley Hansen. No credit rating. No felony or misdemeanor convictions or arrests.

There wasn't much in any of it, except for the fact that TRW had no listing on Ashley Hansen. Almost everybody uses credit cards these days, establishes some kind of credit—especially a young woman whose income is substantial enough for her to afford an apartment in one of the city's best neighborhoods. Why not Ashley Hansen?

She was one person who could tell me; another was Gianna Fornessi. Maybe Gianna *had* gone straight to work this morning. . . . Call or drive over to Showplace Square? Drive. It wasn't far, and I'd had enough of the office. Oppressive in here now, with the gray day pressing against the window and skylight. With Eberhardt's anger and bitterness lingering in the air like smoke ghosts.

* * *

SHOWPLACE SQUARE IS south of Market and west of 7th Street, in the shadow of the Highway 101 Skyway interchange, in a once-shabby industrial area that underwent urban redevelopment several years ago and now contains a number of new office buildings, upscale businesses, and the S.F. Concourse exhibition hall. The Square is just that, a block-square complex of manufacturers' showrooms for the interior decorating trade—carpets, draperies, lighting fixtures, and other types of home furnishings. Most of it isn't open to the general public, but I showed the photostat of my license to one of the security men on the door and talked him into calling the Home Draperies showroom and asking that Gianna Fornessi come out to talk to me.

Somebody came out but it wasn't Gianna Fornessi. It was a fluffy-looking little man in his forties named Lundquist, who said in a voice that matched his appearance, "I'm sorry, sir, Ms. Fornessi is no longer employed by us."

"Oh? When did she leave?"

"Eight months ago."

"Eight . . . *months?*"

"At the end of October, last year."

"Quit or terminated?"

"Quit. Rather abruptly too."

"To take another job?"

"I don't know. She gave no adequate reason."

"No one called for a reference?"

"No one," Lundquist said.

"She worked for you two years?"

"About two years, yes."

"As a sales representative."

"That's correct."

"Mind telling me her salary?"

"I'm afraid that's confidential."

"Just this, then: Was hers a high-salaried position? In excess of thirty thousand a year, say?"

Lundquist smiled a faint, fluffy smile. "Hardly," he said.

"Was her work satisfactory?"

"Well, not really. She seemed . . . uninterested."

"With her job or the interior design trade?"

"Both."

"So it's not likely she'd have taken another, better-paying job in the industry."

Another fluffy smile. And another "Hardly."

So why had Gianna quit Home Draperies so suddenly eight months ago, at just about the same time she moved in with Ashley Hansen? And why hadn't she told her family about it? And what had she been doing since to afford a $5000 down payment on a new car and half the rent on a $2000-a-month North Beach apartment?

Chapter **5**

THE SAME WHITE Nissan was parked along the retaining wall across from 250 Chestnut, in the same place as on Sunday. I parked behind it again. It looked new and it was a Sentra—Gianna's? If so, all it meant was that she'd left it here and gone off for her long weekend in somebody else's car. Boyfriend's, maybe. I had my doubts about Ashley Hansen's disclaimer on that issue.

The wind off the bay was cold and blustery up here; it blew me on a tack across the street and up the stoop of her building. In the vestibule I punched the doorbell for apartment four. No answer. Either Ashley Hansen had gone out or she didn't want to deal with callers; and apparently Gianna still hadn't come home. I leaned on George Ferry's bell. No answer there, either. Well, it was a weekday. It figured that he'd be at work.

I tacked back across the street to the Nissan, bent at the driver's window. There wasn't anything to see inside except empty upholstery. That door was locked; but it turned out that the passenger door wasn't. Careless, Gianna, I thought. Don't you know new cars are targets in the city, even cheaper models like the Sentra?

Street and sidewalks both were deserted. Some Nosy
Parker might be peering out a window, but for all anybody knew I had every right to poke around inside the
Nissan. I opened the door all the way and folded myself
into the passenger seat. Cars like this aren't made for
big men; my knees were up around my chin and there
was barely enough room for me to work the glove com-
partment open. At that, I had to haul out the contents
and then hold each item up past my legs so I could see
it clearly.

Owner's manual. Registration card and insurance receipt, both made out in Gianna Fornessi's name. An
open roll of lime Life Savers. A packet of Tampax.
Seven pennies, one nickel. And three Shell Oil credit
card slips. The card owner's name was the same on each
slip, but it wasn't the Fornessi girl's; it was male, and if I
was any judge of handwriting, so was the back-scrawled
signature underneath. Brent DeKuiper. Nice name,
very distinctive—very easy to trace. Gianna's boyfriend?

I wrote it down in my notebook, along with the credit
card number, the date on each slip, and the fact that
Brent DeKuiper had been a customer of Shell Oil since
1971. The dates were widely spaced: one in early April,
one in mid-May, one nine days ago. The 1971 date
made DeKuiper a good deal older than Gianna—unless
one of his relatives had believed in long-range planning
and presented him with a Shell card instead of a teeth-
ing ring on his first or second birthday.

Everything back into the glove box. Then I poked
around a little—as much as my cramped position would
allow—on the floorboards and under the seats. All that

got me was dirty fingers. I hauled myself out of there, grunting as my muscles uncricked again. Before I shut the door I pushed the locking doodad over into the lock position. You're welcome, Ms. Fornessi. Crime prevention, after all, is every good citizen's duty.

FIVE-TEN FREMONT STREET was just off Mission, within shouting distance of the Transbay bus terminal. Busy downtown area, this, so street parking was a virtual impossibility during business hours. The third parking garage I tried had short-term space for my car, at an exorbitant hourly rate—and it was four cold blocks from there to Fremont and Mission.

The building that bore the numerals 510 was a three-story stone pile that had been born not long after the 1906 quake and looked as if it was pretty damned weary of standing around in the same spot after eighty-plus years. Its score or so tenants were all small businesses of the more esoteric variety, from a small jewelry manufacturer to an outfit that sold micrographic equipment. The Ferry Temporary Employment Agency was on the second floor, just down the hall from where a cranky old elevator deposited me.

Ferry had a modest layout, mostly anteroom with one or maybe two small private offices at the rear. Newish if inexpensive furnishings, restful colors, a designer map of the city on one wall and a big sign on another that said SE HABLA ESPAÑOL. At right angles to the sign was a counter, and behind the counter was a desk and a fat woman with lemon-colored hair. The anteroom's other two occupants were middle-aged, tired-looking women, one Latina and one Anglo, perched like mismatched bookends on either end of a row of hard wooden chairs.

The fat woman looked me over and seemed to decide that I was neither a male domestic nor a potential employer of domestics. Maybe she mistook me for a bill collector or one of the less shabbily dressed street people who had wandered in looking for a handout; in any event she fixed me with a hard eye and said, "May I help you?" in a voice that might have been packed in dry ice.

I said, "George Ferry."

"Mr. Ferry is in conference."

"Sure he is. But he'll see me."

I gave her my name. She didn't want it, so when she repeated it on the interoffice phone she mispronounced it—deliberately, I thought. She listened, nodded in satisfaction, and said to me, "He doesn't know you."

I had no patience for this. "He knows me," I said. "Tell him I'm the detective who came to see him on Sunday. And damn it, lady, pronounce my name correctly this time."

She was like a tub of cheap margarine: hard-looking on the surface, all soft on the inside, so when you cut into her a little she melted and ran. She quit looking at me; repeated my message to Ferry in a different voice, and with my name correctly pronounced. As soon as she put the phone down she got very busy with a sheaf of papers stacked in front of her. Some receptionist. Some outfit. I felt sorry for the two job-seekers, who were trying to pretend that they hadn't heard a thing. For all the poor women who needed the Ferry Temporary Employment Agency to make ends meet.

Another Latina, sad-eyed and slump-shouldered, came out through the inner door and lowered herself into a middle chair in the waiting area: bedraggled paperback between the two bookends. Ferry appeared in the doorway, looking nervous and worried, and gestured for me to join him. His office was about a third as large as the anteroom, just as bare and functional. The only visitor's chair was a hardwood job that matched the ones out front. Ferry's desk chair, on the other hand, was an executive model with thick arms and six inches of leather-covered foam rubber in the seat.

"What is it now?" he said when the door was shut. His voice had a whiny tone; it didn't go any better with his chocolate-brown Armani suit than the healing marks on his face. "I explained everything to you on Sunday."

"Did you, Mr. Ferry?"

"Of course I did. I don't see what—"

"Sit down, why don't you? Let's talk a little more."

He sat down, reluctantly. I stayed on my feet, went around on the side of the desk so that I was standing close above him. Some men you can intimidate with that kind of looming posture. Ferry was one of them.

He licked his lips, as if his mouth was dry and he was wishing his old buddy Jack Daniel's was close at hand. Tried to find something to do with his hands and finally folded them together at his chest with his thumbs twitching the material of his paisley tie. Nor could he keep his eyes still; they kept shifting this way and that under blinking lids, never quite meeting mine.

I let him stew awhile before I said, "Gianna Fornessi."

". . . What about her?"

"What does she do for a living?"

Blink. Lick. Twitch. "Do?"

"Her job, Mr. Ferry. Where does she work?"

"I . . . don't know," he said.

"No idea at all? Didn't she fill out a renter's application before she moved into your building?"

"I never saw it. It's not my building. . . . I mean, I don't own it. . . ."

"Who does own it?"

"A man named Chandler, Adam Chandler."

"Where does he live?"

"Back East. Pennsylvania."

"And she sent the application directly to him?"

"Well, no, she . . . I took it. But I didn't read it."

"Just sent it on to this Adam Chandler in Pennsylvania."

"Yes."

"And he checked her out and approved her from back there."

"That's right. Yes."

"What about Ashley Hansen?"

". . . I don't know what you mean."

"What does *she* do for a living?"

Twitch. Lick. "I have no idea," he said.

"Come on, Ferry." I leaned down so that I was right in his face. "What're you trying to hide?"

"Nothing. I . . . nothing."

"Then why won't you tell me what those two women do to earn their rent money?"

"I don't know, I tell you. I don't know!"

He knew, all right. The sweat on his face, the scared-rabbit look in his eyes, made a lie of his words. If I'd been a genuine city-sanctioned officer of the law I would have kept on squeezing him about Gianna Fornessi and Ashley Hansen, hard, until he cracked and the truth seeped out. As it was, I couldn't afford to get too rough with him. He was liable to call his lawyer, or go straight to the Hall of Justice himself and holler police harassment. And then I would be in trouble, even though technically I was not guilty of impersonating a policeman. Technicalities have a way of being over-looked when cops find themselves under fire for something they didn't do.

"All right," I said. "Tell me about Jack Bisconte."

"Who?"

"You heard me. Jack Bisconte."

"I don't know anybody by that name."

"Runs a florist shop on upper Grant."

Headshake.

"Big guy," I said. "Late thirties. Hair on him like fur."

Maybe Ferry didn't know Bisconte's name or profession, but he knew Bisconte: he got even paler and the lick-blink-twitch reaction grew more pronounced. "No," he said.

"No what? You know him."

"No."

"Is he the one who worked you over the other day?"

"Worked me . . . no! Nobody worked me over. I told you how I—"

"Yeah. You're clumsy and you fell down the stairs."

Twitch. Lick. Head bob.

"What's Bisconte's relationship with Gianna Fornessi?"

Blink. Blink.

"Or is it Ashley Hansen he's involved with? Which one?"

"I don't know anybody named Bisconte!"

"Brent DeKuiper, then."

"I . . . who?"

"DeKuiper. Brent DeKuiper."

Headshake.

"That name doesn't ring any bells either, huh?"

"No."

"Friend of the Fornessi girl's. Boyfriend, maybe."

Headshake.

"You've seen her with men, haven't you?"

"Sometimes, yes, but—"

"But you don't know anybody named DeKuiper."

"No."

"What's her boyfriend's name?"

"Boyfriend?"

"Gianna's current boyfriend. What's his name?"

"I don't know," Ferry said. "How would I know that?"

"You just said you've seen her with men."

"I don't ask their names!"

"Any man in particular lately?"

Lick. Twitch. "I can't remember . . . no. No."

"You see her with a man last Friday or Saturday?"

"No."

"Sure about that?"

"I haven't seen her since . . . before I found the money."

"The two thousand dollars you thought she'd stolen."

"The mistake I made, yes."

"So you don't know where she went this past weekend. Or with who."

"I don't know *anything* about Gianna's private life. How many times do I have to say it? I don't know!"

Useless. Something or somebody had him scared spitless—Bisconte maybe. So scared that he wasn't even willing to unburden himself to a man he thought was a cop.

I backed off from him, both physically and verbally. In softer tones I said, "I hope you're not mixed up in anything illegal, Mr. Ferry. For your sake."

Twitch. Lick. "I'm not," he said, and got a handkerchief out and swabbed his wet face. "I swear it—I'm not."

I went out without saying anything else to him. The three job seekers were still perched in the waiting area; the lemon-haired receptionist was again, or still, shuffling papers. None of them looked at me. None of them made a sound as I walked across to the outer door. Funeral parlor anterooms were more cheerful than this damned place.

In the elevator I thought: Ferry might not be mixed

up in anything illegal, but Gianna Fornessi? Starting to smell that way. Even if she's not a thief, even if she didn't steal Ferry's money, she's got some kind of dirt on her hands. Her and Ashley Hansen both.

Chapter **6**

THE BISCONTE FLORIST shop was deserted except for an elderly Chinese woman busily rearranging some floral displays. Mr. Bisconte didn't work on Saturdays or Tuesdays, she said. Sometimes he didn't work on other days, four or five days in a row sometimes. She said this with no little disapproval, as if she considered his habits a violation of the normal human work ethic—maybe even an affront to God. She didn't seem to like her boss much more than I did.

From there I drove up to Greenwich Street, less than a dozen blocks away. The building in which Bisconte made his home was a two-flat converted Victorian on the steep part of Greenwich just below where the street begins its winding ascent to Coit Tower. Two big flats, one on top of the other—at least six rooms each. Expensive digs. Either the neighborhood flower shop business was a lot more lucrative than I realized, or Bisconte had another and possibly suspect source of income.

There were two people on the building's stoop, holding what looked to be an animated conversation, when I drove by; they were still there when I came back down-hill on foot a couple of minutes later. Man and woman, the man wearing Western-style clothing—Levi's jeans, boots, sheepskin jacket, a Stetson hat clutched in one hand—and the woman dressed in a sweater and slacks and a pair of scuffed, too-big slippers. She was in the doorway, hanging on to the edge of the door with one hand, looking bored and irritated at the same time. The guy had his back to the street, talking to her with his hands as well as his mouth. He wasn't trying to be quiet about what he was saying; I could hear him plainly even before I reached the stoop.

"Listen, damn it, I've *got* to see him. Can't you get that through your head? It's important!"

"He didn't tell me where he'd be," the woman said. She was in her twenties, a slender brunette with the kind of mammary development that would hurl some men into fits of passionate fantasizing. Not me. Pretty face, but one without much intellect or character. The face of a mannequin, or maybe one of those pod crea-tures in *Invasion of the Body Snatchers:* not quite fin-ished, no real stamp of individuality.

The guy said, "You must have *some* idea, for chris-sake."

"Well, I don't. I told you."

"Don't give me that. Where is he, where can I find him?"

"Bugger off, okay?"

She started to back up, to shove the door closed. The guy moved forward, fast, and caught her arm with one hand and used the other to hold the door open. "You're not going anywhere," he said, "not until you quit jerking me around."

"Let go, goddamn it."

"No. Where is he?"

I was up the stairs and onto the landing by then. He didn't know I was there until I took hold of his shoulder, pulled him around gently but firmly. His mouth came open; he glared at me with hot, dark eyes. He was about thirty-five, short and wiry, with thick curly black hair and eyebrows like clumps of black nettles. He might have been handsome except that he had a mean, spoiled look about him.

"The lady asked you to let go," I said.

"Who the hell are you?"

"Somebody who doesn't like to see women manhandled. Let her go."

Stare-down. He may have been mean but he wasn't tough: I won in five seconds flat. He released the woman's wrist, at the same time shrugging free of my hand so he could pretend that averting his eyes and backing off a step was his idea.

"All right," he said to the brunette. Nastily. "But when he comes home you tell him I was here. You tell him I need to talk to him right away."

"Yeah, yeah," she said.

Without looking at me again he went down the stairs, stalked across the street to where a dusty blue Ford Ranger was parked. He didn't burn rubber when he pulled away, headed downhill, but he came pretty close.

I turned to the brunette. She said, "Thanks. But I

could've handled him. He doesn't hurt women in public, just in private."

"Nice guy, huh?"

"Prime asshole," she said.

"Friend of Jack Bisconte's, maybe?"

"Don't tell me you're looking for Jack too?"

"I am."

"Well, you're out of luck. I really don't know where he is."

"Or when he'll be back?"

"Or when he'll be back. You want me to give him a message?"

"No. I'll catch him later."

"You and Mr. Asshole," she said.

When she was gone inside I took a look at the two mailboxes near the door. Bisconte had the upper flat; his was the only name on the box. Well, whoever the brunette was, she knew him pretty well. She was not only occupying his flat while he was out, she was wearing what were probably his slippers.

So much—for now—for Jack Bisconte.

Next up: Brent DeKuiper.

GIANNA'S GASOLINE-BUYING FRIEND—or at least somebody named Brent DeKuiper—was listed in the city directory, with an address on Balboa. The high street number told me that it was all the way out on the northwestern rim of the city, close to the ocean and Cliff House.

Going out there always gives me pangs of nostalgia. It's where Playland-at-the-Beach used to be, and Play-

land—a ten-acre amusement park in the grand old style
—was where I'd spent a good portion of my youth.
Funhouses, shooting galleries, games of chance, the Big
Dipper roller coaster swooping down out of the gaudily
lit night, laughing girls with wind-color in their cheeks
and a mischievous sparkle in their eyes . . . and all of
it wrapped in thick ocean fogs that added an element of
mystery to the general gaiety. All gone now; closed
nearly twenty years ago and then allowed to sit aban-
doned for several more before it was torn down; nothing left of it except bright ghost-images in the memories
of graybeards like me. Condo and rental apartment
buildings occupied the space these days: Beachfront
Luxury Living, Spectacular Ocean Views. Yeah, sure.
Luxuriously cold, gray weather and spectacular weekend views of Ocean Beach and its parking areas
jammed with rowdy teenagers and beer-guzzling adult
children.

It made me sad, thinking about it. Getting old. Sure
sign of it when you started lamenting the dead past everywhere you went, glorifying it as if it were some kind
of flawless Valhalla, when you knew damned well it
hadn't been. Maybe so, maybe so. But nobody could
convince me Beachfront Luxury Living condos were
better than Playland and the Big Dipper, or that some
of the dead past wasn't a hell of a lot better than much
of the half-dead present.

I'd expected the address on Balboa to be a house or
an apartment building, but it turned out to be a narrow
storefront in a little neighborhood business district a
couple of blocks from the Great Highway. Script letter-

ing on its dirt-smeared front window said VORTEX PUBLI-
CATIONS. And below that, in smaller letters, JOB PRINTING.

Wrong address? No, I was sure I'd copied it down
correctly; and the directory I'd consulted had been Pac
Bell's most recent. Well, maybe this was DeKuiper's
business and he lived on the premises. I pushed open
the door and walked in.

Narrow space containing a counter that ran from wall
to wall lengthwise. Behind the counter, a closed door
and some shelving partitioned into little cubicles, a few
of which held finished letterheads and envelopes and
business cards waiting to be picked up. On the counter,
a stack of newspapers. That was all. Nobody in sight,
but from behind the closed door a printing press was
making a hell of a racket.

I stepped to the counter and whacked a big handbell
with the palm of my hand. It made a loud noise, but it
didn't summon anybody; the printing press kept right
on clattering away. I decided to try shouting the thing
down. A couple of "Hellos!" at the top of my voice did
the trick. The press shut down almost immediately,
though it was a minute or so before I had company.

While I waited I picked up one of the newspapers,
casually, the way you do. Eight sheets, shopping-news
size. But it didn't look like a supermarket or neighborhood sheet; liberal or alternative press maybe. *Vortex.*
Some name for a newspaper. Across the top half was a
headline that read: SOUTH OF MARKET HOT SPOTS. Article
on trendy comedy clubs or nightclubs, I thought. I was
about to glance through it when my host put in an appearance.

He was big—pro-football big. Six and a half feet high, a solid 250, with linebacker shoulders and not much neck. Linebacker eyes too: wide and a little wild. Dirty-blond hair, full beard to match, both worn long and shaggy. Paul Bunyan in a printer's leather apron, with hands so heavily ink-stained at the moment that they looked tattooed.

I was more impressed with him than he was with me. Quick scan with a pair of bright blue eyes, just long enough to determine that he'd never seen me before. And: "Do for you, my man?" in a voice made for backwoods roaring.

"Brent DeKuiper?"

"Guilty."

I told him my name but not my profession. "I understand you're a friend of Gianna Fornessi's."

Nothing for a couple of beats. Then a slow half-smile, wry and not too pleasant. "Told you that?"

"Nobody in particular. Word gets around."

"Yeah. So?"

"Close friends?"

"Uh-uh," he said.

"How well do you know her?"

"Uh-uh. Question, man—your question. Uh-uh to that."

"Meaning it's none of my business?"

"Meaning not the way it's done."

"Not the way what's done?"

"You walkin in here like this. What you think I am?"

"I don't know," I said, "what are you?"

"Publisher, printer—period. Got it?"

"We don't seem to be connecting, Mr. DeKuiper. I'm trying to track down some information about Gianna Fornessi—"

"Sure," DeKuiper said, "information." He sneered at me. "You old guys hand me big pain."

"What's that supposed to mean?"

"Hundred names in friggin paper, box numbers, phone numbers, but no, got to come suckin around after some chick somebody told you about. Bullshit, man."

I shook my head. "You're not making sense."

"Think you are, pops? Get lost, I got work to do."

We were like two guys in alternate universes, on either side of a borderline between them, looking across at each other but unable to communicate. His habit of chopping up his sentences, leaving out articles and verbs and modifiers, only made it harder to try to understand him.

I said, "Suppose we back up and start over. How long have you known Gianna Fornessi?"

"Out," he said.

"What?"

"Out, man. Good-bye."

"Not just yet. How long have you known her? How long have you been dating her? Simple questions, simple answers. Okay?"

He opened his mouth, closed it again, and stared at me for three or four seconds—the way you'd stare at a funny-looking fish in a tank. Then he put his head back and cut loose with a booming noise that might have been an imitation of Paul Bunyan calling Babe the Blue

Ox, but was probably his version of laughter. "Dating her," he said when his primal howl was finished. "Grins, pops, that's what you are."

"Well?"

"Think she's high school kid? *I'm* one? Man oh man."

I didn't say anything. Just looked at him.

His good humor melted away and I got the nasty sneer again. "That what you like, pops? High school kids? Maybe even younger, huh?"

"I don't—"

"Real young. Wouldn't be one of those?"

"One of what?"

"Pedophiles."

"Pedo— Christ!"

"Hate pedophiles, man. Unnatural bastards."

"I'm not a pedophile!"

"Just dirty old man, huh?"

"Don't call me that either." Rage had crawled into my throat, dark and combustible—the kind of choking rage over which I'd had little enough control the past couple of years. "Just what the hell do you think I came here for?"

"Old lady won't give you any, lookin for one last fling, lookin for kinks, need young meat help you get it up . . . heard it all before, man."

"For Christ's sake I'm not after sex."

"Everybody's after sex."

"Information." I had to force the word past the constriction in my throat. "About Gianna Fornessi, goddamn you."

He didn't like being cursed; his wild eyes got wilder. "Out. Now."

"I'm not going anywhere until you—"

"You're goin," he said.

He came up and over the counter in one quick, fluid motion, like an actor performing a bar-vault in an old Western film. But there was nothing theatrical about the way he did it; it was the action of a genuine barroom brawler. He landed a couple of feet to my right, facing me, leaning my way with his shoulders squared. I held my ground without flinching.

"Don't put your hands on me," I said.

For a second I thought he was going to do it anyway. If he had we'd have been into it and it would have been ugly. As it was, we stood motionless, matching hot-eyed glares.

"Out," he said again. "Or get thrown out."

"You could try," I said.

"Five seconds, pops. Better not fuck with me. Like man says, I'm your worst nightmare."

I wanted to hit him. Badly. Muscles twitched in my shoulder, my arm; I could feel the strain all through my body. A year ago, even six months ago, the rage might have short-circuited my reason. Today, at least, common sense prevailed. Hitting DeKuiper would be stupid for a couple of reasons. This was his place of business; technically I was an interloper. He could have me tossed in jail for aggravated assault, or sue my ass and my assets down to a nubbin. Or—just as likely, given his bulk and agility—he could beat the hell out of me, put me in the hospital.

"Time's up," DeKuiper said.

I went. Struggling to make my legs move, struggling to hold myself in check, but I went. He waited until I had the door open and was passing through it before he said loudly, "Old fart," as a parting shot; if he hadn't waited, I might still have lost the struggle. I slammed the door behind me to cut off his voice, and immediately wished I hadn't. It was such a damn feeble gesture.

I kept on walking past my car and out to the Great Highway and along there for a ways before I turned around and came back: working off some of the rage in hard, fast strides. It wasn't until I was at the car again, about to open the driver's door, that I realized I was still carrying the copy of *Vortex.* It was all twisted and crumpled in my hand; I must have been working on it as if it were DeKuiper's throat.

I did not quite trust myself to drive yet, so I uncrumpled the paper and opened it out against the steering wheel. At first I wasn't even seeing it. Then my eyes focused on the newsprint—and my internal temperature began to climb all over again, only this time the anger was partly directed at myself. For being naive, for not telling DeKuiper who I was first thing, for letting him rag me the way he had without tumbling to his reasons. For being a horse's ass.

Vortex wasn't a liberal or alternative newspaper, any more than it was a shopping or neighborhood sheet. It was a sex tabloid—the borderline hard-core type you can buy from vending machines and news dealers in the Tenderloin, Polk Gulch, and the city's other sleazy neighborhoods.

On the front page below the fold was a photograph of a naked woman suggestively eating a chocolate-covered banana; on the inside pages were more photos, mostly of interracial couples in poses that left little to the imagination. The South of Market Hot Spots headline didn't herald an article on comedy clubs or nightclubs, for Christ's sake; it headed one on sex clubs and leather bars. And the classified ads . . .

FALL IN LOVE WITH MY BEST FRIEND. He's big, sensitive, responsive, all muscle, solid as a rock, likes to party all night long. And best of all, he's an adorable Nine!

I LOVE FAT WOMEN! The bigger the better. Good-looking male, funny, financially secure, sincere in his wish to meet very heavy women black or white, or women willing to grow. Big appetites a plus.

HINDU MONK seeks liberal atheist who likes snuggling, Kam-Shastra. Serious applicants only.

WHIP IT GOOD! Old man will train submissive middle-aged woman to be his love slave. Write DeSade, Box 829, this paper.

Old man—dirty old man. No wonder that was what DeKuiper had accused me of being. He thought I was a regular reader of his scummy tabloid; that I was asking about Gianna Fornessi because I wanted to have sex with her.

He was a pornographer. The quasi-legitimate variety, but a pornographer just the same.

And Pietro Lombardi's granddaughter, who kept company with DeKuiper? What was she?

Hundred names in friggin paper, box numbers, phone

*numbers, but no, got to come suckin around after some
chick somebody told you about.*

Dating her. Grins, pops, that's what you are.

Think she's high school kid? I'm one?

*Old lady won't give you any, lookin for one last fling,
lookin for kinks, need young meat help you get it up . . .
heard it all before, man.*

Yeah. Right.

Gianna Fornessi was a hooker, a high-priced call girl.
Full-time pro for the past eight months; probably a
part-timer before that, while she was working for Home
Draperies.

Ashley Hansen. Same damn thing.

Jack Bisconte. Bisconte was their pimp.

Chapter 7

WELL, ALL RIGHT. Now what?

Two options . . . make it three. One: Go straight to Pietro, tell him what I suspected, walk away clean. Two: Keep quiet until I could talk to Gianna personally and confirm my suspicions, and then lay it out for Pietro. Three: Don't tell him at all. George Ferry's complaint had been dropped; I had already fulfilled my commitment to the old man. Let him go on believing his granddaughter was the innocent apple of his eye, *la bellezza delle bellezze.*

I didn't like any of them.

He had a right to know the truth. But did I have a right to force it on him, either as a suspicion or as a confirmed fact? Maybe he'd find it out eventually, some other way—and maybe he wouldn't. I did not want to hurt him; I did not want her to hurt him. The whole damn thing was a no-win mess.

I drove downtown, taking the traffic slow and careful, and went up to the office. No Eberhardt; no sign that he'd been back since this morning. He's not going to walk, I thought again. How could I have scarred his pride that deeply? And yet, I kept remembering the hard look in his eyes, the conviction in his voice when he'd said he was dead serious. . . .

Among my telephone messages was one from Dominick Marra. Had I found out anything about this man Bisconte? Pietro still had *la miseria,* better call him up and let him know, hah?

Pushing it. And they'd keep right on pushing it until they got answers that satisfied them.

They were some pair. Dominick the aggressor, the spokesperson; Pietro the quiet brooder. Good men, good friends, watching out for each other now as they had for most of their lives. Not asking much, really, even if what they did ask was on the pushy side. All they wanted, when you got right down to it, was to live out what remained of their lives in peace, with their families and their traditional values intact.

So what happens? Pietro's favorite granddaughter turns out to be a *ficona,* a *puttana,* a *scopona*—the worst kind of disgrace to an Italian family.

He'll take it bad, I thought, if I tell him or he finds it out some other way. Personally, as if it's his fault. As if Gianna were laughing at him, spitting on his love and devotion, saying to him, *"Qual' rincoglionito di mio nonno!"*—what an old fool my grandfather is!

I can't tell him, I thought.

Damn it, I *can't.*

I ARRIVED AT Kerry's apartment at a quarter to seven that night, freshly showered and shaved and dressed in a new shirt and my best sport jacket. I wanted this meeting with Cybil to go well; I wanted to make just the right impression. For her sake, as well as for Kerry's and my own. My involvement with Pietro Lombardi and his family problems had made me all too aware of what it was like to be elderly, and hurting, and alone.

I rang Kerry's bell from downstairs in the foyer, rather than letting myself into the building with my key. She buzzed me in right away, and when I got upstairs she was waiting with the door open. I kissed her before I went in—hard. And held her for a few seconds after I was inside. It had been that kind of day.

"You smell nice," she said. "Is that the cologne I gave you for Christmas?"

"Yup."

She stood off from me, looked me over. "Look nice, too, you big hunk."

"Big hunk of what?"

She laughed. Good. Now if I could just get a smile out of Cybil.

"I figured I'd better get cleaned up," I said, "try to make a good impression. Where's Cybil?"

"In the living room. Waiting for you."

"Already?"

"Since six-thirty. You'd better go in."

"Aren't you coming?"

"She wants to see you alone."

"Oh boy."

"Go on. It'll be okay."

I headed down the hall to the living room. Kerry went the other way, into the kitchen, where she would no doubt establish a listening post. She has a bundle of good qualities, my lady, and only a few suspect ones. Nosiness is among the latter, not that I was in any position to be judgmental on that score.

Cybil was sitting on the big sofa facing the fireplace. Not doing anything, just sitting there. She must have heard me coming, but she didn't turn her head. I took a deep breath, let it out silently, and walked around in front of her.

At first glance she appeared frail, shrunken, as if I were seeing her through the wrong end of a not-very-powerful telescope—the same impression I'd had the last time I had seen her, the week before Christmas, when Kerry and I picked her up after her flight from L.A. But if she wasn't the same healthy, strong woman I'd first met several years ago, neither was she the withered, haunted caricature I had driven here from the airport. Some of her former beauty seemed to have been restored, the once-striking resemblance to Kerry. Same long, willowy body type; same generous mouth; same thick-textured hair, though hers was now mostly gray. Only the eyes were completely different. Kerry's were green, and sometimes hazel, and sometimes almost brown—chameleon eyes that seemed to change color in different shadings of light. Cybil's were big and tawny, alert again now, penetrating—her best feature, one that had led a fellow pulp writer and unrequited lover named Russell Dancer to nickname her Sweeteyes.

Some of her former serenity and self-possession had been restored too. Attributes nurtured by growing up poor and working hard for everything she'd attained; that had allowed her to take on the man's world of pulp fiction in the late thirties and throughout the forties, and to conquer it by writing better, tougher detective stories (the Max Ruffe private-eye series, as by Samuel Leatherman) than 95 percent of her male colleagues; that had kept her from ever having to lean on anyone, including her husband, until Ivan's fatal heart attack last October had shattered her defenses.

"Hello, Cybil," I said. "You're looking well."

"So are you. You've lost weight."

I'd lost it long before last Christmas, but she had not been in any shape to internalize the fact, if she'd even noticed it. I said, "Forty pounds, give or take."

"Diet? Exercise?"

"Both."

"Don't put it back on."

"I won't."

"Sit down," she said.

There may have been some nervous stiffness in my tone, but there was none in hers. Her voice was strong, with a little of the old imperiousness. She had no smile for me, but that did not have to mean anything. Her gaze was direct, without animosity. Almost friendly, in fact.

I sat on one of the chairs between the sofa and fireplace, turning it so that I could face her. She watched me without speaking. Outside, I could hear the wind yammering, the way it does most of the time up here on the Heights. The drapes were closed; otherwise I could have seen gray evening shadows beginning to settle over the cityscape below.

I was trying to find something to do with my big, awkward hands when Cybil said, "I asked to see you because I owe you an apology."

"Oh?"

"I've treated you badly since I've been here. It wasn't right to try to keep you and Kerry apart—it wasn't fair."

"No," I said, "it wasn't."

She nodded; an honest response was what she'd wanted from me. "I haven't been myself since Ivan passed away. These past few months . . . I look back at them and they're not quite real, as if someone else lived them in my place. You understand, I think."

"I do, yes."

"Ivan and I . . . well, when you live with someone for so many years, you try to ignore his faults and his prejudices. He had plenty of both, God knows."

I didn't say anything to that.

"But sometimes they affect you just the same, like a seed that sprouts in a place you can't see. Intolerance was Ivan's worst fault, the one I hated most. Yet I've been guilty of the same thing, the same intolerant attitude toward you that he had."

"I understand that too," I said. "I'm sure he must have railed against me pretty strongly."

"Oh yes. He thought you weren't good enough for Kerry."

"No man would have been good enough for his daughter."

"I suppose that's true. He idolized her."

"So do I. What he couldn't accept was the competition."

"He hated you," she said. "Did you hate him?"

"No." Small white lie; there had been times when I'd hated him very much. But the rest of what I said was the truth: "I never wished him ill, Cybil. He was Kerry's father; I could never wish ill on any man who helped bring her into the world."

The words moved her; her tawny eyes glistened. "You love her deeply—I've known that from the first. I don't know how I could have forgotten it."

I was silent.

"She loves you just as deeply," Cybil said.

"I hope she does."

"Oh, she does." She sighed, shook her head. "I've been a foolish old woman," she said.

"No you haven't. You've been grieving, that's all."

Pretty soon she said, "I know you've asked Kerry to marry you."

"Several times."

"Recently?"

"The last time was about a year ago."

"Why won't she say yes?"

"Marriage has become an evil concept to her. Confining, restricting. She believes she can make and keep a commitment without legal encumbrances. Fundamentally, I agree with her. But I'm old-fashioned enough to want the ceremony as well as the commitment."

"God knows she has reason to feel as she does," Cybil said, "after the mistake of marrying that Ray Dunston person. But not all husbands are like him."

"That's what I tried telling her."

"Two people in love should live together, be together. They should be married."

"I tried telling her that too."

Kerry, I thought, I hope you're getting an earful out there in the kitchen.

"She's a stubborn woman sometimes," Cybil said. Small, wry smile. "Just like her mother."

"Exactly like her mother. I wouldn't have it any other way."

We looked at each other—and we were allies. Just like that. Enemies for more than six months, at least as far as she was concerned; and now, in the space of ten minutes, we were a united front against the Kerry Wade Antimatrimonial League. Go figure.

Abruptly Cybil called, "Kerry. Come in here, dear."

Kerry was there in five seconds, looking half relieved and half determined. "You're not going to change my mind," she said, "either of you."

"About what, dear?"

"About marriage. I'm not getting married again."

Imperturbably Cybil said to me, "My daughter, you know, is an eavesdropper," and I realized that she'd been aware all along that Kerry was listening in. This was followed by a second realization: She'd deliberately steered our conversation around to the marriage issue. Well, well. The old Cybil, all right. The old spirit.

Kerry said, "I wasn't eavesdropping. The walls in this apartment aren't thick, and you weren't exactly whispering."

"You were eavesdropping," Cybil said.

Kerry looked at me for support. I didn't give her any. Didn't say anything, just smiled at her—blandly.

"I think I'd like a cup of decaf," Cybil said, and then asked me, "Will you join me?"

"A pleasure," I said.

Muttering to herself, Kerry went back into the kitchen. As soon as she was out of sight, Cybil winked at me. Damned if she didn't.

NOT LONG AFTER we had our coffee, Cybil said she was feeling tired and excused herself and retired to her bedroom. Kerry and I sat in companionable silence. It was a comfortable room, if a little too feminine for my taste—a good, familiar place where you could sit with someone you loved and do nothing and be perfectly content. I had missed coming here to be with Kerry. Missed it even more than I'd realized.

At length she said, "Well, I'm glad *that's* over."

"It wasn't so bad. In fact, I enjoyed it. Cybil seemed almost her old self again."

"I'm glad you think so."

"Don't you?"

"Well, she's a lot better than she was. Except that she's done a complete about-face where you're concerned and I can't quite figure out why."

"Gremlins," I said.

She ignored that. "All that marriage nonsense . . . it isn't the first time she's brought it up with me, you know. In the past few days."

"No?"

"No."

"Why didn't you tell me?"

"Why do you think. I do not want to get married again."

"Have I asked recently?"

"No, but that doesn't mean you won't."

I sat enjoying the quiet.

"Well?" she said. "Are you going to?"

"Going to what?"

"Propose to me again."

"Not if you don't want me to."

"I *don't* want you to."

"Then I won't."

"No argument?"

"Nope. I respect your feelings."

"Well, good. So you've given up on the marriage issue?"

"Sure. But I don't think Cybil has."

"What does that mean?"

"It means I don't think Cybil has."

"She doesn't have any influence on me."

"I didn't say she had."

"So don't count on her changing my mind—"

"I'm not."

"—because it's not going to happen."

"All right," I said.

The good quiet for about a minute. Then Kerry said, "Coconspirators. That's how the two of you acted. My God, she didn't want you anywhere near her or me for six months and now she's conspiring with you to get me back to the altar."

"Conspiring?" I said. "You sound paranoid."

"Maybe I have a reason to be paranoid."

"I don't think you do."

"No?"

"No."

"Mm," she said.

Neither of us had anything more to contribute. We sat close together, listening to the night. I wasn't thinking about Cybil then, or about marriage; I was thinking what a nice room this was, what a good place to spend time with the woman I loved. I felt, sitting there, as I had the day I'd come back from Deer Run.

I felt that I was home again.

Chapter **8**

CRISES—BIG ONES, little ones—are the weeds of human existence. You do battle with one kind or another all your life, uproot a stubborn variety only to find a new one just as stubborn, and no matter how diligent a gardener you are, the best you can hope for is to keep them down to a manageable level. The last root-pieces of the Cybil crisis had been dug up, the ground there finally smoothed out. So of course the Eberhardt weed was now growing fast and sprouting thorns.

Surprisingly, he was at his desk when I got to the office Wednesday morning. The big converted loft was already blue with carcinogens from his lousy pipe tobacco. He was thumping on his computer terminal with two hard, blunt fingers; he didn't say hello, didn't even look up. I thought that if he bit down any harder on the stem of his stubby briar, he would wind up picking hard plastic slivers out of his molars.

He hadn't made any coffee, which was just as well; he made worse coffee than I did. I went and put up a pot. When I was done I said, "Early bird this morning," taking care to keep my tone light and cheerful.

Nothing at first. Then, "Lot of work to do." His tone was about as light and cheerful as a morgue attendant's.

"You free for lunch?"

Another pause. "Why?"

"I thought maybe we could have a burger and a beer."

"Why?"

"Because we haven't done that in a while."

No response.

"All right," I said. "So we can talk."

"We got nothing to talk about."

"Does that mean you've made up your mind?"

"About what?"

"Not to bust us up," I said.

Silence.

"Or is it the other way around?"

Silence.

I said evenly, "I'll ask once more. How about lunch?"

"I got a lunch," he said.

"Drinks after we close up, then."

"I'm meeting Bobbie Jean."

"Lunch tomorrow."

"Busy then too."

"Okay. Okay. You name it, whenever you're free."

"Quit bugging me, will you? I told you I got work to do—didn't I just tell you that?" He began to bang the computer keyboard again, violently this time.

I started some work of my own, but I couldn't concentrate. The atmosphere in there was oppressive again: Eberhardt's attitude was as foul as his frigging tobacco. After ten minutes I got up, got ready to leave.

At the door I said, "I'll be back sometime this afternoon, if anybody wants me."

He didn't look up, didn't speak.

"Put my answering machine on when you go. Or you want me to do it now, so you don't have to deal with my calls?"

"It's your machine," he said. "I'm busy."

Weeds. High, getting higher, and full of thorns.

PIETRO LOMBARDI? Or another try at an audience with his granddaughter?

I debated the issue with myself as I got my car out of the parking garage down the block. The first thing I decided was that I could not face Pietro cold on this cold morning, even to tell him a benign lie of omission. The mood I was in, I would probably make a slip of some kind, or just blurt out my suspicions about Gianna; there was about as much tact in me right now as there was in an elephant. Talking to him would have to wait until later in the day. Or until tomorrow.

As for Gianna, I didn't have to talk to her at all. I was pretty sure she was selling her body, and to confirm it I could try Bisconte again, or get in touch with a couple of street people I knew who could find out anything about anybody on the shady side, given enough time and the right amount of grease.

The sticking point was that neither of those approaches would quite satisfy my professional curiosity about Gianna Fornessi. What kind of person was she? What kind of young woman, with a goombah like Pietro and a rock-ribbed, traditional Italian family upbringing, turns to hooking to make her living? I wanted to know that before I talked to Pietro; it might make lying to him a little easier. And to know it I had to know her at least a little—I had to meet her face-to-face, ask her some hard questions.

GIANNA'S WHITE NISSAN was still sitting in the same spot along the retaining wall opposite her building. The wind had been working hard up here; bits and pieces of litter were shaped around its tires, as if the elements were using it to build some kind of nest. Not that the unmoved Nissan had to mean she was still missing. If she'd returned from her long weekend sometime yesterday or last night, she could have been dropped off here and elected not to go out again.

Double-parked directly in front of 250 was an appliance store delivery truck, its rear doors open and its tailgate lowered to the pavement. The entrance door to the building also stood wide open. I parked a couple of spaces ahead of the Nissan this time, let the wind blow me over past the truck.

Nobody was in the vestibule or lobby, but the murmur of voices filtered down from the third floor. One of them, I thought, belonged to George Ferry. Not working today? Well, maybe he just hadn't left yet; it was not quite ten, still early, and he was his own boss.

If I'd been a burglar I would have rubbed my hands together in glee at the wide open entrance and empty lobby: Welcome, prowlers, one and all. As it was, I walked in as if I belonged there and climbed the inside staircase.

When I swung into the second floor hallway I came face-to-face with Jack Bisconte.

He was hurrying toward me from the direction of apartment four, something small and red and rectangular clutched in the fingers of his left hand. He broke stride when he saw me; and then recognition made him do a jerky double take and he came to a halt. I stopped, too, with maybe fifteen feet separating us. That was close enough, and the hallway was well-lighted enough, for me to get a good look at his face. It was pinched, sweat-slicked, the eyes wide and shiny—the face of a man on the cutting edge of panic.

Frozen time, maybe five seconds of it, while we stood confronting each other. There was nobody else in the hall; no audible sounds on this floor except for the quick rasp of Bisconte's breathing. We both moved at the same time—Bisconte in the same jerky fashion of his double take, shoving the red object into the pocket of his safari jacket as he came forward. Then, when we had closed the gap between us by half, we both stopped again as if on cue. It might have been a mildly amusing little pantomime, if you'd been a disinterested observer. It wasn't amusing to me. Or to Bisconte, from the look of him.

I said, "Fancy meeting you here. I thought you didn't know Gianna Fornessi or Ashley Hansen."

"Get out of my way."

"What's your hurry?"

"Get out of my way. I mean it." The edge of panic had cut into his voice; it was thick, liquidy, as if his vocal chords were bleeding.

"What did you put in your pocket, the red thing?"

He said, "Christ!" and tried to lunge past me.

I blocked his way, getting my hands up between us to push him back. His eyes went wild; he made a noise in his throat and swung at me. It was a clumsy shot and I ducked away from it without much effort, his knuckles just grazing my neck. But then he got his shoulder down, into my chest before I could sidestep, and his pumping legs drove me hard into the wall.

The force of the collision hammered the breath out of me, made me see double; I might have gone down if his body hadn't been pinning mine. He hit me in the rib cage, weakly, then tried to throw me aside, but I had hold of the rough material of his jacket and he couldn't yank loose. He was almost sobbing now, more with fear than exertion, the panic raking him.

We hung there against the wall, him sobbing, me trying to get my breath back—bodies jammed together, legs and feet twined and scrabbling like a couple of drunks performing a lunatic jitterbug. Somewhere people were yelling; I could hear that over the blood-pound in my ears. Bisconte got one arm loose, short-punched me on the ear without doing any damage. I hit him in the belly with the same result. We clinched again, danced some more. But not for long.

The son of a bitch got a leg back far enough to kick me, hard, on the left shinbone. I yelled and relaxed my grip enough for him to tear loose, and this time I did go down. He kicked out again, at my head; didn't connect because I was already rolling away. I fetched up tight against the curve of the stair banister and by the time I got myself twisted back around, Bisconte was on the stairs, running.

I used the banister to get on my feet, almost collapsed again when I put weight on the leg he'd kicked. Hobbling, wiping pain-wet out of my eyes, I chased after him.

People were on the staircase above me, coming down from the third floor; the one in the lead was Ferry. He called something that I didn't listen to as I started to descend. Bisconte, damn him, had already crossed the lobby and was charging out through the open front doors.

Hop, hop, hop down the stairs like a contestant in a one-legged race, clinging to the railing for support. When I reached the lobby, some of the sting had gone out of my shinbone and I could put more weight on the leg. But I still couldn't move very fast, because my breathing wasn't right.

Out into the vestibule, with a hobble-stagger gait, looking for him. He was across the street and down a ways, fumbling with a set of keys at the driver's door of a new silver Mercedes. But he was too wrought up to get the right key into the lock, and when he saw me pounding across the street in his direction, the panic goosed him and he ran again. Around behind the Mercedes, onto the sidewalk. And up and over the concrete retaining wall. And gone.

I heard him go sliding or tumbling through the undergrowth below. I lurched up to the wall, leaned over it. The slope down there was steep, covered with trees and brush, strewn with the leavings of semihumans who had

used it for a dumping ground. Bisconte was on his but-
tocks, digging hands and heels into the ground to slow
his momentum. For a few seconds I thought he was
going to turn into a one-man avalanche and plummet
over the edge, where the slope ended in a sheer bluff
face. But he managed to catch hold of one of the tree
trunks and swing himself away from the precipice, then
crawled in among a tangle of bushes where I couldn't
see him anymore. I could hear him—and then I
couldn't. He'd found purchase, I thought, and was easing himself down to where the back side of another
apartment building leaned in against the cliff.

There was no way I was going down there after him. I
turned from the wall, bent to massage my shin; most of
the sharp hurt was gone now, in its place a thin, pulsing
sting. I was able to walk more or less normally to where
the Mercedes was parked. And to breathe more or less
normally, too, thanks to the cold wind.

The Mercedes had a vanity plate, the kind that makes
you wonder why somebody would pay $25 extra to the
DMV to put it on his car: BISFLWR. If the car had had
an external hood release I would have popped it and
disabled the engine; but it didn't, and all four doors
were locked. All right. Chances were, Bisconte wouldn't
risk coming back here soon—and even if he did run the
risk, it would take him a good long while to work his
way up the hill from below.

I recrossed the street to 250. Four people were clustered in the vestibule, staring at me—Ferry and a couple of uniformed deliverymen and a fat woman in her
forties with her hair up in curlers. Ferry said as I came

up the steps, "What happened, what's going on?" I didn't answer him. There was a bad feeling in me now; or maybe it had been there from the moment I'd first seen the look on Bisconte's face upstairs. I pushed past the four people—none of them tried to stop me—and went on up to the second floor.

Nobody answered the bell at apartment four. I tried the door, and the knob turned freely, and I walked in and shut it again and locked it behind me.

She was lying on the floor in the living room, sprawled and bent on her back near a heavy wood-and-glass coffee table, peach-colored dressing gown hiked up over her thighs. Her head was twisted at an off angle, blood and a deep triangular puncture wound on the left temple. The blood was still wet and clotting. She hadn't been dead very long at all.

In the sunlight that spilled in through the undraped front windows, the blood had a kind of shimmery radiance. So did her hair—her long platinum-blond hair.

Good-bye, Ashley Hansen.

Chapter 9

I CALLED THE Hall of Justice and talked to a Homicide inspector I knew slightly named Harry Craddock. I told him what I'd found, and about my little skirmish with Bisconte, and said that yes, I would wait right here and no, I wouldn't touch anything. He didn't tell me not to prowl through the apartment and I didn't say that I wouldn't.

While I was talking I took a good look at the living room. Expensively furnished in a modern southwestern style—white-wood tables, chairs and a sofa with muted blue and salmon-colored fabrics, set against a white background. But it hadn't been done by a decorator, or by anyone with much taste. None of the four wall decorations—two darkish paintings, an Indian-style rug thing, some kind of ceremonial mask—complemented one another; the big rococo mirror over the fireplace was both ugly and out of place; there were too many overstuffed pillows strewn around. Stains and scuff marks marred the hardwood floor and two of the walls. The place was none too clean, either. And the dead woman in the middle of it all gave it a tawdry, pathetic aspect.

Poor Ashley Hansen. All that quick cash for selling her body, and what had it bought her? Death at twenty-two or twenty-three in a room that wasn't much larger or fancier, when you got right down to it, than a Tenderloin crib.

Somebody had started banging on the door. Ferry, probably. I went the other way, into one of the bedrooms.

Ashley Hansen's: There was a photograph of her prominently displayed on the dresser, and several more rococo mirrors to give her a live image of herself. A narcissist, among other things. The room smelled of expensive perfume and shower damp, but it wasn't any cleaner than the living room. Clothing and lingerie littered it; there was a dustball peeking out from under a corner of the bed. The fact that it had been searched, with what apparently had been frantic haste, added to its unkempt appearance.

Drawers in the dresser were pulled out, one lay upended on the floor in front of it; the nightstand drawers were open too. Things had been tumbled out of the closet. And on the unmade bed, tipped on its side with most of its contents spilled out, was a fancy beaded leather purse.

I used the backs of my two index fingers to stir around among the spilled items and the stuff still inside. Everything you'd expect to find in a woman's purse. And one thing that should have been there but wasn't— a personal address book. The kind, say, that was small and red and rectangular, like the object Bisconte had shoved into his pocket.

On one nightstand was a powder-blue combination telephone and answering machine. With a knuckle I switched the machine on, pushed the PLAY button. The last recorded message was still on the tape, which meant that Bisconte had overlooked this angle in his panicked hunt through the apartment. If he'd thought of the answering machine, he'd sure as hell have taken the time to erase the tape.

Man's voice, friendly, cheerful, but with a smarmy edge to it: "Hi, babycakes. Dave here, Big Dave from Colma. Like to see you again Thursday night. Give you a ride in one of my new demos, then give you a *real* ride, ha ha. Just come on down to the lot if you're available, usual time. I'm feeling spry, maybe we'll party all night. See you then."

Not this Thursday, babycakes, I thought. Not any Thursday with Ashley ever again.

I reset the machine, went across the hall into Gianna Fornessi's bedroom. The decor in there was different from the rest of the apartment: frilly, done mostly in pink brocade and pink satin and white lace, like a little girl's room. Full of cute little porcelain knickknacks, even a big stuffed koala bear propped against the bed's headboard. Gianna was tidier than Ashley had been; the bed was made, all her soiled clothing picked up, all the cosmetics in order on her vanity table. Even so, there was disorder in the room now: it had been searched in the same rough, hurried fashion.

A telephone and a Panasonic answering machine sat

on one of her nightstands; the number on the phone dial was not the same as her roommate's. The message light on the machine was lit; Bisconte had missed that too. I worked the REWIND button—three messages, judging from the amount of tape that reversed—and then hit the PLAY button.

First message. Soft, older voice: "This is Everett, from Fresno. Remember me? I'll be in the city again Friday, checking into the usual place around six. If you're free, pencil me in. I'll call again later to confirm."

Second message. Younger, angry voice: "Gianna . . . Bud. What the hell's the idea standing me up this afternoon? Don't I pay you enough? Don't I always treat *you* right? You want any more of my business, you better have a good excuse."

Third message. This voice was so shrilly nervous it cracked like sheet ice on a couple of syllables: "Gianna, my name is Tom . . . Tom from Fairfax. Dick from San Rafael gave me your name and number. He said . . . well, he said you wouldn't mind meeting somebody new. You can give him a call, he'll tell you I'm okay. I run my own business and I've got plenty of money and I . . . I can be generous. Maybe you'd be willing to come here some night next week, to my home? Paul's told me a lot about you and I . . . well, I'd really like to get together. Okay? Best night for me would be Friday . . . next Friday, if you can make it. My number is 555-2897, I'm home most evenings after six, it's okay to call anytime because I live alone. Thanks. I look forward to hearing from you and meeting you, Gianna."

Jesus.

My teeth were set so tightly now I could feel ridges of pain along my jawline. I reset the machine, moved around to where a spindly writing desk stood against one wall. All the drawers had been yanked open; papers littered the top, the floor underneath. But Bisconte in his frenzy had overlooked something here, too, something that caught my eye almost immediately: one of those loose-leaf calendars in a little molded plastic tray, with each date on an individual sheet that you can pluck out and throw away. The top sheet had nothing written on it, evidently the reason Bisconte had passed over it; but the date was last Thursday's, and when I lifted that sheet to reveal Friday's date, I found inked words in a childish, feminine hand.

The Old Cocksman!

Saturday's sheet had the same words on it. With two exclamation points and curlicue underlining, as if the phrase—or maybe the individual it referred to—was some kind of private joke. Sunday's sheet was blank. Monday's bore the notation: *Bud, Skygate Motel, 4:00.*

The Old Cocksman. Her weekend date, probably; reference to his sexual prowess, or lack of it. Fine, dandy, and wouldn't her goombah be delighted by such charming wit? But she'd written the phrase just twice, which indicated that it was a two-day shack job and she'd expected to be home by Monday. Only she hadn't come home on Monday; and she'd missed her afternoon date with Bud at the Skygate Motel. Nor had she shown up yesterday or yet today, so far as I knew. Why not?

The little-girl room, with its taint of big-girl corruption, was wearing badly on me. I took myself out of there, back into the living room. Faint acrid odor in the air . . . or was there? I thought I smelled it, but when I stopped and stood sniffing, all I could smell was the drifting scent of Ashley Hansen's perfume. Imagination. Phantom whiff of brimstone . . .

The door-knocking had started up again. Bang, bang, bang. And now I heard Ferry's voice, rising querulously. "Hey! Hey in there! What's going on?"

I walked over there, threw the bolt lock, yanked the door open. "Quit making so much noise."

Ferry blinked and backed off a step; he didn't know whether to be afraid of me or not. Behind and to one side of him, the two deliverymen and the fat woman looked on with hungry eyes. They would have liked seeing what lay inside. Blood attracts some people, the gawkers, the insensitive ones, the same way it attracts flies.

"What's happened?" Ferry asked me.

"Come in and see for yourself. Just you."

I opened up a little wider and he came in past me, showing reluctance. I shut and locked the door again behind him. Before I turned he said, "Oh, my God," in a sickened voice. He was staring at the body on the floor, one hand pressed up under his breastbone.

I moved around in front of him. "Not pretty anymore, is she."

". . . Dead?"

"Very."

"Gianna . . . is she all right?"

"You tell me."

"She's not here?"

"Not since Friday, the way it looks."

Headshake. "What happened to Ashley?"

"What do you think happened?"

"Accident . . . an accident?"

"I wouldn't want to bet on it."

"Somebody . . . did that to her? Who?"

"You know who, Ferry. You saw me chase him out of here."

"I . . . don't know that man. I never saw him before."

"The hell you never saw him. He's the one put those cuts and bruises on your face."

"No," Ferry said, "that's not true." He looked and sounded even sicker now. "I told you how that happened—"

"You told me lies. Bisconte roughed you up so that you'd drop your complaint against Gianna. He did it because she and Ashley are call girls and he's their pimp and he didn't want the cops digging into her background and finding out the truth."

Ferry leaned unsteadily against the wall, facing away from what was left of the Hansen woman. The lick-blink-twitch reaction had set in again. He didn't speak.

"Nice quiet little operation they had," I said, "until you got wind of it. That's how it was, wasn't it? You found out and you wanted some of what Gianna's been selling."

More twitchy silence. Then, "It wasn't like that, not at first. I loved her . . . thought I loved her."

"Sure you did."

"I *did.*" Lick. Blink. "But she wouldn't have anything to do with me."

"So then you offered to pay her."

". . . Yes. Whatever she charged."

"Only you wanted kinky sex and she wouldn't play."

"No! I never asked for anything except a night with her . . . one night. She pretended to be insulted; she denied that she'd been selling herself to men. She . . . she said she'd never go to bed with a man as . . . ugly . . ." He moved against the wall—a writhing movement, as if he were in pain.

I said, "And that was when you decided to get even with her."

"I wanted to hurt her, the way she'd hurt me. It was stupid, I know that, but I wasn't thinking clearly. I just wanted to hurt her . . ."

"Well, you succeeded. But the one you really hurt is Ashley over there. If it hadn't been for you, she'd still be alive."

He started to say something to that, but the words were lost in the sudden summons of the doorbell.

"That'll be the police," I said.

"The police?" Twitch. Blink. "But . . . I thought you were—"

"I know you did. I never told you I was, did I?"

I left him holding up the wall and went to buzz them in.

I SPENT TWO HOURS in the company of the law, alternately answering questions and waiting around. I told Inspector Craddock—a heavyset, intense black man who went about his job with a kind of missionary zeal—who I was working for and how I happened to be there. I told him how I'd come to realize that Gianna Fornessi and Ashley Hansen were call girls, and how George Ferry and Jack Bisconte figured into it. I told him about my encounter with Bisconte in the hallway, about the small red rectangular object Bisconte had shoved into his pocket—the probable address book with the names and numbers of some of Hansen's johns. There was nothing that I didn't tell him; Harry Craddock was not a cop you withheld information from, not if you wanted to maintain an amicable relationship with him.

He said, "So Bisconte and the Hansen woman had some kind of hassle, he shoved her or smacked her one, she fell and hit her head on that table over there. Second-degree homicide. That how it looks to you?"

"That's how it looks."

"Complications?"

"Gianna Fornessi, maybe."

"You think Bisconte did something to her too?"

"I don't know. But she does seem to be missing."

"*Seem*. She could be off with a john."

"I know it. But five days is a long time."

"Some guys got big sexual appetites," Craddock said. He grinned around one of the plastic-mouthpiece cigarillos he favored. "I used to have one myself. Wore my wife out when I was a young stud."

"I'll bet you did."

"Fact is," he said, "nobody's filed a missing persons

report on the Fornessi girl. I had one of the men call in to check."

"She's not close to her family anymore; she couldn't afford to be, in her profession. They don't know she's been away so long."

"Not close to her grandfather?"

"Especially not him."

"She told him about Ferry's robbery complaint."

"He called her up to see how she was doing," I said, "because he hadn't heard from her in a while. That was right after Inspector Cullen talked to her. She was upset and she let it slip; she wouldn't have told him otherwise."

"Uh-huh."

"And Hansen wouldn't file a missing persons report, even if she had any personal feelings for Gianna. Bisconte would see to that."

"Could also be," Craddock said, "Hansen knew all along where Gianna went last Friday and with whom and wasn't worried. Maybe the only one who's worried is you."

"Ask Bisconte when you find him. Ask him who 'the Old Cocksman' is."

"Oh, I will. I'm curious, too, being an old cocksman myself. Anything else? Theories, suggestions?"

"Just a favor. A small one."

"Department owes you a favor, does it? I know I don't."

"It's not like that, Inspector."

"Your client, right? The Fornessi girl's family?"

"Yes."

"Keep the prostitution angle out of the media. That it?"

"That's it," I said. "The Lombardis and the Fornessis are good people, respectable—old-fashioned Italian families. They don't have any idea what she's into and it'll hurt like hell if they find out."

"Uh-huh."

"Besides, it's minor-league stuff. A second-degree homicide, probably—you said that yourself."

"Yeah. Pimps and whores, one killing the other. Happens all the time in the city."

"That won't stop the media from making a thing out of it. Sex sells papers and attracts viewers, especially when the victim is a pretty young blonde. Might even make it harder for you to find Bisconte."

"Might," he conceded.

"So what do you say?"

Craddock thought it over, chewing on the mouthpiece of his cigarillo. "Nobody else in the building knows about the hooking?"

"I doubt it, but you can ask Ferry. He knows. And he won't want it to get out any more than I do."

"All right. I don't see why it can't be handled that way, at least until we find Bisconte. But if he makes more trouble, resists arrest, say, there might not be any way to keep it under wraps."

"As long as possible, that's all I'm asking."

Now that the coroner's assistant had finished his preliminary examination, a pair of white-coated morgue attendants had come into the flat and were loading the dead woman's remains into a body bag. Craddock glanced over there, shook his head. "Pimps and whores," he said again.

Sure. Pimps and whores. One killing the other, happens all the time in the city. Old, old story, as old as sin. Simple. Cut and dried.

Maybe it was. It looked like it was. So why wasn't I satisfied too?

Chapter **10**

SPIAGGIA'S WAS A VENERABLE, hole-in-the-wall North Beach saloon on Vallejo off Broadway. Not just another saloon, though; not even one strictly for the *compaesani*. A saloon in the old tradition, the kind of private club for working-class men that was once referred to as a drinking parlor or a public resort. It had even been a speakeasy during Prohibition, or so legend had it.

Narrow, dark, comfortingly womblike. Battered hardwood tables and chairs, a few settees and armchairs with puffy, dust-laden upholstery, which looked as though they had come out of somebody's grandfather's attic. Thick musty smell composed of tap drippings and tobacco and dust and dry rot and body odor and all manner of old things, built up over three quarters of a century until it was as tangible a part of the place as the walls and fixtures. Placard on the back bar: DON'T ASK FOR CREDIT. Another, crusty with age: MIND YOUR MANNERS OR THEY'LL BE MINDED FOR YOU. Rack of communal clay and corncob pipes, left over from the days when the purchase of a pint of draft entitled you to a free smoke.

There weren't many customers in attendance when I walked in a few minutes past two. Too early for all but the dedicated drinkers and the lonely ones. It was so dark in there that I had to wait several seconds for my eyes to adjust before I could make out the faces at the bar and tables. Not more than half looked Italian; there were two Nordic types, a WASP, an African-American, and an elderly Chinese. Spiaggia's was nothing if not democratic. Most of the patrons were past fifty and all were male.

Three weekend bocce players were having a game of pedro at a rear table, one of them Dominick Marra. There was no sign of Pietro Lombardi. As soon as I was sure that Pietro was absent I felt relief, a subtle easing of tension. I wasn't here to face him if it could be avoided; I was here to talk to Dominick. Hell, I was here to take the coward's way out.

When Dominick saw me he said something to his companions, got to his feet, hitched up his baggy trousers, and reached out to grasp my arm. "Hey," he said, "detective. Where you been, hah? We don't hear from you."

"Working," I said.

"You want Pietro? He's not here."

"No. It's you I want to talk to. One of your neighbors said I'd find you here."

"Sure, I'm here, where else I got to go at my age?" He said this with a certain irony, but without bitterness. "What you want to talk about?"

"In private, Dominick, okay?"

Before we went to an empty table farther back, Dominick insisted on buying drinks—beer for me, a glass of Lambrusco for him. The beer tasted good, a lot better than the words I had to say. And it went down much easier than the words came out.

Dominick listened without interruption, without expression. When I was done he stared at me silently, hard-eyed, intense. Then he said, "No." Just the one word, half disbelief and half denial.

"It's true, Dominick."

"Pietro's Gianna—a *puttana?* Gianna?"

"For at least eight months. Probably longer."

The long stare. Then, "You got proof, hah?"

"I saw proof, I listened to proof."

"You tell me what."

I told him. Gianna's lie about her employment, my talk with Brent DeKuiper, *Vortex,* the things I'd heard on Gianna's answering machine, the truth behind Ferry's theft charges. Not glossing over any of it—giving it to him straight.

"Ah, *Dio,*" he said, "ah, *Dio.*"

"I'm sorry, Dominick."

"This Bisconte . . . he's do this to Gianna?"

"She works for him, yes."

"Gianna, her roommate, how many others?"

"I don't know. Maybe just the two of them."

"Somebody, he should kill Bisconte. Man like that . . . pah!"

"He'll go to prison. The law will see to that."

"Prison." Dominick made a spitting mouth; an angry gesture with an upraised fist. *"Dead he should be."*

I didn't agree with that. But I didn't say so.

In the new silence I was aware of the bar sounds: men shifting on cracked leather and dusty brocade, ice clicking in glasses, bottles thumping against wood, the low murmur of voices. No TV noise; there was a set in one corner of the back bar, but it would mostly remain dark. No jukebox or video games or pinball machines—not even a pool table. If you craved distractions you went somewhere other than Spiaggia's.

Dominick had been brooding into his wine. Now his shoulders jerked and he sat up straight, as if a sudden thought had struck him. "Pietro," he said. "You don't tell Pietro?"

"No."

"You gonna tell him?"

"No."

"It's hurt him bad," Dominick said mournfully. "He's love Gianna like nobody else."

"So you won't tell him either?"

"Me?" The long stare again. "That's why you come to me? You want I should tell this terrible thing to Pietro?"

"No. That's your decision. But somebody close to him has to know the whole truth, and you're his best friend, blood of his blood. If he ever has to find out, better from you than a stranger."

"I don't hurt Pietro that way. Never."

I nodded. "Let's hope nobody ever hurts him that way."

Pretty soon he said darkly, "Ah, *cacchio!* I got to tell him. Before he's hear it on TV, read it in the newspapers. Pietro, Gianna's mama . . . everybody, he's gonna know."

"It won't be on TV or in the papers, not about Gianna. The police are keeping quiet about the prostitution. Ferry won't say anything either."

"Why they do that? Keep quiet?"

"I talked to the policeman in charge. Gianna's shame has nothing to do with her roommate's death."

"This policeman, he's promise you?"

"He promised me."

Dominick sat focused inward; then abruptly he picked up his glass, drained it. The heavy red wine made his lips and the edges of his white mustache look bloody in the dim light. "Maybe Gianna, she change now," he said. "You say Bisconte, he's go to prison and the other one, the roommate, she's dead. Maybe Gianna, she's stop being *puttana.*"

"Maybe."

"But what you think? Yes or no?"

What I thought about a woman I knew little enough about and had never set eyes on was irrelevant. But I said, "Yes. If this whole thing, Ashley Hansen's murder, scares her enough."

"I got to talk to her myself," Dominick said, "scare her little bit myself. Where she is now?"

"I don't know. The only one who does is Bisconte."

"What you mean?"

"Nobody's seen her since last Friday."

"Friday? She's go away last Friday?"

"That night, evidently."

"With somebody, hah? Some man?"

"Yes." I wasn't about to mention the Old Cocksman to him.

"And she don't come back since then?"

"No. Her car hasn't been moved."

"Cristo bello," he said. "You think something's happen to Gianna? That *stronzo* Bisconte, he's hurt her too?"

"It's possible."

"He's hurt her, I kill him. For Pietro, I kill him dead!"

His voice had risen; a few of the other drinkers turned their heads to look at us. I said, "Easy now. We don't know that anything's happened to Gianna."

"Then where she is since Friday?"

I shook my head.

"You got to find her," Dominick said.

"Not me. That's a job for the police now."

"No. You, *'paesan.'*" He caught hold of my arm, tight-fingered. "The police, they come around, they ask questions, they talk to Pietro and Gianna's mama; Gianna's shame, it's all come out."

"It doesn't have to be that way. The police—"

"You find her," he said adamantly. "For Pietro. For Gianna's mama. For me too."

"Dominick, I—"

"You find her," he said again.

His eyes bored into mine, full of fire. I tried to look away from them; couldn't seem to manage it. *Com-*

paesani—Dominick and Pietro, and me. Blood of the blood.

"I'll find her," I said.

THE REST OF THE DAY was a bust.

I went back to the office—no Eberhardt, big surprise —and did fifteen minutes of work on the personal-injury case before I ran out of interest. On impulse I opened the San Francisco Yellow Pages, which includes Colma, to the section marked Automobile Dealers— New Cars. *Big Dave from Colma . . . give you a ride in one of my new demos, then give you a* real *ride, ha ha . . . just come on down to the lot if you're available.* No listing under Dave or Big Dave. Easy enough to identify him, though, if he did in fact run or work for a car dealership in Colma; three or four phone calls would do it. But was it worth the effort? His message had been on Ashley Hansen's machine, not Gianna's.

Gianna, my name is Tom . . . Tom from Fairfax . . . my number is 555-2897, I'm home most evenings after six . . .

Two ways to get somebody's home address when you have nothing more than a telephone number: contact in the telephone company, contact in the police department. I used to know somebody who worked for Pac Bell, but she'd left about a year ago and I hadn't found anyone else to cultivate. Jack Logan or one of the other cops I knew would trace the number for me—but not today, not yet. Despite my promise to Dominick, I had no real desire to continue poking around in the sad, painful lives of Gianna Fornessi and her grandfather;

I'd had enough of *la miseria*. And it might not be necessary. Gianna might come back home tonight, of her own volition, or the law might locate her in their hunt for Bisconte. No use dipping my oar into it prematurely, was there? Besides, it was a homicide case and that meant I would have to get Harry Craddock's permission to mount an independent investigation, even though Gianna was not directly involved. Just a formality, the permission, but one that had to be taken care of before I did any work.

So the hell with it for today. Talk to Craddock in the morning, find out how things stood then, and proceed accordingly.

THE EVENING WAS A bust too. I called Kerry, to see if she could get away for dinner, and got her machine. Out with Cybil somewhere, apparently. Good for both of them, if not good for me. I hunted through the refrigerator and the sparse items in the pantry, didn't find anything I wanted to eat. I drank a beer—my second of the day, one more than my usual allotment, but I figured I was entitled—and tried to watch the Braves and Dodgers on TBS. Dull game, or maybe it was the watcher who was dull tonight. I shut it off, put on a Pete Fountain record, got restless listening to all that throbbing New Orleans brass, finally went out and into my car and drove down to the Safeway at Fort Mason. I spent twenty minutes wandering the aisles before I found something I felt like eating that wasn't fattening —a Weight Watchers frozen lasagna.

Back home, I tried to read while I ate. Gave that up

as a bad idea halfway through the lasagna, which I also gave up as a bad idea; it seemed to have the taste and consistency of the spitballs we used to make when we were kids. A lot of food tasted that way to me lately. I'd read somewhere that there are 9,000 taste buds on the human tongue; that they all die within a twelve-day period and new ones take their place, but that the older you get, the longer it takes for the new taste buds to grow. Maybe the aging process in me was accelerating; maybe mine had died for good. *Sic transit gloria* buds.

I decided to take a hot bath. But the plumbing wouldn't cooperate; it's old in my building, older than I am and just as cranky sometimes, and tonight it refused to provide enough hot water. I gave the bath up, too, crawled into bed. I was tired enough to get to sleep right away, but just as I was dozing off the telephone rang. A hairy male voice wanted to know if I was Harlow. I said no, not too pleasantly. The voice said, "Stupid schmuck," as if it were my fault I wasn't Harlow, and banged the receiver in my ear.

Perfect end to another perfect day.

FROM THE OFFICE in the morning I called Harry Craddock. He didn't sound annoyed to hear from me again so soon, maybe because he thought I was calling to find out if he had a statement ready for me to sign—which he didn't. Or maybe I'd just caught him on a good day, one in which his workload was not quite as jammed up as usual. In any event, he was willing enough to respond when I started asking questions.

"Bisconte turn up yet?"

"Not yet," he said. "Might take longer than I figured. He's got cash to run on, thanks to Melanie Harris."

"Who?"

"His lady friend. He called her half an hour after you had your run-in with him. Told her where his stash was and to bring it to a bar on the Embarcadero. She did it. Afraid not to; he threatened her."

"How much was in the stash?"

"Couple of thousand, she says."

"He didn't give her any idea where he was planning to go?"

"None. No ideas of her own either. Says she doesn't know him real well, only met him three months ago, didn't have a clue that he was pimping."

"She knew him well enough to move in with him," I said. "Assuming she's the same one I met at his apartment the other day."

"Probably is, but she hadn't moved in yet. Still has her own apartment in the Marina." There was a pause, as if Craddock had switched his phone from one ear to the other. In the background I could hear a muted version of the usual squad room racket. "You're not trying to pump me about Bisconte, are you? For reasons of your own?"

"Uh-uh. I never horn in on police business."

"That's good. I wouldn't like it if you did."

"It's Gianna Fornessi I'm interested in," I said. "She show up last night or this morning?"

"Not as far as I know. There's a seal on the door of her flat, we had a Denver boot put on her car just in case, and Ferry has instructions to call us if she contacts him."

"Still missing, then. Six days now."

"And you want to go looking for her."

"If you have no objections."

"Still working for her granddad, or is this your own idea?"

"Still working for him." Technically, anyway.

"She your only interest in this business?"

"One and only."

"Okay, then. But if you turn up anything on Bisconte or the Hansen homicide, anything at all, I want to hear about it first thing. Agreed?"

"Agreed."

So I was still in it, like it or not. Gianna, Pietro, and more *miseria*.

After Craddock and I disconnected, I rang the Hall of Justice right back and this time asked for Jack Logan. He wasn't in. But Marty Klein was. Klein was an old pal and former partner of Eberhardt's and we'd had some friendly dealings in the past, played a little poker now and then.

I caught him in the right mood too. He agreed to run a check on Tom-from-Fairfax's telephone number, find out the full name and address of the subscriber for me. Call him back after lunch, he said.

"How's Eb doing?" he asked then. "Don't see much of him anymore."

"That makes two of us. He still blames me for his marriage plans falling apart."

"Oh," Klein said, "so that's what's behind it."

"Behind what?"

"Him talking about quitting partners with you, maybe opening up his own agency."

"Where'd you hear that?"

"Frank Plutarski in the D.A.'s office," Klein said. "Eb talked to him about it a couple of days ago."

"The hell he did."

"Don't tell me he hasn't said anything about it to you?"

"He's made some noises, yeah. But I didn't know he'd been making them to other people. What exactly did he say to Plutarski?"

"I'm not sure. Better give Frank a call, ask him yourself."

"I'll do that."

"Probably nothing in it. Just noise, like you said."

"Yeah. Just noise."

I called the D.A.'s office. Frank Plutarski wasn't in; he was one of the staff investigators and out on a case. The woman I spoke to said he was expected back late in the day. I asked her to have him call me at home tonight.

I sat there in the empty office, listening to the ping of the radiator and the faint chatter of sewing machines from the Slim-Taper Shirt Company on the floor below. Just noise, damn it. Just noise. But then, why had Eberhardt talked to Frank Plutarski? Only reason I could think of was that he was trying to line up prospective clients for himself, his own agency. Plutarski knew a lot of people in the Bay Area; he'd thrown a little business our way in the past.

Who else had Eberhardt talked to? Barney Rivera? Try to get Barney to give him Great Western's freelance claims investigation business instead of me? Christ, would he stoop that low? I called Great Western. Barney wasn't in either. I left the same message for him that I'd left for Frank Plutarski.

There was a bleak, simmering anger in me now. It built a need to get out of there before Eberhardt showed up, before I suffered claustrophobia or an anxiety attack—legacies of the Deer Run episode that still plagued me in times of stress. I dragged the Yellow Pages out again, started calling automobile dealerships in Colma. Paydirt on the third one I tried, Grissom Dodge Chrysler Plymouth on Serramonte Boulevard: their general manager and vice president was Big Dave Edwards.

I was on my way in ten seconds. To Colma and Big Dave Edwards, giver of rides.

Chapter 11

COLMA IS A PLACE San Franciscans wouldn't be caught alive in.

Local joke, not very funny. Coined because Colma is a community of the dead—a nontown attached to San Francisco's southern boundary and bordered on its other three sides by Daly City, South San Francisco, and the San Bruno Mountains, where most of the West Bay's cemeteries are located. Upwards of a dozen different marble orchards, in fact, large and small: Italian, Chinese, Japanese, Catholic, Jewish, nonethnic and nondenominational.

There isn't much else in Colma. A few hundred residences for the living, and some scattered business establishments of which most are automobile dealerships stretched out along Serramonte Boulevard. So if a San Franciscan actually does find himself visiting Colma, you can make book that it's for one of two reasons: to bury or to pay respects at the grave of a friend or loved one, or to buy a car.

Grissom Dodge Chrysler Plymouth was a medium-size outfit that sold both new and used cars. Emphasis on used, judging from the size and content of their lots and showroom. When I got there I was told that Big Dave Edwards was in conference with a customer. So while I waited I wandered around the showroom, looking at the new models. Be nice if I could afford one, maybe a Dodge Shadow or Colt—something small, economical. My car was twenty years old, had 147,000 miles on it, and used gas and oil as if it were leased out by OPEC. Not this year, though; the investigations business wasn't *that* profitable. Maybe next year.

But probably not.

I had been there fifteen minutes when Edwards put in an appearance. He homed in on me instantly—I was the only nonemployee on the floor, so he couldn't miss —and pumped my hand while we traded names. Ashley Hansen's Big Dave, all right; same faintly smarmy voice I'd heard on her telephone tape. I asked if we could talk in private, and he said, "Sure thing," and clapped me on the shoulder and ushered me into his private office, crowding me all the way. He was that kind of salesman: aggressive, overfriendly, mock-complaisant. He could get away with it, too, because he was three or four inches over six feet, weighed a good two-thirty, most of it paunch, and had a smooth, baby-pink face and a winning smile. Everything about him said he was a sweetheart of a guy, born to serve. Everything except his eyes. They were shrewd, calculating, and feral—a con man's eyes. If I'd had a daughter of any age, I would not have trusted her alone with Big Dave for five minutes.

We sat down and he said, "Well now, what can we do for you? New Chrysler, maybe? Terrific buy on a Le-

Baron, you won't find a better deal anywhere. Just tell me what you're looking for, I'll do my best to fix you up."

"Gianna Fornessi," I said.

". . . How's that again?"

"I'm looking for Gianna Fornessi. Ashley Hansen's roommate."

He didn't ruffle easily; men who are all facade seldom do. His smile stayed in place, with only a little congealing at the edges. "Don't think I know either of those folks," he said.

"You read this morning's paper, Mr. Edwards?"

"No. Why?"

"Then you don't know that Ashley Hansen was murdered yesterday."

This time the smile slipped, went crooked; he had to work to get it back in place. "Murdered?"

"In her apartment. By Jack Bisconte, apparently."

Nothing from Edwards.

"You know him?" I asked. "Bisconte?"

"No."

"Ashley Hansen's pimp."

There was a wooden box on Edwards's desk, Oriental-looking, with an intricate inlaid design; he popped it open, took out a cigarette, lit it with a gold lighter. His hands were steady. He took three deep drags, watching me through the exhaled smoke, before he spoke again.

"Who are you?" he said. "Not a cop, or you'd have said so."

"Private investigator."

"Some kind of shakedown, is that it?"

"You watch too much television, Mr. Edwards."

"Yeah? Then what do you want?"

"Information."

"About what?"

"Gianna Fornessi. I told you, I'm looking for her."

"Why come to me? I don't know her."

"You knew Ashley Hansen."

"Did I? How do you figure that?"

"Message you left on her answering machine, yesterday or the day before. Asking for a date tonight. Offering her rides."

"Message with my name in it? I don't think so."

"Big Dave from Colma."

"Lots of Big Daves in the world," he said.

"Come on, Edwards. If I can track you down, the police can track you down. You want them to show up here?"

No reply.

"You're wearing a wedding ring," I said. "You want your wife to find out you've been seeing a call girl?"

"That a threat?"

"I don't make threats. I'm just telling you that things can get nasty if you let them."

He smoked the rest of his coffin nail in silence, thinking about it. When he crushed out the butt he said, "Why'd this guy Bisconte kill Ashley?"

"The police don't know yet. Some kind of argument, maybe."

"What a waste," Edwards said. He shook his head. "Best fuck I ever had."

"Is that all you've got to say about her?"

"What do you want me to say?"

"You don't seem to care much that she's dead."

"She was a whore," he said, and shrugged.

I'd disliked him on sight; I disliked him a whole lot now, to the point where I would have enjoyed mating my fist with his baby-pink face. Some of what I was feeling must have showed in my face, because for the first time cracks showed in his facade, began to ooze worry.

"All right," he said. "But there's nothing I can tell you. I don't know anything about Ashley getting killed and I don't know where you can find Gianna. I never made it with her. I only met her once and that was three months ago."

"Ashley talk much about her?"

"No. Hell, you think I paid her two bills a pop to *talk?*"

"So you don't know any of Gianna's johns."

"No."

"Any of Ashley's other johns?"

"No. None of my business."

"The term 'Old Cocksman' mean anything to you?"

Shrug. "Why should it?"

"The time you met Gianna—where?"

"Her place, hers and Ashley's."

"North Beach. Upper Chestnut."

"Yeah. Ashley brought her car in that day for some repair work—I made a deal with her to take it out in trade. So she needed a ride, so I rode her and then I rode her home." He grinned at me, saw the look on my face, and wiped the grin off his fat mouth. His eyes shifted away from mine; he busied himself lighting another weed.

I said, "Gianna was there when you brought Ashley home?"

"Out front, yeah. Just getting home herself."

"You talk to her?"

"No. Ashley said she was her roommate, that's all."

"Was Gianna alone?"

"With a guy."

"I don't suppose Ashley identified him."

"Hell no."

"What did he look like?"

"I only got a glimpse. He didn't get out of his truck."

"Truck?"

"Pickup. Ford Ranger. 'Ninety, I think."

"What color?"

"Blue."

"Give me an idea of the man. Anything you can remember."

"Dark, like you. Not too old—thirties."

"Black hair? Thick, curly?"

"Think so. What I could see of it under his hat."

"What kind of hat?"

"Cowboy hat," Edwards said. "Big Stetson."

The guy who had been giving Melanie Harris a hard time on Tuesday afternoon, who'd been looking for Jack Bisconte. Connection—but how far did it go?

I got to my feet. Edwards squinted at me through a haze of smoke. "That it?" he said.

"That's it."

"Not too painful after all." Some of the jaunty arrogance was back; his ass and his bank account were secure again. I pitied the woman he was married to, any woman who would hook up with a man like Big Dave Edwards. "Do me a favor, okay? You ever want to buy a car, go someplace else. Don't come here."

"Count on it," I said.

I STOPPED AT A service station two blocks from Grissom Dodge Chrysler Plymouth and checked the San Francisco White Pages. There was no listing for Melanie Harris, but among the several M. Harrises was one with a Marina address, on Cervantes Boulevard. I rang the number; no answer. It was unlikely that she would still be at Bisconte's flat, given what Harry Craddock had told me, but I looked up the number and tried it. No answer there either.

I drove back into the city, ate a light lunch at a place on Van Ness, and then went up to the office. Empty; and as far as I could tell, Eberhardt hadn't been in at all today. I made short work of mail and messages, rang up the Hall of Justice. Marty Klein was at his desk in General Works, and he'd done the Fairfax telephone trace for me.

"Number belongs to a Thomas Duchaine," he said. "D-u-c-h-a-i-n-e. Seventy-nine Raven Hollow Road, Fairfax."

"Got it. Thanks, Marty."

"Sure. You talk to Frank Plutarski yet?"

"Not yet. I called him but he wasn't in."

"Let me know how it goes, will you? With Eb, I mean."

"I'll do that."

"I'd hate to see you two bust it up after all these years. You know? I hope like hell it works out."

"It will if I've got anything to say about it."

But I was beginning to think that I didn't.

THE MARINA IS AN affluent neighborhood along the northern lip of the bay, where the Small Craft Harbor and some of the city's older and finer homes are located. But it was all landfill, and the area had been hit hard during the October '89 earthquake. Half a dozen apartment buildings had been shaken loose of their foundations; a lot of other multiunit structures and private homes were badly damaged, some beyond repair. Gas mains had burst and fires had raged through the Marina, with the result that much of the national and international news coverage had been focused on the district. Even now, scars from that devastating night are still visible. And here and there repair work is still going on.

The Cervantes Boulevard address for M. Harris was a four-story wood-and-stucco apartment building not unlike a couple of those that had collapsed in the quake. This one showed no outward signs of damage, but it might have undergone structural restoration and/or cosmetic surgery. You can't judge how stable a building is by its outward appearance, particularly not in the Marina. Which is why a large number of the neighborhood's residents, some of whom had lived there for decades, had fled to safer locales since October 17, 1989. FOR SALE and APARTMENT FOR RENT signs are still common sights; there was one of the latter on the front of M. Harris's building.

According to the mailboxes in the foyer, M. Harris occupied 3C. I rang the bell. Nobody responded.

I gave it another try, finally went back out to the sidewalk. A car had pulled up behind mine; a fat woman about my age, hennaed hair flaming in the sun, was getting out of it with a cake box balanced in one hand. I waited to see if she was coming here. She was, with a mildly curious glance at me in passing. I let her get all the way into the foyer before I turned back in after her.

"Excuse me, ma'am."

She turned, a little startled. "Yes?"

"Maybe you can help me. I'm looking for Melanie Harris."

"Who?"

"Young woman, slender, dark hair. Lives in Three C, I think."

"Oh," the fat woman said, "her."

"You know her, then?"

"As well as I want to, which is hardly at all."

"Don't like her much?"

"What's to like? Snotty, foul mouth, morals of a rabbit." She paused. "Uh, you're not related to her, are you?"

"No."

"One of her 'friends,' I suppose."

"Not that either. I'm here on business."

"Uh-huh."

"Truly," I said. "She's not home and I need to talk to

her. You wouldn't happen to know where I can find her?"

"How should I know? You think I keep track of my neighbors' comings and goings?"

"No, ma'am. I thought you might know what she does for a living, where she works."

"You don't know where she works and you got business with her?"

"I've only spoken to her once, briefly."

"What kind of business?"

"Insurance."

She studied me, frowning. Pretty soon she said, "Well, she doesn't work days. Little Miss Harris works nights."

"Oh?"

"In North Beach." She made the words sound like Sodom and Gomorrah.

"Whereabouts in North Beach?"

"One of those sleazy clubs on Broadway. High Hat or Top Hat or something like that. One of those topless places."

"Dancer? Singer? Waitress?"

"Bartender," the fat woman said. "Can you believe it? A bartender in a sleazy topless club. What kind of job is that for a young woman?"

"A job is a job," I said. "It probably pays pretty well."

She sniffed. "My daughter took a job like that," she said, "I'd disown her. You'd better believe I would."

I believed it.

Back in the car, I used the mobile phone to call directory assistance. No High Hat or Top Hat listed, but there was a Top Cat Club on Broadway. I called that number and got a male voice that had to shout to make itself heard above a blare of heavy-metal music. Yeah, the voice said, Melanie Harris worked there. No, she wasn't there now—why the hell would she be there now? Her shift didn't start until six.

Six o'clock. The same time I could expect to find Thomas Duchaine at 79 Raven Hollow Road, Fairfax. Nearly three hours to kill. If I stayed in the city and went to see Melanie Harris first, I couldn't figure any productive way to dispose of the interim time. But if I drove over to Marin County, there was a worthwhile stop I could make between now and six o'clock, somebody in San Rafael I needed to talk to.

Bobbie Jean Addison worked over there. And if anybody knew what was going on inside Eberhardt's head these days, it was Bobbie Jean.

Chapter **12**

COMMUTER EXODUS FROM the city starts early; the north-bound lanes on the Golden Gate Bridge were already beginning to clog as I drove across. Traffic moved at more or less normal speeds until I got to Sir Francis Drake Boulevard, south of San Rafael. Then it commenced to snarl again, as it sometimes does along there, because of the arteries leading to and from the Richmond Bridge. So it was after four by the time I pulled into San Rafael and found a place to park on Mission Avenue downtown.

San Rafael is an old town, built in the early 1800s around one of the original California missions. Mission San Rafael Arcángel has been well preserved, and the area surrounding it still retains some of the town's once-strong Spanish flavor. The realtor Bobbie Jean worked for had her offices here, in a building on A Street whose front windows offered a partial view of the mission's tile roofs and buff-colored bell tower.

Bobbie Jean was alone at her desk when I walked in. It was a much warmer day over here, summery, and her brown, angular body was encased in a sleeveless yellow dress. She looked cool, fresh, as some people manage to do at the tag end of even the hottest day. Not all men would find her attractive at first inspection, but the perceptive ones did when she smiled; she has an exceptional smile, incandescent and infectious. She favored me with it as soon as she spotted me. We've gotten along well, Bobbie Jean and I, during the two-plus years she and Eb have been together. She'd even come to do a little crying on my shoulder after his too-elaborate wedding plans had pushed her into calling the whole thing off in April. We hadn't seen much of each other since, thanks to Eberhardt's tight-held grudge.

"Well, this is a surprise," she said. "What brings you over here?"

"Some business in Fairfax. I thought I'd stop by for a few minutes."

"I'm glad you did."

"Can we talk, Bobbie Jean? It can wait until after five, if you're busy . . ."

"I haven't been busy for half an hour. This is slack time around here." Bobbie Jean is from South Carolina and when she says things like "slack time" you can hear the Deep South in her voice. Mostly, though, after twenty-some years in California, her accent is barely noticeable. "Some coffee? There's a pot on in back."

"I wouldn't mind a cup."

She went away and I rolled a padded chair from the waiting area over next to her desk and put myself down in it. I was trying to find the most tactful frame for my questions when she came back and made it easy for me.

She said as she handed me one of the cups she carried, "It's Eb you want to talk about." It wasn't a question.

I nodded. "Do you mind?"

"No. He's one of my favorite subjects." But her smile wasn't quite as bright now; there was a pensive quality to it. Even after all that he'd put her through, her love for Eberhardt hadn't diminished any. If anything, it was stronger than ever.

"Has he said anything about me, about his plans?"

"How do you mean?"

"Dissolving our partnership. Opening his own agency."

"Oh, Lord," she said, and now the smile was gone completely. "You mean he's *serious* about that?"

"Seems to be."

"I didn't think so, or I'd have called you."

"How long has he been talking about it?"

"Not long. And just one time."

"When?"

"Last Sunday night."

"What did he say?"

"His exact words?"

"They won't hurt my feelings."

Bobbie Jean drank some of her coffee, spoke with her eyes on the cup. " 'I'm tired of taking orders from him. He thinks he knows everything—he's a goddamn little tin god. It's time I was my own boss again.' "

"Uh-huh. That's about what he said to me on Tuesday."

"Was he angry? You know, fulminating the way he does?"

"No. He was calm enough."

"Damn," she said.

"Yeah," I said.

"But he wasn't definite? About quitting?"

"Well, he didn't quit on the spot. But he's been talking to people, I think maybe trying to line up clients for himself."

"You don't mean trying to steal them away from you?"

"I don't know yet," I said. "I hope not."

"He wouldn't do a thing like that—"

"As angry at me as he is? He might."

"What're you going to do?"

"Too soon to decide that. Before I do anything I wanted to talk to you. And to the people he's been seeing, find out exactly what he's said to them."

"What if he is trying to steal clients?"

"I won't lie to you, Bobbie Jean. If that's the case, then I'm through with him. In every way."

She sighed. "He's so damn stubborn . . . he makes me crazy sometimes, and I've only known him a short while. I can imagine what it must be like for you."

Bobbie Jean's telephone rang. She picked up, spoke briefly, made a note. I was working on my coffee when she disconnected. It was good coffee, much better than what I made.

"If Eb did open his own agency," she said, "what do you think would happen?"

"You mean could he make a go of it?"

"Yes."

I hadn't let myself think much about that; I thought

about it now, weighing the probabilities. "He might," I said at length, "if he applies himself. He has sloppy work habits. He's chronically late getting to the office, he sloughs off paperwork and routine phone calls. . . . Hell, I don't have to tell you. You know how he is."

"All too well."

"He'd have to get out and hustle work too. Regularly. Even if he swipes clients, the ones he can get won't be enough to support him. Neither will favors from old friends. There are a lot of private investigators in the Bay Area and only so much work to go around. It's a damn grind. I've been in the business more than twenty years and I still have to scratch part of the time."

A couple of beats, and Bobbie Jean said, "He'd fail." It wasn't worried reflection; it was a flat statement of fact.

"Yeah," I said. "In the long run he probably would."

"Then what would he do? He's almost sixty."

"Get a job with one of the bigger agencies, maybe. If he was lucky."

"Doing what, at his age? He wouldn't let himself be tied down to a desk job—what else is there?"

"Electronic surveillance, but he's never had any training in electronics and it's not his kind of thing anyway. No experience in high-powered corporate shenanigans either. Besides, that sort of specialized investigating is a young man's game."

"What's left?"

"Security work. Guard duty, private patrol."

"Wearing a uniform? Like those old men in banks?"

"Like that."

"It would drive him crazy," Bobbie Jean said. "A proud, stubborn, active man like Eb . . . he couldn't stand it."

I didn't say anything. But she was right: It would drive Eberhardt crazy, maybe even put him into an early grave. Just as it would me.

RAVEN HOLLOW DRIVE, according to my Marin County map, was in the well-to-do residential section of Fairfax called Sleepy Hollow. Wooded countryside out there—a narrow valley bounded by low, craggy foothills. Lots of oak and madrone and eucalyptus, and in the summer months, sweeps of dry brown grass that made fire an ever-present danger. Lots of short, twisty, dead-end streets with names like Van Winkle Drive, Legend Road, and Catskill Lane to complete the Washington Irving, New York Dutch theme.

The higher up on the hillsides the streets went, the more expensive the homes. Raven Hollow Drive was not one that climbed to ridge heights; it was a valley street, angling a short ways upward off Butterfield Road, the main drag. Even so, it didn't lack much in either affluence or bucolic appeal. Dark-red plum trees lined it thickly, as did a little creek on one side, and the homes and lots were large—probably in the $300,000 to $400,000 range. Whatever Thomas Duchaine did for a living, he was pretty successful at it.

Well, maybe he was and maybe he wasn't. Number seventy-nine turned out to be a sprawling ranch-style house, partially hidden behind plum trees and pyracantha hedges; it also turned out to be for sale, with a big realtor's sign on the front lawn. Along one side was an unoccupied carport. Nobody home yet: chimes echoed emptily inside when I rang the bell.

I waited in the car, trying not to brood about Eberhardt. After fifteen minutes a teal-blue BMW came up the street, turned into Duchaine's drive, and stopped under the carport. A medium-size man in a business suit got out, let himself into the house through a side door. I gave him three minutes before I went back to the front porch and worked the bell.

He opened up right away, with the door on a chain. The head and face framed in the gap was early forties, balding, sad-eyed, and nondescript.

"Mr. Duchaine? Thomas Duchaine?"

"That's right, yes. May I help you?"

I had my wallet out, and as I identified myself I showed him the photostat of my license. The look he gave it and then me was bewildered.

"A private detective?" he said. "What do you want with me?"

"We can talk better inside, if you don't mind."

"Not until I know why you're here."

"Gianna Fornessi," I said.

He blinked at me. Then he said, "Oh my God."

"A few minutes of your time, that's all I'm after."

"How did you know I . . . how did you find me?"

"The message you left on her answering machine."

"But I didn't . . . just my first name . . ."

"And your telephone number."

"You heard . . . everything I said?"

"I heard it."

His face screwed up: embarrassment, something that might have been self-hatred. Without looking at me he said, "I still don't know what you want."

"I'm trying to find Ms. Fornessi."

"Find her? Is she missing?"

"It looks that way. Since last Friday."

Headshake.

"Her roommate was killed yesterday," I said. "Murdered in the flat they shared. That fact may not be related to Ms. Fornessi's disappearance; then again, it might be."

"My God," Duchaine said.

He shut the door, not fast, not hard. To take the chain off, I thought, but it stayed shut. Only he didn't lock it or move away from it. I could hear him on the other side, the faint, irregular sibilance of his breathing—trying to make up his mind what to do, or maybe just trying to get himself under control.

"Mr. Duchaine? You have a choice—talk to me or talk to the police."

Nothing for ten seconds. Then I heard the chain rattle and he pulled the door all the way open. Most of the color had gone from his face, leaving it paper-white and splotchy; he looked stricken. "I don't know where Gianna Fornessi is," he said dully. "I don't know anything about her or her roommate. I didn't even know she had a roommate."

"All right," I said. "May I come in?"

"I just told . . . yes. Yes, all right, come in."

The living room he led me into was well-furnished, comfortable enough, but as nondescript as he was—like a furniture store's bland showroom display. He sat slump-shouldered on the arm of a couch and looked at his hands, turning them over and back in front of him, as if examining them for marks or stains. I stood off from him, giving him space, waiting.

Pretty soon he said, "I shouldn't have done it. I knew that from the start."

"Done what, Mr. Duchaine?"

"Called her. I almost didn't. But I . . . it's been such a long time. Almost a year now since my wife left me. There's been no one else and a man . . . a man gets lonely. You can understand that, can't you? How a man can get lonely for a woman?"

"Yes," I said.

"This house . . . all the memories. It wouldn't be so bad if I were somewhere else, if I could sell it, but the real estate market these days . . ." He squeezed his eyes shut, popped them open again. "My son moved out right after my wife. He blames me for the divorce. Katherine lives in Milwaukee now, her hometown—she doesn't have to deal with this place or the memories, she has her family. . . ." Another headshake, sharper this time, angry, but with all the anger directed at himself. "I'm talking too much," he said.

"Don't be so hard on yourself. There's nothing terrible in trying to buy a little companionship."

"Sex," he said. "I wanted sex."

"Either way, it's not a mortal sin."

"Isn't it? A lot of people think it is."

"And a lot of people don't."

"But a prostitute, a call girl . . . I must have been crazy. I've never been with a prostitute in my life."

"All right," I said. "Who gave you Gianna Fornessi's name and telephone number?"

". . . I can't tell you that."

"Concealing information that may have bearing on a homicide case is a felony, Mr. Duchaine."

"Homicide . . ." He shuddered. "What happened to her roommate?"

"Ashley Hansen," I said. "There was a struggle of some kind and she died of a blow to the head."

"Do the police know who did it?"

"They think it was Jack Bisconte."

No reaction.

"Name's not familiar to you?"

"Bisconte? No."

"Gianna Fornessi's pimp. Ashley Hansen's pimp."

Headshake.

"Who's Dick from San Rafael?" I asked him.

"How did . . . oh. The message I left."

"Who is he? One of Gianna's johns?"

"Johns?"

"Customers."

"I . . . yes. But he's married, he has children. . . ."

"Friend of yours? Close friend?"

"Just someone I know. A business acquaintance."

"And over lunch or drinks you happened to mention to him how lonely you are and he told you about Gianna. That how it was?"

"Not exactly, but . . . something like that."

"What's his last name?"

"I just . . . I don't know if—"

"His last name. Don't make me call the police."

Three-beat. "Morris," Duchaine said miserably. "Dick Morris."

"He lives in San Rafael?"

"I think so. . . . My God, you won't say anything in front of his family?"

"Not if I can help it. The address, Mr. Duchaine."

"I don't have it. I've never been to his home."

"His place of business, then. Where does he work?"

"Jeffcoat Electric."

"Which is where?"

"San Rafael. On Lincoln Boulevard. He's their sales manager. He . . . I've known him for years, casually. I buy a fair amount from Jeffcoat . . . I have a small manufacturing company and they . . . Dick is . . ." The jumble of words seemed to congeal in his throat; he swallowed them down.

"Is Dick Morris the only person you know who bought Gianna's services?"

"The only one, yes."

"Did he mention anyone else, any friends of his?"

"I don't . . . no, I don't think so."

There was nothing more he could tell me; I had bled it all out of him. I left him sitting there with his head bowed and his eyes shut, shaken and oppressed—another case of *la miseria.* I felt bad for him, bad about having had to push my way into his sad, empty life. And yet all I'd done was confront him with his own weakness and vulnerability. There really wasn't anything immoral in being lonely and needing a little love, even if it was the kind that cost a couple of hundred bucks an hour. Thomas Duchaine had had to convince himself of that before he was able to telephone Gianna Fornessi; now he had unconvinced himself of it, probably once and for all. In any case, he kept on suffering. He had been wearing a crown of thorns for some time now and he would go right on wearing it.

The things we do to ourselves, I thought as I let myself out. They're as bad as the things we do to others, and sometimes even worse.

Chapter **13**

THE HUB OF NORTH BEACH is the intersection of Broadway and Columbus. That is also the hub of San Francisco's modern Barbary Coast, where the city's more notorious nightclubs and sin palaces are located. Topless, bottomless; female impersonators; jazz, heavy metal, reggae, rap, musical revues, comedy shows. Fun and frolic in a sea of booze and babel and blazing neon. The tourist brochures tell you about that side of the Silicone Alley strip; the side they don't tell you about is the wide-open drug dealing and flesh peddling; the pickpockets and muggers, the roving gangs of kids looking for action and trouble, the aggressive panhandlers and belligerent drunks, the unstable mental patients turned loose on the streets by the closure of most of the city's outpatient psychiatric clinics. You can find fun and frolic on the North Beach strip, all right, but you can also find several different qualities of hurt. I have enough hurt to deal with during the daylight hours; I don't go to Broadway and Columbus at night unless I have to.

This was a weeknight, so the crowds were not as heavy or as unruly as they are on Friday and Saturday.

Even so, and even though it was just a little past seven-thirty when I got to North Beach, the Portsmouth Square Garage was already full. I had to park on the street in the deserted Financial District and hoof it a dozen blocks to Broadway.

As early as it was, most of the clubs seemed to be moderately crowded and the Top Cat was no exception. Outside was a billboard advertising the current attraction, a heavy-metal rock group called The Fat. Inside, the noise level was on a par with a couple of jet planes taking off: people thumping and gyrating on the dance floor, people clapping and smacking tables, and up on the stage, five scruffily dressed, obese white males with hair and beards dyed different colors, abusing piano and drums and electric guitars to create a sound like cats being tortured in an echo chamber. Their combined weight must have been about a ton. The five of them, jiggling and bouncing and sweating greasily, was the best advertisement for a crash weight-loss program I'd ever seen.

All the tables surrounding the stage and dance floor were taken, but the bar area was less crowded. The bar itself was L-shaped, with one bartender working each section of the L. Both bartenders were women and both wore tuxedo outfits with little black hats that were supposed to simulate cat ears. Cute. Cuter than The Fat, anyway. The portion of the L farthest from the stage was Melanie Harris's domain. There was one empty stool at the very end, next to the wall; I wedged in there and parked my hams on it.

Melanie was busy; it took her the better part of ten

minutes to get around to me. Which was all right, because I would have had difficulty trying to talk to her
above the din. As it was, The Fat quit their dissonant
caterwauling just before she moved my way, and a
gross, wheezing voice boomed out that they were taking
a ten-minute break. Thank you, Lord, I thought.

"What'll you have?" Melanie, in a voice only a couple
of decibels above normal.

I said, "Remember me?"

She rolled her eyes; she'd heard that one several hundred times before. "Not too likely, gramps. I'm busy,
okay? What'll you have?"

"Bud Lite."

She got a bottle out of the cooler, banged it and a
glass down in front of me. "Five," she said.

"Dollars?"

"No, Japanese yen. What do you think? Somebody's
got to pay for the entertainment."

What entertainment? I thought. I laid a ten on the
bartop. "I wasn't giving you a line a minute ago. The
other day, up at Jack Bisconte's place. The guy who was
hassling you—I chased him off. Remember?"

She looked at me, actually saw me, for the first time.
"Oh, yeah," she said. "But that doesn't buy you any
grateful favors."

"I'm not trying to buy any favors. Not the kind you
mean."

"No, huh? Well, I don't know where he is, if that's
what you're after."

"Who?"

"Jack. He can drop dead for all I care."

"I'm not looking for Bisconte."

"So I'm wrong twice? All right, what *are* you after?"

"The guy who was hassling you. The cowboy."

"What do you want with that asshole?"

"Personal matter."

"Yeah? Who are you anyway?"

"Does that make a difference?"

"It might." She leaned closer. "Cop?"

"No."

"You sure look like one."

"I can't help the way I look," I said. "You know the cowboy, right? His name, where I can find him?"

She shrugged, a gesture that made her cat ears twitch. "I don't want anything to do with him," she said. "I don't like his type."

"What type is that?"

"Rough trade. I don't play those games."

"What games?"

"S&M bullshit."

Somebody from down the bar called loudly, "Hey, sweets, you work here or what? I need a fresh drink."

She called back, "Yeah, yeah, hold your horses," and then muttered under her breath, "Assholes galore." She moved away, taking my sawbuck with her—taking her time.

I waited, nibbling on the five-buck Bud Light, fidgeting a little. It was smoky in there—cigarettes, cigars, grass—and the smoke was irritating my lungs. Fresh air was what I wanted. And home, my flat, where it was quiet and Fat-free.

Melanie served three customers, put up orders for

two topless waitresses in kitty costumes. Back to me then, with my change—five singles. I pushed them back her way, all five of them.

She gave me a look. "What's that for?"

"The cowboy's name and where I can find him."

"Oh, hell," she said, and made the bills disappear. "Chet. His name's Chet."

"Last name?"

"Who knows? Chet's the only one I ever heard."

"Where does he live?"

"I think out in Bolinas."

"But you're not sure?"

"Well, Jack took me to a party out there once, a couple of months ago. This Chet acted like he owned the place, so I guess maybe he did."

"You wouldn't remember the address?"

"Who remembers addresses? I was only there once."

"The name of the street?"

"Main drag, I guess. Whatever that's called."

"His place is right downtown?"

"A little ways beyond the stores. Not too far."

"Anything distinctive about the house?"

"It wasn't a house," Melanie said.

"What is it, then?"

"Kind of a cottage. You know, a beach cottage."

"On the lagoon there?"

"On the water, yeah. Behind a fence that runs along the edge of the street."

"Anything else about the cottage? Size, color, shape?"

"Well, it was pink," she said.

"Pink."

"Real pink. Like a fag would have."

"Is Chet a homosexual?"

"I doubt it," she said, wry-mouthed.

"What kind of party was it?"

"Just a party. At first, anyhow."

"What happened?"

"Things started to get kinky."

"Kinky how?"

She leaned close again. "Chet wanted to put on a show. D&S for starters. One of the other girls was stoned and willing to do the slave bit. You didn't have to be a genius to figure out what he was trying to promote."

"Orgy?"

"The S&M kind—whips and chains, probably. I don't go for that crap. I like my sex one-on-one. I told Jack, if he knew what was good for him he'd take me out of there, fast."

"Did he?"

"Sure he did. He knew what was good for him."

"He ever try to talk you into anything himself?"

"D&S, S&M? No."

"How about turning tricks?"

The wry mouth again. "You know about those bimbos he had up on Chestnut, huh? What happened to the one yesterday." I nodded. "Yeah, well, he never tried to turn *me* out. If he had I'd have fixed his wagon. I'm no whore. I wouldn't have had anything to do with him if I'd known he was pimping."

"I believe you, Melanie."

"I don't care if you do or not. It's the truth."

"This Chet character," I said. "You think Bisconte was procuring for him?"

Another of the waitresses called to Melanie from the slot farther down. Melanie straightened, hesitated, then yelled that she'd be right there. To me she said, "How should I know what Jack was doing for Chet?"

"I'm just asking your opinion. Could their relationship be that kind—business? Or would you say they're friends?"

"Not friends," she said, "at least not close friends. Chet never called or came around Jack's while I was there."

"Why did he want to see Bisconte the other day? What was he so exercised about?"

"Who knows? He didn't tell me. Listen, I don't care about Chet any more than I care about Jack, okay? I don't want anything more to do with either of them. I got enough assholes smelling up my life."

There was a sudden shrill, vibrating shriek that set my teeth on edge. Microphone feedback? No: electric guitar. The Fat was back, and with a vengeance. The shriek rose to a screaming pitch, was joined by other shrieks—more poor felines being brutalized in the echo chamber.

Melanie mouthed something that might have been, "Thanks for the five bucks," and then made a shooing gesture to indicate our discussion was finished. It would have been finished in any case, thanks to The Fat. They had begun to sing something that had the words "love" and "crazybone" and "death's door" in it, while they continued abusing their instruments and the crowd roared and stomped its pagan approval.

I got the hell out of there.

I HAD A SURPRISE VISITOR waiting for me when I got home. Sitting in a dark-colored Caddy smack in front of my building, on the passenger side with the window rolled down. He hailed me as I came walking toward him—I'd had to park on the next block—and passed under the streetlight diagonally across from the vestibule.

"Hey," he said, "hold up, pops."

Brent DeKuiper.

I held up, with leftover anger kicking up in me, and watched him hoist his massive body out of the Caddy. When he shut the door I said, "So now you know who and what I am. And that I'm not a goddamn pervert."

"Yeah. Guy in Gianna's building told me."

"George Ferry?"

"Him, yeah."

"Uh-huh. You didn't push him around, did you?"

Lopsided grin. "Flexed muscle. All it took."

"What do you want, DeKuiper?"

"Bad scene other day," he said. "Sorry, man. But hell, didn't say who you were."

"Your fault or mine—which is it?"

"Said sorry, man."

"Sure. Except that guys like you don't hang around places waiting to apologize for your mistakes. What do you really want?"

"Gianna," he said.

"Why?"

"Worried about her, what happened to Ashley."

"Found out she's missing and Ferry told you I might be looking for her and now so are you. That the way it is?"

"Yeah. Find her yet?"

"No."

"Leads?"

"No."

"Tell me you knew anything, huh, pops?"

"Sure thing," I lied. "Why would I hold back?"

"Still pissed, maybe."

"I don't hold grudges."

"Me neither. Think Bisconte hurt her too?"

"I don't know. Police'll ask him when they catch him."

"Better catch him before I do."

"But you don't know where he might have gone."

"No," DeKuiper said.

"Tell me if you did, huh?"

The lopsided grin again. "Sure thing, pops."

"How well do you know Bisconte?"

"Well enough. Prick."

"Why? Because he had his hooks into Gianna?"

"Hooks? Shit, he's her pimp. So what?"

"That didn't bother you?"

"Why should it?"

"You like her, maybe you've got a thing for her. Don't you care that she's been selling it with Bisconte's help?"

"Hell no. Everybody's a whore these days, one way or other. You, me, everybody."

"So then why don't you like Bisconte?"

"Reasons. Killed Ashley, didn't he?"

"Let's talk about Gianna. When did you see her last?"

"Week ago."

"Before the trouble with Ferry?"

"Yeah. Would've fixed that myself, she'd asked."

"But she asked Bisconte instead."

"Her choice."

"When you saw her, she tell you anything about her weekend plans?"

"No. Never talked about her tricks."

"Or mentioned the names of any of her johns?"

"Hookers know better," he said, and shrugged.

"So you don't know any of them."

"No. How about you? Find out any names?"

"Not yet," I lied. "Bisconte took Ashley's address book—Gianna's, too, for all I know. There wasn't anything in the apartment to give me a line on her johns."

DeKuiper raked fingers through his dirty-blond beard. His eyes were bright and hard in the reflected shine from the streetlamp. "Sure not holding out on me?"

"I'm sure."

"Bust your ass, find out you are."

"Stuff your threats, DeKuiper. You don't scare me."

"No? Not much fight in you, other day."

"You're wrong about that," I said thinly. "There was plenty of fight in me but it was your turf. This is mine.

You want to find out how much fight I've got in me right now?"

"Tough talk for old man."

"Talk's cheap. Well?"

He tried to hurt me with his eyes.

"Okay, fine," I said. "I'm going inside now . . . unless you want to try to stop me."

I put my back to him, walked into the vestibule. He didn't try to stop me. Behind me he said, "Find Gianna, find out anything about her, better let me know. Mean it, pops. Know what's good for you, let me know."

I didn't answer. Didn't bother to look at him again as I unlocked the door and let myself inside.

THREE CALL-BACK MESSAGES: Kerry, Frank Plutarski, Barney Rivera. I rang Kerry first, but her line was busy. Plutarski was next. His line was clear and he was the one who answered.

"Yeah, Eb and I had a talk," he said. "He came into the office on Monday, said he was thinking about going into business for himself. He wanted me to keep him in mind if I heard of anybody who needed private work done."

"He tell you why he was thinking of going out on his own?"

"Just that he needed a change."

"Mention me at all?"

"No. I figured he must've talked it over with you, got your blessings. That's not the way it is?"

"No. How definite was he?"

"Pretty definite."

"Already a done deal in his mind?"

"Sounded that way to me."

"He mention having an office yet, an agency name, anything along those lines?"

"I got the impression he hadn't gone that far," Plutarski said. "Asked me to call him at home if I had anything for him."

"Meaning right away? Anytime?"

"That's how I took it."

"Okay, Frank, thanks."

"What is it with you two?" he asked. "You have some kind of falling out?"

"Yeah," I said. "Some kind of falling out."

I punched up Barney Rivera's number. He was home alone for a change; he bemoaned the fact as soon as I identified myself. Twenty-four hours without a woman is a lifetime to guys like Barney, who walk around with perpetual erections. He and JFK would have made good partying buddies.

"Eb's thinking about going solo?" he said, sounding surprised. "No, not a word to me about it. When'd he make this decision?"

"Not too long ago. But I guess he's been building to it ever since the wedding fiasco."

"Hell, maybe he's not serious. . . ."

"That's what I thought at first. But he's serious, Barney. You'll see that when he gets around to you."

"Don't think he'd try undercutting your fees, do you?"

"I hope to Christ he doesn't. What'll you do if he suggests it?"

"Ream him out good. I don't do business that way."

"I didn't think you did."

"Fact is, though," Barney said, "he's an old friend just like you are. If he's straightforward about it, I'd have to throw a bone his way now and then too."

"Sure, I know that."

"Not that there are all that many bones to throw, this damned economy. Eb must know that. Alone, just starting out, he'll be in for some lean times."

"He's either ignoring the fact or it doesn't matter to him," I said. "You know how stubborn and shortsighted he is. He always thinks he can beat the game."

"Which is why he's such a patsy at the poker table, drawing to inside straights and three-card flushes. Nine times out of ten he winds up losing his ass."

"It's his ass," I said. "I got enough worries looking out for my own."

"Don't we all," Barney said. "Don't we all."

Kerry's number again. This time it was free; she picked up on the second ring. "I just got off the line with Bobbie Jean," she said.

"She call you or you call her?"

"She called me. She said you'd stopped by to talk about Eb. She also said she called him after you left, to try to pin him down. He wouldn't discuss it with her."

"Wouldn't say anything at all about his plans?"

"Not a word."

"Another bad sign." I told her about my conversations with Marty Klein earlier in the day and Frank Plutarski a few minutes ago.

"Even so," she said, "couldn't he just be testing the

waters? I mean, if he was really going to go through with it, wouldn't he have told you straight out by now that he was leaving? And when?"

"Not necessarily."

"I can't believe he'd just walk out cold."

"I wouldn't have believed it either, last week. Now . . ."

"Maybe if I talked to him," Kerry said.

"And said what?"

"Asked him point-blank if he's leaving. And if he admits that he is, appeal to him as a friend not to do it."

"Uh-uh. If he won't discuss it with Bobbie Jean, he won't discuss it with you. Besides, he'd think I put you up to it. That's the way his mind works."

"I guess you're right."

"The only person who can get this settled with him, one way or another, is me. I'll handle it."

"When?"

"Soon." I did not want to talk about Eberhardt anymore tonight; I'd had enough aggravation for one day. I changed the subject to why she'd called earlier.

"To tell you that you're in solid with Cybil again," she said. "Now she'd like you to come with us to Larkspur on Saturday."

"Chauffeur and another strong back to help with the move?"

"No, it's a family thing with her—she considers you family again."

That touched me and I said so.

"So will you join us?"

"Wouldn't miss it. What time?"

"Nine," Kerry said. "The moving company is due from L.A. at noon and Cybil wants to be 'settled in' by then."

"Nine it is."

"Just do me one favor. No marriage talk. If Cybil brings the subject up, don't encourage her. Deal?"

"Deal."

I COULDN'T SLEEP.

I lay staring up at the dark, with Eberhardt in my head—chasing him round and round in there. Thirty-five years of friendship, five years of partnership, plenty of good times and not too many bad ones. Big memories: the day we graduated from the police academy, the day he married Dana and I was his best man, the day I quit the force to open my own agency and we got drunk together on English pale ale to celebrate, the day we were both shot and seriously wounded in his house in Noe Valley, the day he confessed to me—the only person he'd ever told—that he'd taken a bribe after thirty years of being a dead-honest cop, the day he took his early retirement and I brought him into the agency as a full partner, the day I returned from the Deer Run kidnapping after three long months and tears came into his eyes when he saw me, saw that I was still alive. All of that and so much more . . . and now, all of a sudden, he wanted to end it, throw it all away. Because of a few angry words and a stupidly impulsive punch in the belly that I had apologized for a dozen times? It didn't make sense to me. Worse things than that had happened between us in thirty-five years, uglier things, and much

harsher words, even other blows, had been exchanged—
and none of them had snapped the bond of our friendship. If anything, to my mind and in the long run, they
had made it stronger. Why, then, would he let this thing
rip us apart, this minor, foolish disagreement?

You have to tell me that, Eb. If you go ahead and
bust us up, you owe me that much explanation at least.
Why *this* thing, out of all of them? Why now?

Chapter **14**

ON FRIDAY MORNING I left the city just before eight-thirty, traveling against the sluggish flow of commute traffic on the Golden Gate Bridge. Twenty minutes and I was in downtown San Rafael. I stopped at a café on Lincoln Boulevard, the industrial part west of the freeway, and ate a light breakfast and drank three cups of coffee. It was just nine-thirty when I walked into the newish, block-wide building that housed Jeffcoat Electric.

Dick Morris was in, but he didn't want to see me— not even on what I told the receptionist was an important personal matter. He sent word back with her that he was too busy; perhaps this afternoon. No, not this afternoon—now. I volleyed the receptionist back to him with that message, and the fact that my visit concerned the Gianna matter in San Francisco. Gianna was the magic word: It bought me quick entry into Morris's private office.

Physically he was a well-dressed, white-collar version of the farmer in Grant Wood's "American Gothic." Tall, lean, knobby, with a sharp nose, a long face, long wrists and hands, and a protuberant Adam's apple that made his tie look as if it were tied with two knots instead of one. He stood ramrod stiff alongside his desk, one hand on the telephone, and gave me a fast, hard once-over. His pale eyes were morgue cold.

Without preamble he said, "If you're here to try to extort money from me, I'll call the police. I mean that. I won't pay you or anybody else a dime."

"Good for you. Blackmail's an ugly business."

That didn't relieve him any. "Well?"

"The answers to some questions is all I want, Mr. Morris."

"What questions?"

"About Gianna Fornessi, the people you and she know. She's missing and I'm trying to find her."

"Why? Who are you?"

I opened my wallet and poked it up under his nose. He stared at the license photostat for half a minute before he raised his cold eyes to mine again.

"Who told you about me?" he said.

"What makes you think somebody told me? I'm a detective; detectives have all sorts of ways of finding out things."

"Who are you working for?"

"Gianna Fornessi's grandfather. My turn now."

". . . What?"

"To ask the questions. Your turn to answer them."

"I don't admit to knowing Gianna Fornessi."

"We'll get along better if you don't deny it."

"Maybe I should call my lawyer, have him come over."

"Go right ahead."

We held a stare-down. There was a fan on a table under the office's single window, turned to a low speed; the motor made little ticking, pinging noises in the stillness. I was prepared to stand there listening to that motor for ten minutes or more. Morris wasn't, so he lost the contest. Abruptly he turned, went around behind his desk, sat down, and rested his bony hands edgewise on the blotter as if he were measuring something approximately eight inches in length and invisible.

"Ask your questions," he said stiffly.

"When did you last see Gianna?"

"Three weeks ago."

"Where?"

"In San Francisco."

"Talk to her since then?"

"No."

"She had a date last Friday night," I said. "A weekend date, at least two days, with somebody she referred to as the Old Cocksman. That name mean anything to you?"

"No."

"How about Jack Bisconte?"

"No."

"Bolinas resident named Chet?"

"No," Morris said.

Faint eye flick on each of the last three negatives. Lies? I thought so; he wasn't the nervous type.

I said, "Who told you about Gianna?"

No answer to that one.

"You didn't get her name out of the Yellow Pages," I said. "Somebody put you on to her. Who, Mr. Morris?"

"I don't have to tell you that."

"Right, you don't. Would you rather tell the police?"

"Why should the police be interested in me? I didn't have anything to do with her disappearance, if she really has disappeared. No one can say I did."

"How about the murder of her roommate? You have anything to do with that?"

His mouth came open about an inch; otherwise, no reaction.

I said, "News to you? It was in yesterday's papers."

"I don't read crime news. When did it happen?"

"Wednesday afternoon. The police think Jack Bisconte was responsible; they're looking for him."

Morris didn't ask why—maybe because he already knew who and what Bisconte was.

"Did you know Ashley Hansen?"

"Who?"

"Gianna's roommate."

"No."

"Never met her or talked to her?"

"No."

Eye flicks again on both negatives.

"How long have you been seeing Gianna?"

"About four months."

"Regularly?"

"Once or twice a month."

"Who gave you her name?"

Silence.

"I meant what I said about the police, Mr. Morris. If they get into it, you're not going to be able to keep a lid on your involvement with Gianna. Maybe you don't care if your family finds out. But if you do care, I suggest you cooperate with me. I'm a whole lot more discreet than the law."

His eyes were glacial now. He was one cold bugger. I'd come here to make him sweat a little; all I was getting was frost.

"Call your lawyer," I said, "ask him what he thinks. Or let me lay it out for him. My guess is he'll tell you to cooperate."

Morris put his hands flat on his desk, lifted himself slowly to his feet. With the same slow movements he paced the width of the room, twice, making almost military turns at both ends, not looking at me in the process. It wasn't until he came to a standstill that he laid his icy gaze on me again.

"John Valconazzi," he said.

"Who would he be?"

"Rancher. West part of the county."

"Cattle rancher?"

"Dairy cattle, horses, other things."

"Exact location?"

"Petaluma–Marshall Road, three miles west of Hicks Valley Road. But it won't do you any good to go out there."

"No? Why not?"

"He doesn't see strangers."

"Why not?" I asked again.

"He has his reasons."

"Which are?"

"He's reclusive, fanatical about his privacy."

"How is it you know him?"

"He's a customer of ours."

"Good friend too?"

"Of mine? No, I barely know him."

"Then why would he give you Gianna's name?"

No response.

"Well, Mr. Morris?"

"He . . . didn't give me her name."

"How did you get it, then?"

He was standing so stiffly now, it was as if the coldness in him had frozen his joints. "No one gave it to me," he said. "I met her at the Valconazzi ranch."

"Uh-huh. Under what circumstances?"

"At a . . . gathering out there."

"Gathering. You mean a party of some kind?"

"You could call it that."

"I thought you said Valconazzi was reclusive."

"He is. Where strangers are concerned."

"So it was a party for his friends."

"That's right, his friends."

"Funny you were invited, then."

"Funny?"

"You hardly know him, so you said."

Silence.

"What was the occasion?" I asked.

"I don't . . . occasion?"

"The party. Must have been a reason for it."

Cold silence.

"Does Valconazzi have these gatherings often?"

More of the same.

"Did he have one last weekend?"

"I don't know. If he did I wasn't invited."

"Sex parties, are they?"

"You . . . what?"

"The kind Valconazzi throws. Orgies?"

"Good Christ, no."

No eye flick that time.

I said, "But Gianna was at the one you attended. As a guest or what?"

"A guest, yes."

"Was she with Valconazzi? His date?"

"I don't remember."

"He introduce you to her?"

"Yes."

"Any other hookers there?"

The cold stare.

"Mr. Morris?"

"I don't know. I only met Gianna."

"Was Ashley Hansen there?"

"I've never met Ashley Hansen."

"But was she there?"

"Not as far as I know."

"Gianna attend any of Valconazzi's other gatherings?"

The stare again.

"You've been at more than one, right?"

No reply.

"Who else attends these parties? Give me the names of some of Valconazzi's friends."

"No," Morris said. "No, by God. I've said enough— I'm not going to tell you another damn thing."

It wasn't bluff; he meant it. You can prod a man just so far, no matter how much leverage you happen to have. I'd pushed Dick Morris smack up against something—some kind of secret—that he was more afraid of having revealed than his paying for high-priced sex. Another, tawdrier vice? Some illegality connected with John Valconazzi? Whatever it was, I wasn't going to find it out from him.

Even so, I gave him back some of his own cold silence. Just to see if he had anything else to say. He did, but it wasn't much.

"I don't know where Gianna is," he said. "I haven't seen or talked to her in three weeks. I don't know anything about her disappearing or the death of her roommate. That's the truth. Go ahead and sic the police on me if you think I'm lying, create a public scandal, harm my family—it'll be on your conscience if you do."

Right. My conscience. I pitied his wife as much as I pitied Big Dave Edwards's.

I let him have a little more of the silent treatment, but he was all through talking. He was not going to squirm or melt any either. He just stood there waiting for me to go away.

OUTSIDE, IN THE CAR, I called Eberhardt's line at the office. Not without reluctance and half hoping I would get his machine. I got him instead, on the third ring.

"It's me," I said. "You got a little time?"

"What for?" Civil, but just barely.

"I need you to do something for me."

"I'm busy," he said.

Anger rose in me; I put a cap on it. Business, damn it,

this is business. I took a couple of deep breaths before I said, "Eb, I'm on the road and in the middle of a job and I've got to have background on a Marin County resident. You know a guy in the Marin sheriff's office; I don't. Barker, is that his name?"

Five seconds went by; six, seven, eight—

"Barkley," he said.

"Right, Barkley. Call him for me, will you? Get him to run a check on a West Marin rancher named Valconazzi, John Valconazzi. Lives on the Petaluma–Marshall Road. You got a pencil? I'll give you the probable spelling."

Shorter pause this time. "Hold on." Then, "Go ahead."

I spelled the name for him. Italian names are easy enough to spell, and not just for another Italian; you can work out most of them phonetically with no trouble. Too many non-Italians don't even bother to try.

"Anything else?"

"While Barkley's at it, he might see if there's any criminal record on a Dick—probably Richard—Morris, works for Jeffcoat Electric in San Rafael."

"Morris, yeah."

"Thanks, Eb. Have Barkley call me when he's got the dope, on my car phone or at the office. That way you won't have to hassle with it. I need it as fast as he can oblige."

"Don't you always?"

I let that go. "Any calls, anything going on this morning?"

"Nothing for you."

"Eb . . . listen, you know we have to talk. If we could just sit down together—"

"I got to go," he said.

"Wait, don't hang up—"

He hung up.

Chapter **15**

BOLINAS IS SOME thirty miles from San Rafael, the shortest route to it from there being due west out Sir Francis Drake Boulevard to Olema and then south through the Olema Valley. It's a pretty drive, past redwood forests and over rolling hills and through fir and eucalyptus groves—or it is when your head isn't clogged with business and personal matters. Today the road could have wound across the cratered surface of the moon for all the attention I paid to the surroundings.

Once you come out of Olema Valley, the Bolinas Lagoon—a sanctuary for marine bird life, thanks to the Audubon Society—opens up straight ahead. The main road skirts the lagoon to the east and takes you into Stinson Beach; a branch to the right leads out onto a two-mile-long sandspit, at the tip of which is Bolinas. The village is well over a century old, a long-ago lumber and shipbuilding center from which schooners ran a regular schedule to and from San Francisco. Nowadays it's the kind of moldering isolated seacoast hamlet that tourists refer to as quaint, that attracts artists and societal misfits and dropouts of one stripe or another, and that breeds distrust of outsiders. Bolinas's provincial attitudes are such that there are no road signs in West Marin telling you how to get there or when you've arrived. Whenever the county puts one up, some local goes out and rips it down.

It had been years since I'd been out there, but nothing much had changed. The scattershot architecture looked the same: Victorian cottages, beach cottages, sagging frame and brown-shingle houses, sea shanties, an occasional newer ranch-style home, and just plain shacks. There is a certain charm to the place on days like this one, when the sky is darkly overcast and the wind blows hard and wet with salt mist and few people are out and about. Come here on a sunny summer weekend, though, when it's packed with gawking sightseers and packs of teenagers and beer-guzzling surfers and sullen residents, and you won't find it half so engaging.

Once the Olema–Bolinas Road passes through the two-block business section, it narrows considerably and undergoes a name change to Wharf Road. A fifth of a mile is all there is of Wharf Road; it ends at a narrow beach where the lagoon meets Bolinas Bay. Funky cottages and shanties line it on the lagoon side, most of them built on pilings, some set behind a high, continuous board fence. Only one of the dwellings was pink, a kind of deep-rose pink—the last of the ones hidden behind the fence.

The opposite side of the street was reserved for parking. I found a space and walked back to where a doorway was set into the fence in front of the pink cottage.

The door was shut, but not locked; I went on through, into a tiny yard bloated with weeds and brush and a single gnarled buckeye tree in full bloom. The cottage was old and run-down and badly in need of a coat of paint, pink or otherwise. A shutter hung at a drunken angle from one window, flapping a little in the rough wind. The tide was out and the smell of mudflats came up sharp and fishy from underneath.

There was no porch, just a single step up to a warped pink door. I looked for a bell push, didn't find one, and worked my knuckles against the door panel. When that failed to bring anybody I pounded the wood with the heel of my hand, hard enough to rattle the door in its frame. No one responded to that either.

I did a slow turn to check the immediate vicinity. Right-angle extensions of the fence enclosed the yard and the cottage on its two sides, down to where a low bank sloped to the waterline. To the north, the upper story of a doddery Victorian was visible above the fence, but its windows were all blind with shades. I moved around on that side of the cottage, to where I could see its back side. Rectangular deck on barnacled pilings, with stairs leading down to a short, empty pier. Nobody on the deck, nobody on the pier, nobody on a narrow boat channel dredged through the mudflats beyond.

At the front door again, I tried the knob. Locked— but the lock wasn't much. I had it open in less than a minute. There had been a time when breaking-and-entering a stranger's empty house was something I would not have done. The three-month Deer Run ordeal had lowered some of my loftier principles. Maybe the loss of patience and certain scruples have made me a lesser man, but ironically it may also have made me a better detective.

I shut the door behind me, stood looking into a long, narrow living area that extended the cottage's full length. Sliding glass doors at the far end gave access to the deck; through them I could see all the way across the lagoon to the Stinson Beach road and the hills beyond. Man's place, this—a man who had Western-style tastes. Navajo rugs on the bare floor, horse prints and riding paraphernalia as wall decorations, square-block furniture with slung leather seats and backs, an old-fashioned potbellied stove complete with a Rube Goldberg flue arrangement, a big wet bar faced with half a dozen hand-tooled leather stools, a stereo system and a rack of CDs that would no doubt be mostly country and western. All very casual and haphazardly arranged, pieced together by the kind of individual who has no interest in how a place looks to anyone other than himself.

It wasn't warm in here, but neither did the room contain any of the day's chill. I laid a hand on the stove's rotund side. Warmish. A fire had been built inside earlier this morning.

Off the living room at the rear was the kitchen. Dirty dishes in the sink, bread crumbs and morsels of some kind of yellow cheese on the dinette table. I picked up one of the cheese things and rubbed it between my thumb and forefinger. Soft, not hard—not more than a couple of hours old. Bread and cheese: some breakfast.

A hallway led from the kitchen to two bedrooms separated by a bathroom with ancient plumbing and a huge clawfoot tub that left little room for the other fixtures. In the larger of the bedrooms was a rumpled king-size bed and a nightstand that held a half-empty bottle of bourbon, a finger-marked glass, and an ashtray jammed with cigarette butts. Along the baseboard was a space heater. I bent to feel it. Cool to the touch. Used earlier today, though; the room still retained the warmth from it—

Sudden banging noise out front.

At first I thought it was the door slamming; I stood up tense, listening. Then the sound came again, and this time I recognized it: the wind smacking that broken shutter against the outer wall.

Still alone in here . . . but for how long?

I searched the cottage quickly but thoroughly, room by room, opening drawers and closets, examining the few pieces of paper I found. There was nothing in the place to link Chet with Gianna Fornessi. Or with Ashley Hansen or any other woman. No cosmetics or lingerie or other items of female apparel. Not even the lingering scent of perfume in the bedroom to indicate that he'd shared the rumpled bed with anyone last night. Melanie Harris had said that Chet's sexual tastes ran to D&S and S&M, but I found no evidence of that either—no bondage equipment, no autoerotic devices. The only item of a sexual nature was an unopened package of French-tickler condoms.

Surmise: The women he brought here were one-night or one-weekend stands. If he had a wife or steady girl-friend, she had either never been here or he controlled her visits to the point where she was not allowed to leave even a whisper of herself behind.

Another surmise: Chet was not a full-time resident. There were no bills or canceled checks or receipts or any private papers—nothing with his full name on it. The wet bar was well stocked, but the refrigerator and pantry weren't. The bedroom closet contained a minimal amount of clothing: two shirts, one pair of Levi's jeans, one pair of slacks, one light jacket, one battered Stetson hat, one pair of old leather boots. This was a beach cottage all the way: weekend retreat, hideaway, party house.

So why did he stay last night, a Thursday? And why the solitary drinking in the bedroom?

I went back in there, without any conscious realization of why until I was standing next to the nightstand. The overflowing ashtray, the crushed-out butts . . . Kools. Every one of them was a Kool.

Bisconte, I thought.

Not Chet—Bisconte.

The Kools, the liquor, the bread-and-cheese breakfast . . . it made sense, it felt *right*. And not just last night; the past couple of nights. Instead of skipping the Bay Area on the cash Melanie had brought him, he'd talked Chet into letting him hole up here for a while—give the heat time to cool, figure out what he was going to do. Maybe Chet owed him a favor, or maybe he had something on Chet, or maybe it was strictly a cash deal.

But where did he go this morning? Short trip, returning before long? Day trip, coming back tonight?

Done hiding and gone for good, on his way to parts unknown?

Check here again later, I thought. That's one way to find out.

I quit the cottage, resetting the front door lock on the way. The wind seemed colder now, damper, with a taste of rain in it. The black-edged clouds confirmed that it might rain a little out here later on. Wharf Road was still empty when I stepped through the gate in the fence. I pulled my coat collar up and walked the short distance to the village's business district.

The first two merchants I tried were uncooperative; one said in surly tones that he didn't know who owned the pink cottage, the other seemed to take me for a salesman and wouldn't talk to me at all. Number three, the elderly proprietor of Bud's Liquors, was the one I was looking for: talkative, not too inquisitive, and not so mistrustful of strangers.

"Sure," he said, "I know Chet. You a friend of his?"

"No. He may have something I'm looking for."

"Wouldn't be surprised. He's a promoter, Chet is."

"How do you mean?"

"Oh, you know, knows a lot of people, gets around pretty good. You want something from him, he can probably help you out."

"Married, is he?"

"Seems I heard divorced."

"Likes the ladies?"

Toothy grin. "Who doesn't?"

"You ever see him with a young, dark, Italian girl? Early twenties, name's Gianna?"

"No-o. Can't say I have."

"How about with a tall blonde, same age—looks Scandinavian, wears a lot of gold jewelry?"

"Don't sound familiar."

"Man named Jack? Big guy, late thirties, thick hair on his arms and chest, smokes Kools."

"Don't sound familiar," Bud said again.

So Bisconte, if Bisconte was hiding out at the cottage, hadn't bought his bourbon or his cigarettes from Bud. One of the other stores in the village. Or Chet had bought them for him.

I asked, "Chet been in lately—past couple of days?"

"Nope. He's a weekender."

"Never shows up during the week?"

"Not so's I remember. Doesn't come every weekend neither. Just when it suits him."

"He have any close friends in town?"

"Don't know who they are, if he does."

"Where could I find him on a weekday?"

"His old man's ranch up the coast," Bud said. "That's where he lives and works."

"The Valconazzi ranch?"

"That's the one."

I wasn't surprised, not even a little. "Chet Valconazzi —John Valconazzi's son."

"Right. You know John?"

"Not yet. Soon maybe."

"Well, if Chet hasn't got what you're looking for, could be John does."

"Yeah," I said. "Could be."

* * *

SOMETIMES ON A CASE—not nearly often enough— you get caught up in an avalanche effect. You muddle around not finding out much, going from one lead to another, working through a blockage of small truths, half truths, outright lies, and dead ends. Then finally you get hold of something and it turns out to be a keystone: yank on it and the whole thing begins a fast tumble into place.

I was driving past Samuel P. Taylor State Park, on my way back to San Rafael, when the car phone buzzed. Phil Barkley, Marin County sheriff's department. He had the information I'd requested through Eberhardt, though first he wanted to know if what I was working on was anything he should know about. I said it might be, but that I didn't have enough facts yet, and sketched out the basic details for him. When I promised to notify him if and when I uncovered any evidence of illegal activities within his jurisdiction, he was satisfied.

He said, "Okay, here's what I've got. First—Richard Morris, Jeffcoat Electric. No arrest record of any kind, not even a parking ticket. Officially, he's a model citizen."

"John Valconazzi?"

"Him, we got a jacket on. Six arrests dating back twenty years, the last one eight years ago. Six convictions, four stiff fines but no jail time. All the same misdemeanor violations—California Penal Code 597, 597b, and 597j."

"Which are?"

"Cruelty to animals; fighting animals or birds; possession of gamecocks for fighting purposes. Valconazzi is a cockfighter, and I mean in a big way. Raises high-class birds, sells them all over the country, fights mains and hacks on his ranch most weekends during the summer and off and on the rest of the year. He's got a national reputation in cockfighting circles."

I digested this before I said, "How come eight years since his last arrest?"

"He's smart, that's why," Barkley said. "Our office has set up raids more than once since then, acting on tips from animal rights people. None of them netted us a thing."

"How come?"

"Valconazzi has a tight security setup. Guards on the main entrance gate, guards patrolling his property lines whenever there's a match in progress. All the guards are outfitted with walkie-talkies; they see a raiding party coming, they call a warning to the ranch. The way the place is built, the condition of the roads, it takes a good fifteen minutes to get to the ranch buildings from any direction—and by then they've shut down the fighting and masked or hidden everything illegal. They've got cover-up procedures down to a science. The officers in the raiding parties couldn't find so much as a single gaff or dead rooster. All they found was a bunch of people having a picnic and coops full of live chickens. And there's nothing illegal about raising gamecocks in California, unless you can prove the raiser is fighting them."

"So in effect Valconazzi's an untouchable."

"Unless we raid him with helicopters and thirty or

forty men, and that's not going to happen. Cost-prohibitive on a misdemeanor; we'd never get county permission. Or unless the animal rights activists provoke him into making a mistake someday. There've been a couple of confrontations at his ranch. But Valconazzi's got the trespassing law on his side; we've had to arrest half a dozen people who were on his property illegally, trying to break up mains."

"Valconazzi's son, Chet," I said. "He a cockfighter too?"

"Like father, like son."

"Jacket on him?"

"Nothing major," Barkley said. "Couple of DUIs, one assault charge that didn't amount to anything."

"What were the circumstances of the assault?"

"Just a minute, I'll check. . . . Woman claimed he beat her up, busted her arm. Six years ago. But she dropped the charges two days later. Paid off, probably."

"Prostitute, by any chance?"

"Good guess. You want her name and address?"

"Local?"

"L.A."

"Maybe later. Is John Valconazzi still married to Chet's mother?"

"No. She died several years ago."

"He remarry?"

"No."

"How about Chet? Is he married?"

"Divorced."

"Either of them living with a woman, would you know?"

"No. Nothing in our records on that."

"How old is John?"

"Early sixties. Let's see . . . yeah. Sixty-three last month."

The Old Cocksman. Not much doubt of that now. In her calendar notation Gianna hadn't been referring to her weekend john's sexual prowess, except maybe in a sly secondary fashion. The reference was to his passion for raising and fighting gamecocks.

All right, so she'd evidently gone out to the Valconazzi ranch last Friday to attend another of his weekend cockfights and to ply her ancient trade. And not for the first time, because Dick Morris had met her at an earlier "gathering." Something must have happened to her during or after her visit, probably Saturday night or early Sunday. But what? And at the ranch or somewhere else? And who was responsible? John Valconazzi, the Old Cocksman? His son, who was into S&M and who had broken a hooker's arm once? Jack Bisconte? Or somebody else who'd been at the ranch watching a bunch of poor brainless birds rip each other into bloody shreds?

Chapter 16

DICK MORRIS WAS NO longer at Jeffcoat Electric. Gone for the day, the receptionist said; not expected in again until Monday. She had a nice face and she wasn't unpleasant to me, so I believed her. I didn't even make things difficult for her by trying to pry loose Morris's home address. She wouldn't have given it to me anyway.

I drove to a Shell station near the freeway on-ramp and communed with the Marin County telephone directory. There were no Dick Morrises and not too many Richard, D., or R. Morrises. Assuming he lived somewhere in the county, if not in San Rafael proper, and if he didn't have an unlisted number, he shouldn't be too difficult to track down. I copied all the likely Morris listings into my notebook, then sat in the car and went to work with the mobile phone.

The fourth Richard Morris I tried was the right one. A female voice—young, fifteen or sixteen—answered, and I asked if this was the number for Dick Morris of Jeffcoat Electric, and she said yes it was, but he wasn't home. Did I want to talk to her mom? No, I didn't, but could she tell me what time Dick was expected? Sup-

pertime, probably, she said. Any message? No message,
I said—and she hung up before I could say good-bye
and without saying good-bye herself. Cold father, cold
daughter.

The address that went with the correct number was
5977 Woodland Avenue, San Anselmo. I looked it up
on my Marin County map. Woodland Avenue climbed
one of the hills off Sir Francis Drake Boulevard, not
more than three miles from where I was. I pumped
some gas into the car and drove on over there.

Morris's house was at the top of Woodland—a big
old redwood-sided place guarded by trees and fronted
by a lawnless garden that was one-third crushed rock
and wood chips, one-third flowering shrubs, and one-
third leaf mold. In the driveway sat a plain white station
wagon into which a plump blond woman in jogging
clothes was loading baseball equipment and three kids
in Little League uniforms. There was no other car in
sight. Evidently the cold daughter had been telling the
truth about her father's absence.

I made a U-turn, drove back downhill to Sir Francis
Drake. Now where? There didn't seem to be much
point in going back to the city, since I still had business
over here. But it was only a little after two, and Morris
wasn't expected home until suppertime, whenever that
was in his household. Another swing through Bolinas,
see if anybody had showed up at the pink cottage? Or a
ride out to the Petaluma–Marshall Road to reconnoiter
the Valconazzi ranch?

I tossed a mental coin. Bolinas lost.

* * *

NOVATO, A DOZEN MILES north of San Rafael, used to be a sleepy little farm town. One of my cousins had had a ranch up there when I was a kid, half a mile outside the village; he'd sold it off in the late fifties, for what he considered a handsome price. If he'd hung on to his 120 acres for another couple of decades, his two sons would be millionaires today. Over the past twenty-odd years Novato has grown into a minicity of fifty thousand residents, with sprawling subdivisions and luxury countryside homes—the bedroom community of choice for large numbers of San Francisco cops, firemen, office workers, and professional people.

Thousands of acres of Marin farmland have died as a result. Thousands more are doomed to the ever-rapacious developers, who have already consumed nearly a million acres of Bay Area croplands since 1950—forty percent of the total that year. All in the name of progress, yes sir. More and more folks coming into the state, more and more folks born in the state, we've got to have more and more housing, right? More and more *cheap* housing, right? Never mind how we're going to feed all the new and old citizens if there's no land left to plant crops on. Never mind all the agricultural jobs, thousands of them, that have already been lost and will continue to be lost. The buck's the thing. The Big, Big Buck.

So one of these days, sure as death and taxes, all of Hicks Valley Road will be lined with tracts—and most of the Petaluma–Marshall Road will be too. For the time being, though, once you reach the intersection of the two, you're more or less back in unspoiled Marin. Rolling hills patchworked with summer-browned grass and stands of dark green trees; dry creeks and rocky meadows and long stretches of bottomland spotted with dairy cattle; ranches few and far between, their buildings nestled in hollows or pressed back against the hills. Not many cars or people. Quiet. A place to go when you're tired of having your senses assaulted by your fellow man. A place without distractions; a place where you can afford to think and drive at the same time.

The Petaluma–Marshall Road is even more sparsely populated. Narrow, twisty, it follows a slender valley with steep wooded hillsides to the left and rumpled meadowland to the right. Buckeye trees in full bloom grow thickly out here; Spanish moss beards the branches of dusty old oaks.

After a couple of miles, low rounded hills closed in to compress the cattle graze. The land on that side took on a broken, eroded aspect, creased by shallow ravines and stream beds. At 2.5 miles by the odometer, the fencing that bordered the road appeared newer, sturdier. I had not passed any ranch buildings or access roads in more than a mile, and as the odometer reading neared 3.0 I began to look for one or the other. Even so, I didn't spot the half-hidden intersection until I was almost parallel to it.

The turning was screened by pepper and buckeye trees, and I had to brake sharply to make the swing. The pole sign mounted there was even less conspicuous: small, made of metal suspended on chains, dark red lettering on a crisp white background. VALCONAZZI, it said; and below that, HOLSTEIN-FRIESIAN CATTLE—MORGAN HORSES. The ranch road was unpaved, dusty, rutted. Ten yards in from the county road, it made a sharp right-hand loop and dipped down behind the trees, so you couldn't see the gate blocking it until after you'd completed the turn.

I had to brake sharply a second time and the car slid a little, sideways, in the dust. The gate was tall, of tubular metal, painted white like the sign; a thick chain and padlock secured it to an iron stanchion. Barbed-wire fencing ran off on both sides. Beyond, the serrated roadbed snaked down through a hollow, up over a rise, and out of sight. None of the ranch buildings was visible from this vantage point.

For no good reason I got out of the car and walked up to the gate. The weather was better out here than it had been at Bolinas—no fog, the overcast torn apart in places by high-altitude winds. The wind blew strong at ground level too: cold, and this close to Tomales Bay, smelling faintly of salt. I stood with it billowing my hair and clothing, looking through the gate and along the empty road.

An odd feeling of disconnection came over me. What am I doing here? I thought. John Valconazzi, Chet Valconazzi, Gianna Fornessi . . . I didn't know any of them, had laid eyes only on Chet and then for about two minutes. Ranches and cockfighters, a hooker with a probable heart of stone—and a fifty-eight-year-old detective who likely was not going to realize a dime from his involvement with any of them. All the probing and running around I'd been doing did not seem to have much point when you looked at it that way. Dead or alive, Gianna was a bad seed; dead or alive, her grandfather and the rest of her family were going to suffer if and when they found out the truth. What the hell was there for me in any of that? White knight on another crusade for truth, justice, and the American way? Bullshit. Small truth, tiny bit of justice, absolutely no effect on the American way. She was a hooker, for Christ's sake.

She was a human being, for Christ's sake.

Hookers sell their bodies; private eyes sell another kind of expertise. What's the difference, really, when you get right down to it. DeKuiper last night: *Everybody's a whore, one way or other.* The son of a bitch was right. Profoundly right. Everybody's a whore, everybody sells *something* in order to survive. And survival is the key—every person's inalienable right to survive.

That was what I was doing here. The same thing I'd been doing most of my life, the only thing I know how to do, poor old whore that I am: selling myself on the side of what I believe is just, trying to protect people's right to survive.

The Valconazzis and the Biscontes of the world were playing God; so was I. The difference was, I was trying to play a better one.

IT WAS FOUR O'CLOCK when I drove back up Woodland Avenue in San Anselmo. I'd figured I might as well give Morris another try, even though it was not suppertime yet by anybody's reckoning. Bolinas was another long drive and San Anselmo was more or less on the way.

Good choice: Parked in the driveway of 5977 now, in place of the station wagon, was a new dark blue Buick Electra. And sitting alone on the front porch, with his coat and tie shed and a drink in his hand, was Dick Morris.

He got up in a hurry when he saw me park and step out of the car. He came down off the porch in long, stiff-legged strides. I stayed on the sidewalk, waiting for him. He had to be angry, upset, but none of that showed in his face or in those morgue-cold eyes. The iceman cometh.

He stopped a pace away and thrust his bony snout to within three inches of mine. "How dare you," he said.

I don't like people invading my space uninvited. I backed him off by squaring up my shoulders and crowding forward, fast and aggressive. "I'm doing a job," I said, "and you're not cooperating. Blame yourself, Morris. If you'd told me everything this morning, I wouldn't have had to look you up again."

"For God's sake keep your voice down. My daughter's in the house."

"Sure," I said. "If you don't withhold any more facts."

"What do you think I withheld?"

"The cockfighting, for one thing."

"How did you—" Surprise had opened his mouth; cold will closed it again.

"I told you this morning—detectives have ways of finding out things. You claimed you don't know anybody named Chet; John Valconazzi has a son named Chet. You claimed you didn't know who the Old Cocksman could be. You didn't tell me the truth about the 'gatherings' at the Valconazzi ranch. You also didn't tell me that you're mixed up in an illegal bloodsport. Do you just watch, Mr. Morris? Or do you bet on cocking mains too?"

"All right," he said.

I waited.

Slow inhale; slower exhale. He was caught and he knew it, but he wasn't contrite. Or afraid. Or angry or upset, either; I'd mistaken that. He wasn't anything. The man had about as much interior as an empty freezer. "I didn't tell you about the cockfighting because it *is* an illegal sport," he said. "Consorting with a prostitute is scandalous enough. If it should come out that I attend and gamble on cockfights, I could lose my job as well as my standing in the community."

Job first, standing in the community second. Family third—or fourth or fifth. Mr. Wonderful. I waited some more, not giving him an inch.

"All right," he said again. "You have more questions. Go ahead, ask them."

"Did Valconazzi hold a cocking event last weekend?"

"Nearly every weekend during the summer."

"Friday, Saturday, Sunday?"

"Saturday and Sunday."

"Did you go?"

"Only on Saturday. I had other plans for Sunday."

"Was Gianna Fornessi there?"

"Yes."

"All day?"

"All day."

"Still there when you left?"

"I think so. There was a big crowd."

"So the last time you saw her was sometime Saturday evening."

"Yes."

"What do you think happened to her?"

"I have no idea."

"You said John Valconazzi introduced you to her. Truth or another lie?"

"The truth."

"Was she always with him at the ranch?"

"I never saw her with anybody else."

"How about Chet? He ever buy her services?"

"I don't know."

"Never said anything to you along those lines?"

"No."

"But he does use hookers, same as his father?"

"Sometimes."

"Ashley Hansen?"

"Once. I saw him with her once."

"At the ranch?"

"Yes."

"How many other times did you see Ashley there?"

"Just that once."

"But Gianna was a regular, right?"

"I saw her out there four or five times."

"Enjoying herself? Into the cockfighting?"

"Yes. Women like the sport—some women. All the blood. It gets them . . . excited."

"You too, huh?"

No reply.

I said, "I hear Chet's into S&M and D&S. That what you hear?"

Shrug.

"What about John? He like to hurt women too?"

"I have no idea. Other men's preferences are none of my business."

"You, then. What's your sexual bag?"

"That's none of *your* business," Morris said. Then he said, "Damn you."

His bearing and his voice were very stiff now. He didn't like talking about sex, not with a stranger and probably not with anybody, including his wife. At the core of Richard Morris there was a little dry-ice ball of prudishness.

I asked, "Lot of women attend Valconazzi's cock-fights?"

"Not many. A few."

"Respectable women?"

"Most of them."

"How many people altogether, on a typical day?"

"Anywhere from fifty to a hundred and fifty."

"Mainly locals?"

"Quite a few out-of-towners."

"Heavy betting?"

"Yes."

"You bet heavily yourself?"

"No," he said.

Eye flick. The hell he didn't.

"Things ever get out of hand? Fights? Weapons?"

"Of course not. What do you think cocking enthusiasts are?"

I didn't tell him what I thought they were.

"The only trouble we've ever had," Morris said, "is with the damned animal rights activists. A band of them tried to break up a main last year and there were some scuffles. John had them arrested for trespassing."

"Uh-huh. What about hard drinking, drugs?"

"Not that either. Cockfighting is a serious sport, a civilized sport. My God, we're not pagans. Men have been breeding and fighting gamecocks for three thousand years—decent men, important men. George Washington and Thomas Jefferson were both cockers. Abe Lincoln was a referee in Illinois."

"That doesn't make it morally right."

Icy zealot's stare.

"Let's talk about Jack Bisconte," I said.

"What about him?"

"You still deny that you know him?"

"No. I've met the man."

"At Valconazzi's?"

"He's been at some of the mains."

"Pimping for Gianna and Ashley?"

"No. Gambling."

"But you do know he was their pimp."

"Yes, I know it."

"You buy your time with Gianna through him?"

A car was grinding its way uphill. Morris turned his head abruptly to watch it come into sight; then he put his eyes on me again. He'd thought it might be his wife's car, but it wasn't.

He said, "What did you ask me?"

"Bisconte. You make your arrangements for Gianna through him?"

"Just the first time. I didn't have anything to do with him after that."

"No? Why not?"

"He . . . I thought he was asking too much for Gianna's favors."

Favors. Christ.

"And you argued about that?"

"Yes."

"What happened?"

"Nothing happened. I had no choice—I paid his price."

"Then what? You called Gianna direct whenever you wanted to see her?"

"That was the arrangement, yes. The price had been fixed. There was no need to go through Bisconte again."

"Were they charging Valconazzi the same amount?"

"I don't know. Probably."

"You ever try to negotiate a lower price with her?"

"No. She . . . Gianna is worth the money. Every penny."

"Yeah," I said.

"I don't care what you think of me," he said.

"Morality is in the eye of the beholder, right?"

Nothing from him.

I said, "Is Valconazzi fighting cocks again this weekend?"

"Mains scheduled for both days."

"Starting times?"

"Tomorrow at two, Sunday at four."

"How late do they run, usually?"

"Fairly late on Saturdays. Eleven or twelve. That's the day for big mains—at least a dozen hacks. You know what mains and hacks are?"

"Suppose you enlighten me."

"Mains are tournament competition," Morris said. "Usually the Valconazzis versus breeders from other parts of California or out of state. Hacks are individual contests, one cock owned by each breeder. Whichever breeder wins the most hacks wins the main."

"Uh-huh. And on Sundays?"

"Smaller mains and grudge or special hacks. They seldom run later than about eight P.M."

"You planning to be there this weekend, both days?"

"Just tomorrow."

"How does Valconazzi work things with his guests? Notify them by phone or what?"

"Written invitation."

"So only people he knows personally get to attend?"

"No, not necessarily."

"This written invitation—you have to show it at the gate to get onto his property?"

"Yes."

"It have the guest's name on it?"

"No. It's a plain card with dates and times."

"Sent through the mail?"

"Yes."

"This weekend's card," I said. "You have it on you?"

"In my car."

"I'd like to see it."

Morris hesitated, couldn't find a way to refuse, and in his stiff-legged gait moved off to the Buick. When he came back he handed me a blue rectangular card, like a library card, with rounded corners and tomorrow's and Sunday's dates and times typed on it with a red-inked ribbon.

"So you drive up to the gate," I said, "and show this card to the guards. Does it buy you automatic entrance? Or do they have to know you or your car license?"

"The card is all that's necessary."

"They don't ask to see any ID?"

"Just the card," Morris said.

I tapped it against my thumbnail. "Tell you what, Mr. Morris. Suppose you spend tomorrow with your family. Weather should be better than it is today; you could go on a picnic or something."

"You want the card," he said.

"Like I told you, I have a job to do."

"If John ever finds out where you got it—"

"He won't find out from me. And you won't have to worry about me showing up at your office or your house again either. We never have to see or talk to each other after this. Sound reasonable?"

"If you mean what you say."

"You have my word. That is, if you keep the exchange confidential. And if you haven't told me any more lies or withheld any more information."

The front door of his house opened just then and a pudgy teenage girl came out on the porch. "Father!" she yelled. "Telephone!"

Morris didn't move, didn't speak for about five seconds. Then he said to me, "Take the card," and executed one of his military about-faces and left me standing there. He didn't look back.

The iceman goeth. To hell with the iceman.

Chapter **17**

RAIN WAS NO LONGER threatening to dampen Bolinas. The sky out there was still overcast, but now it was with thickening patterns of fog that had already blurred the outlines of the hilltop homes. There were more people in the village center, moving in and out of the grocery and liquor stores—commuters home from their jobs and stocking up for the evening or the weekend.

A parking space was free in front of one of the art galleries; I claimed it, rather than taking a chance on Wharf Road. Before I quit the car I unclipped the .38 from its hiding place under the dash. Smith & Wesson Bodyguard, Airweight model, with a two-inch barrel and a five-round cylinder capacity. Not much of a gun, really, for any use other than sport shooting—but I didn't want much of a gun. I don't like the things, never have; hadn't owned one in several years, before this one. I'd bought it after the incident in the Salinas Valley in April, when I had needed a firearm and hadn't had one and as a result, with perfect irony, I had killed a man in another way. If I'd had a gun that day I might

not have his death on my conscience now. So I'd bought
the .38, gotten the proper permits for it. It was strictly
for emergency service, to be carried only as a safeguard
and used only under extreme duress.

I checked the loads, slid the piece into my jacket
pocket. It weighed less than a pound, with its light-
weight frame; there was no telltale sag as I walked down
to Chet Valconazzi's pink cottage.

The .38 turned out to be unnecessary. So did the second trip out here. Bisconte wasn't in residence. No
smoke came out of the chimney, no lights burned in the
windows against the encroaching fog, and nobody answered when I banged on the door.

Back in the car, I considered my options. Run a
stakeout? The cold and fog said no; so did the dull
weariness behind my eyes. Long day already, and I still
had a fifty-mile drive back to the city.

Call Harry Craddock, relay my suspicions to him?
Not that either, not just yet. I had no proof that Bisconte had been staying here; the Kools and a hunch
weren't evidence. No point in crying wolf—particularly
not if Chet Valconazzi had had anything to do with Gianna's disappearance. Police interest might scare him
into an even tighter cover-up.

Which brought me to the prospect of infiltrating the
Valconazzi ranch tomorrow afternoon. At the time I'd
gotten the invitation card from Morris, it had seemed
like a good way to ferret out information. But was it?
Unfamiliar territory; hostile environment; enemy turf.
Plus I did not know enough about cockfighting to run

much of a bluff. If I wasn't careful I could get myself arrested for trespassing . . . or worse. Worth the risk?

Worth it, I thought. A week nearly gone already since Gianna's disappearance, and the more time that elapsed, the harder it would be to find out what had become of her. Evidence vanishes or gets successfully hidden; people forget or misremember useful details. There would be individuals at the ranch tomorrow who had been there last Saturday, who might know something. And if necessary I could do a little fast shuffling with the Valconazzis, *padre e figlio.*

Maybe then I'd have something definite to pass along to Harry Craddock—and not just about the whereabouts of Jack Bisconte. I had a bad feeling that Gianna was going to turn out to be the same kind of police matter as Ashley Hansen.

DUSK WAS SETTLING when I recrossed the Golden Gate Bridge into the city. As tired and hungry as I was, I drove straight to O'Farrell and the office.

Among the half-dozen messages on my machine were two from Dominick Marra, both worded pretty much the same. He wanted to talk to me; he would either be home or at the Sons of Italy social hall. I called both places and he wasn't at either one, though he'd been at the social hall until about twenty minutes ago. Went to have dinner at Giacomo's, the man I spoke to said. I thought about calling the restaurant, one of the older and better family-style eateries in North Beach, but then I remembered that one of their specialties was *tortelli di erbette*—a spinach-stuffed ravioli prepared the old-fashioned way. The thought of their tortelli made my juices run.

Next stop: Giacomo's.

BY THE TIME I found parking and walked to the crowded, noisy place, it was eight-thirty. Dominick was still there, occupying a table in back near the kitchen. That was the good news. The bad news was that Pietro Lombardi was sitting there with him.

The two of them wore dour expressions and my appearance did nothing to lighten their moods. A half-eaten dish of cannelloni sat in front of Dominick; the spaghetti and meatballs Pietro had ordered was hardly touched. But they'd done all right with the carafe of red wine on the table: it was almost empty.

I said, "All right if I join you?"

"Sure, sure," Dominick said without enthusiasm, "sit down."

I sat down. Pietro turned his seamed face toward me, and the look of his eyes was a shock. Lifeless, moist with pain and disillusionment—the eyes of a dog that has been whipped by a master he adored. I could feel their hurt penetrate deep inside me.

He knows, I thought. Somehow he found out.

Nobody said anything until a waiter had appeared and taken my order for the tortelli and a glass of Chianti. Then Dominick asked, "You got some news for us, hah?" His tone said that he was afraid of the answer.

"No."

"Ah," he said.

"But you have some for me."

He glanced at Pietro and said gloomily, "You already know, I think."

"Who told Pietro? You?"

"*Sì.*"

"Why?"

"I don't want to, but he's get it out of me. Old friends like us, is not so easy to keep secrets."

"Is better I know," Pietro said. Flat, empty voice, belying the words.

I wanted to say something comforting, meaningful. But all I could think of was, "I'm sorry, Pietro. I wish none of it had turned out this way."

"It don't matter." Another lie; it mattered a great deal. The knowledge of what his granddaughter was had shattered him, just as I'd feared. Why the hell hadn't Dominick kept his vow of silence?

There was a short awkward time during which none of us had any words. Dominick ended it by speaking to Pietro in a rapid-fire Neapolitan dialect, so I wasn't able to follow much of it. When he was done Pietro shrugged, pushed back his chair, and went off in the direction of the bar. Old man's stride, more shuffle than walk—old, old man.

"What'd you say to him?" I asked Dominick.

"Leave us alone for little while, go have some more wine."

"So you and I could talk."

He nodded. "The messages I leave for you, I mean I want to see you alone. Just you and me, private."

"I didn't know Pietro was here with you or I wouldn't have come."

"He don't want to stay home, all alone. So we go to Spiaggia's, we go to Sons of Italy, we come here."

"You wanted to tell me Pietro knows about Gianna."

Another nod. "You don't find her yet?"

"Not yet."

"But you know why she's disappear?"

"Part of the reason, maybe, but none of the details."

He waited. I didn't elaborate.

"You don't want to tell me, hah?"

"I don't want Pietro to know."

"You think *I* tell him?"

"You told him the truth about Gianna."

Dominick looked pained. "You think I do that on purpose? *Cristo e Madonna,* I rip my tongue out before I hurt Pietro like that."

"Then what happened?"

"He's smart man, he's hear about Gianna's roommate and he's see in my face something's wrong . . . he's make good guesses. I try to lie, but I can't do it—I can't lie to Pietro."

I was being too hard on him; I squeezed his arm. "I don't blame you, Dominick."

He muttered something in Italian. I let it pass; the words had the sound of a lament that was better left untranslated.

The waiter brought my Chianti and a basket of hot garlic bread. I'd been ravenous when I came in; not anymore. Even the aroma of the garlic bread did nothing to revive my appetite.

"About Gianna," I said. "I'll know more tomorrow or Sunday. Then I'll give you the whole story."

"Could be she's just go away, hah?" he said hopefully. "Nothing bad happen to her, she's just go away?"

"I don't think so."

"You think she's dead?"

"I'm afraid she is."

"Somebody's kill her like the roommate?"

"If she is dead, yes."

"Who? Bisconte?"

"I don't know yet."

He drained the wine in his glass. "Maybe is better we never know," he said. "Maybe is better you don't find out tomorrow or Sunday."

"Better for Pietro, you mean?"

"For Pietro, for Gianna's mamma, Gianna's sisters—everybody."

"You're the one who begged me to find her, Dominick."

"So I make mistake. Now I think is better you stop."

"I can't stop. It's too late for that."

"Why?"

"Justice, my friend. If she was murdered, whoever killed her has to pay for it."

"Justice," he said. "Pah!"

"You'd rather her killer got away free?"

"I tell you—"

He broke off because Pietro was returning, a half-full glass of red wine in one hand.

"In the bar they tell jokes, they laugh too loud," Pietro said when he reached our table. "I can't listen to that. So I come back." He sat down, heavily. "You talk about her, hah?"

I said, "Yes."

"You find out where she's go? Why?"

"No."

"But soon, good detective like you."

I had no comment on that.

"You do me favor, hah? When you find her."

"If I can."

"Ask her why she's do this thing, bring disgrace on her family, sell her body for money like that *bionda tintura* she's live with. You do that for me?"

"Don't you want to ask her yourself?"

"No," he said. "I don't want to see her no more. Never. You understand?"

"I understand."

He nodded; drank deeply from his glass; lit one of his black cigars with hands that were not quite steady. And I realized, belatedly, that he was more than a little drunk. He said to Dominick, "You finished talking?"

"We finished?" Dominick asked me.

"Yes."

Pietro got to his feet. "We go now. Too much noise here, too much *ilarità*. We go where is quiet, drink more wine."

Dominick gave me an appealing look, one more silent plea to drop my hunt for Gianna. I gave nothing back to him. Just too damned late for everybody concerned.

Dominick sighed, stood, and I watched the two of them move away. Stooped with the burdens they carried, robbed of the peace that should have eased their last few years; victims of a world they no longer understood. And that was another reason I couldn't and wouldn't quit. Hell, the main reason. Justice was an abstract; victims were reality. I do what I do for the sake of the victims.

The waiter brought my tortelli. At first I didn't want it, just sat there looking at the steaming plate. Then its aroma began to work on me and pretty soon I picked up my fork and began to eat.

I ate it all, scraped the plate clean. Ate all the garlic bread, and asked for more and ate all of that. Drank all my wine too. And ordered a double dish of spumoni for dessert.

Sometimes you can't eat; sometimes you can't stop eating.

Sometimes the human animal makes no sense even to himself.

Chapter **18**

SATURDAY WAS ANOTHER FINE, clear day, with no trace of Friday's mist and low clouds. San Francisco weather: as changeable as a politician's campaign promises. Read my lips . . . no new taxes. Read my lips . . . today we'll have perfect weather except for the possibility of fog by noon, thundershowers by three P.M., and light hail by dinnertime.

The sunny skies helped put me in a more cheerful frame of mind as I drove up to Diamond Heights, and may or may not have had something to do with the high good spirits I found waiting in the occupants of Kerry's apartment. She and Cybil had coffee ready for me, and a plate of hot sweet rolls to go with it. Cybil seemed particularly perky today, with as much animation in her eyes and her voice as on the occasion of our first meeting years ago.

While we were having the coffee and rolls, Cybil sprang a little surprise on me. "I've decided to start writing again," she said.

That was good news and I said so. She knew how

much I admired her work for the pulps. "Short stories again?" I asked.

"At first, to prove to myself I haven't forgotten how to write fiction; it's been more than three decades, you know. Then a novel, I think. I've always wanted to try a novel."

"Detective novel?"

"Well, probably."

"You have an idea in mind?"

Kerry said, "Don't bother asking. She has one, but she won't even tell me what it is."

"It'll just be for my own amusement," Cybil said. "I doubt if I could write a salable novel after all these years." Thoughtful pause. "Then again, Rex Stout was publishing well into his eighties and P. G. Wodehouse at ninety-two. Why not Samuel Leatherman at seventy-seven?"

She could do it. The old Cybil could do anything she set her mind to and it was the old Cybil doing the talking here.

After breakfast we got her luggage loaded into the trunk of my car. Ordinarily, since I had business in Marin later in the day, I would have suggested that Kerry take her car too; but there was a stop I wanted to make in the city before I headed out to the Valconazzi ranch, so I'd already planned on making two trips over and back. Cybil was relatively talkative on the drive, but none of her conversation included the taboo word "marriage." Kerry was no doubt elated.

Larkspur, one of the old pocket communities south of San Rafael, is a pretty little town dominated by redwoods. The seniors complex was near the brief stretch of Magnolia Avenue that serves as the town center, a bigger and lusher setup than I'd expected. Seventy-five individual units, rec room, dining room, small clinic, swimming pool, and nine-hole putting green neatly arranged on five rustic acres. If you didn't know it was a retirement complex you'd take it for a batch of expensive condos—a mitigating factor in Cybil's decision to move there.

We met some of the staff, were given the grand tour. Cybil's apartment turned out to be four large rooms on the ground floor, with a fenced patio shaded by a massive redwood. Nice, private, comfortable.

I did porter duty with the luggage. Then we drove to a small shopping center nearby, within walking distance for the complex's residents who were carless, so Cybil could buy a few staples. It was eleven when we got back, and the movers showed up at eleven-thirty, half an hour early. Kerry and I were on our way fifteen minutes later; we'd have only been in the way if we'd hung around. I got a good-bye hug and kiss from Cybil. In solid again, all right.

We stopped at Larkspur Landing for lunch, at a place where we could sit outside and watch the ferry boats making their slow way across the bay. It was one-ten when I dropped Kerry at her apartment.

"If you get done with business early enough," she said, "come on over. I haven't had a man in my own bed in more than six months."

"Once you get me in, you may not be able to get me out again."

"Oh, I plan to keep you in for a long time. And I'm not just talking about my bed."

Bawdy woman. Hot damn.

I was feeling pretty chipper as I drove over into Noe Valley; it had been a good day so far. But neither the feeling nor the quality of the day lasted much longer. Just until I got to Elizabeth Street. Just until I saw Eberhardt.

BOBBIE JEAN'S SIX-YEAR-OLD Volvo was parked in front of his old two-story house. I'd have been surprised if it wasn't. They spent most Saturdays together here; Eberhardt was a homebody at heart and Saturday was his day to putter, be a couch potato. Daytripping was reserved for Sundays, usually.

Bobbie Jean answered my ring. Ambivalence in her greeting: she was glad to see me, but she knew why I was there without my having to say anything and it started her worrying again.

"Eb's in the backyard," she said.

"What kind of mood is he in?"

"Not too good. He's been . . . distant, moody."

"Still not talking about me, his plans?"

"No."

I went through the house, out the back door. Eberhardt was at the brick barbecue he'd built along the side fence, poking around inside it with an iron rod. In the air was the smell of burning charcoal flavored with mesquite. The smell and the sunstruck look of the yard yanked a grim memory out of my subconscious.

Sunday afternoon in mid-August, five years ago. The

two of us here in the yard, drinking beer, getting a little tight, while Eb prepares the coals for steaks. Down day for both of us: me because I'd had my license suspended for no good reason other than tight-assed city politics, him because he has dark things—the bribe he'd taken—preying on his mind. We step inside to get the steaks and potatoes ready, and that's when the doorbell rings. Eb goes to answer it. I hear his voice exclaim, "What the hell—" and then the two gunshots, and I run in there and he's down and the shooter stands framed in the doorway with the gun in his hand; and before I can react the shooter pops me once, high in the chest, and puts me on the floor too. He runs then and I crawl around in my own blood . . . reach Eberhardt, see the hole in his belly and the wound on the side of his head, and I think he's dead. . . . I think I must be dying too. . . . I think it's finished for both of us . . .

But we're a couple of tough old birds. Too tough and too ornery to let go of life without a hell of a fight. We'd survived that day and the grim days that followed it, and we'd gone on to survive other assaults, other crises. What doesn't destroy you makes you stronger, and stronger still. If we'd come through that bloody Sunday five years ago, we could get through any damn thing. Couldn't we?

He heard me coming across the grass, turned, expecting to see Bobbie Jean. When he saw that it was me his face closed up, hardened; you could watch it happening, like a time-lapse photo of cement drying. He stood with his brows pulled down, the rod aimed at me as if it were a weapon. He was wearing one of those gray and white, vertically striped chef's aprons with the words WORLD'S GREATEST COOK emblazoned on it. Combined with the pointed rod and his scowl, it made him look silly. But I didn't laugh. I did not even smile.

"What're you doing here?" he said.

"I was in the neighborhood."

"Yeah, sure. I don't suppose it's business?"

"No," I said. "Mesquite smells good. Steaks?"

"Burgers. Just enough for Bobbie Jean and me."

"I wasn't going to try wangling an invitation."

"Good."

"But you could offer me a beer."

"You know where the fridge is. Hell, you slammed me into it, remember? Could've ruptured a disc along with my spleen."

I walked away from that. Literally. Took a slow turn around the yard, under the leafy Japanese maple, over past the remains of the vegetable garden he'd put in a couple of years ago and then let die. When I got back to the barbecue he was working at the coals again, shifting them around with the rod.

For a time I watched him do that. And it was as if I was seeing him, really *seeing* him, for the first time in years. You live or work with somebody day in and day out, and after a while you lose sight of him, take him visually for granted. Any radical physical alteration registers, but the subtler changes go unnoticed.

When a man grows older, starts pushing sixty, a kind of weariness settles into and around the eyes. Lines deepen; eye colors fade. The weariness in and around Eberhardt's eyes seemed much more pronounced than my own, the crow's-feet longer and deeper, like fossil imprints in weathered rock. Bitterness was there, too, in his gaze and in the pinched set of his mouth. He looked old, standing there in the sun in his World's Greatest Cook apron, old and tired and squeezed out. As old and tired and squeezed out as Pietro Lombardi, eighteen years his senior, had looked last night. For a shocked moment I wondered if maybe he was sick, had contracted some kind of debilitating disease; he was the type who would tell no one, guard its existence as jealously as a miser guards his hoard of gold. But then I thought: No, it's not like that. It's age, nearly sixty years of hard living taking their toll. Some people get old faster than others and he's one of them. The process accelerated by . . . what? Cynicism? Lost hopes, faded dreams? A sense of failure?

The zest is gone, I thought, that's the thing. Jesus, the zest. Always a man with a big appetite for life, but somewhere in the past year or two or three he's lost it. The World's Greatest Cook isn't hungry anymore.

He felt my eyes probing at him, swung his head my way and then straightened with his shoulders drawn back—a defensive posture. "What the hell you looking at?"

"You."

"What for? Trying to figure out what makes me tick?"

"After thirty-five years? Not much chance of that."

"Funny," he said. "Shit," he said.

I made no comment.

"So what do you want? As if I didn't know."

"I want us to be friends again," I said.

"Bosom pals, huh? Well, forget it."

"Why, Eb?"

"You know why."

"I've told you over and over how much I regret that punch. Why isn't that enough?"

"It just isn't."

"What do you want me to do? Walk through those coals there in my bare feet? Atonement by fire?"

"You always think you're so goddamn funny."

"I wasn't trying to be funny. I'm looking for some way to get things back on an even keel between us. I don't want to lose you as a friend or a partner."

He looked at me. Didn't speak, just looked at me with his tired, zestless eyes.

"Let's get it all out in the open, all right?" I said. "I know you've been talking to people about opening your own agency and you know I know it."

"And *you* don't like it."

"I wish you'd talked to me about it at the beginning, instead of going behind my back."

"I have to clear everything I do with you first?"

"I didn't say that—"

"Didn't have to say it. I want to talk to people, be my own boss, it's *my* business."

"As long as there's no conflict of interest."

"What does that mean?" he said. Then he said, "Oh, I get it. You think I might try to steal your clients."

"The possibility occurred to me, yes. You've been so damned—"

"Jesus Christ."

"—secretive lately. How do I know what's going on inside your head?"

"And I suppose you been accusing me of it, calling up all your accounts, telling them what a shit old Eb is."

"I haven't accused you of anything to anybody."

"I'll bet."

Round and round, round and round. None of this getting us anywhere. I said, "Eb, tell me one thing straight out. No hedging, no bullshit."

"No bullshit in *my* mouth, pal."

"Are you quitting? Straight answer."

"You'll know when I know."

"So you haven't made up your mind yet."

No answer.

"What're you waiting for? More contacts, financing, what?"

No answer.

"Or is it you're afraid it might be a big mistake?"

"Mistake? Why? Can't hack it on my own—that what you think?"

"I never said that."

"But it is what you think."

"We're not high-tech operators, Eb. There's too little skip-tracing and insurance work and too much competition already at our level. Another one-man agency—"

"I'm not stupid," he said. "I know the risks involved."

"All right, Christ, then *why?*"

"Why what?"

"Why take the risks? Why now, all of a sudden?"

He started to answer, changed his mind and said nothing.

"There's more to it than that poke in the belly," I said. "There's got to be."

"Bet your ass there is."

"What? What, then?"

"Freedom," he said.

"From what, for God's sake?"

"From you, your business, your way of doing things. *Your* agency, damn it . . . never was mine or ours, never will be. I'm just a glorified employee."

"That's not true."

"Isn't it? Think about it, buddy boy."

"I don't have to think about it. I've never treated you like an employee—"

"Never? Half the time is more like it. Always telling me what to do and how to do it, like I'm some kind of half-wit. I open my own agency, I'm my own boss. *I* make the decisions, run things my way . . . prove to you and everybody else my way's just as good, maybe better."

Thickness in my throat now like a wad of phlegm; I swallowed a couple of times to work it loose. "Eb, if that's the way you feel . . . I'm sorry. Why didn't you try to talk to me about it, get it out into the open . . . ?"

"I did try. More than once. But you, you don't listen."

"*I* don't listen?"

"Damn right you don't."

"Pot calling the kettle black here."

"Yeah, right. Turn it around, lay it on me. That's your style. Everything's my fault and you never make any mistakes."

I bit back a sharp retort; screwed my temper down tight. "Okay. Okay, I'm listening now, I'm hearing every word you say loud and clear. You want changes in how things are done? All right, we'll make changes—anything within reason. Just tell me what you want done."

Nothing from him.

"Come on, Eb. Give and take."

"It's too late," he said.

"Why is it too late?"

"Still be your agency. And you're too set in your ways, just like I am. Make changes and how long'll they last? A month, two months? Then something comes up, push comes to shove, and who wins in the end? You do."

"I don't understand why it has to be a win-lose thing. There's no competition between us. Or there shouldn't be."

Silence.

"Listen," I said, "we can try, can't we? Start fresh, try to work it out?"

His mouth quirked in a wry, humorless smile. "Know what you sound like? Husband trying to talk his wife out of leaving him."

My immediate reaction to that was anger. But it didn't last long; underwent a transformation into self-mocking humor. "Hell, you're right. Please don't leave me, sweetheart."

"Ha ha," sourly.

"Isn't our friendship worth saving? That much at least?"

He made a meaningless gesture.

I said, "That's not an answer."

"Only one I got for you right now."

"Eb, listen—"

"No. I done enough listening. Cut me some slack, will you? Let me enjoy the rest of my Saturday in some goddamn peace."

What can you say to that?

"Go on," he said, "get out of here."

I nodded. Put a hand on his shoulder, briefly—he didn't pull away from it, but he didn't respond to the gesture either—and went to the stairs. I was halfway up when I heard him say my name. I stopped and turned, thinking that he was going to call me back, that maybe he'd had a sudden change of heart.

"On your way out," he said, "tell Bobbie Jean to bring me a beer."

IN THE CAR I TRIED to remember a time, any time, when I had treated Eberhardt as a half-wit or an employee. I couldn't, but there could have been any number of clashes between us that he'd interpreted that way. We were different people, with different mind-sets and methodologies. I was a workaholic, totally committed to my job; he was a man who separated and compartmentalized his personal and professional lives, who worked to live rather than lived to work. We'd fought often enough about his willingness to let his caseload pile up; and I kidded him mercilessly—jerked his chain too much, maybe—because he was so sobersided, had no sense of humor and was incapable of laughing at himself. But I had never looked down on him, either as a person or as a detective. Never.

Got to be even more to it than that, I thought. Something deeper . . . something he can't or won't talk about. The same something that's aging him so fast, making him so bitter.

Freedom, he'd said, freedom from me. That hadn't seemed a satisfactory answer at the time, but if you looked at it the right way, maybe it was. Opening his own agency, becoming his own boss, as a way to recapture what was lost and missing from his life—I could understand and accept that. The thing I couldn't understand was where I fit into his loss in the first place.

What did he imagine I'd done to him? What was ripping him up inside?

Chapter 19

THERE WERE TWO GUARDS on the gate at the Valconazzi ranch. One perched on a camp stool under a buckeye tree on the outside, the other sat on the fender of a dusty stake-bed truck on the inside. The truck was drawn up tight against the gate so that nobody could get through unless it was moved. Both men were big, young, garbed in work clothing; each had a walkie-talkie clipped to his belt.

When I pulled up, the one on the near side got up and came over to the driver's-side window. He didn't say anything, so I didn't either. Just handed him the blue invitation card. He looked it over, nodded, gave it back to me, and gestured to the other one. Reverse the truck, open the gate, and I was in—easy as pie, as long as you had the invitation.

The road was so badly rutted and unevenly graded that I had to crawl along at under ten miles per hour. Even so, thin plumes of dust rose and hung behind me. Not nearly as much wind out here today, and a good fifteen degrees warmer. Summer smells of the dust and the pepper trees, of dry grass and cattle. Nice day in the country; nice day for spilling a little blood.

The session with Eberhardt had laid a band of tension across my neck and shoulders that had not eased much during the drive from the city. Now I could feel it pulling even tighter, stiffening the muscles all the way down my back.

Up over a hillock, down through a sharp leftward curve at the bottom, around the base of another bare brown hill. Then I could see the ranch buildings, spread out in a long hollow that stretched into a notch between two bigger hills. It was a massive place, all right: two-story white frame house set among ancient oaks dripping Spanish moss, two weathered red barns with sheet metal roofs, horse stables and a network of corrals, a shedlike structure that would probably house farm machinery, three long, low chicken houses, an elaborate wire-fenced chicken run. In a cleared area on the near side of the largest barn maybe fifty cars, pickups, and other vehicles were parked in orderly rows. The barn's double doors were open, I saw as I clattered over a cattle guard and into the sprawling ranch yard; one man stood alone just outside. There was nobody else in sight except for a quartet of women under the oaks near the house, busily setting out trays of food. Buffet supper, complete with a couple of kegs of beer and other liquid refreshments. And two rows of picnic tables to eat it on. Beyond the trees, there was even a clutch of outdoor toilets.

The Valconazzis sure know how to throw a party, I thought. Yes they do.

I swung over toward the barn, found a place to park in the improvised lot. When I got out I could hear the swell of voices from inside the barn—excited voices raised to the level of yells. I headed there at a fast walk, trying to look eager and as though I belonged here.

The guard out front was ten years younger than me, long and lanky, wearing a straw hat; he took the hat off and fanned himself with it as I approached. The glance he gave me was cursory. "Main's already started," he said.

I nodded and moved past him into the barn.

It was brightly lighted, with rows of stalls and gleaming automated milking equipment; fairly clean, but still redolent of hay and manure. It was also empty. All the noise was coming from what looked to be an annex that you got to by way of a passage at the near end.

The annex was sixty-by-eighty and fitted up for only one purpose: cockfighting. High-wattage bulbs hanging from low wooden rafters lighted it even more brightly than the barn. In the exact center was the cockpit—a circle some eighteen feet in diameter, made of rough whitewashed boards two feet high, floored with sand; a strong kleig spot directly overhead threw it into white-glare relief. Inside it now were two cocks and three men. Two of the men, both dressed in overalls, were kneeling at the side walls opposite each other. Handlers, I thought. The third man, on his feet but bent at the waist, his eyes intent on the birds, would be the referee.

Tiers of backless benches rose up on three sides of the pit, jammed with people shouting, swearing, calling

out bets to one another. On the fourth side, straight
ahead from where I stood, was a long table on top of
which were weighing scales and behind which were
three men on folding chairs and a blackboard with
chalked names and numbers on it. Beyond the table, at
the far wall, were rows of wood-and-wire cages filled
with more cocks noisily issuing challenges to one another.

Hot in there, the atmosphere so electric you could
almost feel it crackle. All eyes were on the pitted cocks,
one a vivid red-gold, the other a creamy gray with a
thick neck ruff. Circling each other at the moment;
feathers crimson-streaked, the gray bird with a broken
wing and one eye hanging out of its bloody socket.
More blood glistened on the sand, on the wall boards,
on the handlers' overalls. The long steel gaffs affixed to
the backs of the birds' legs threw dazzling glints of light.

I started to move ahead, my eyes on the crowd, so I
didn't see the start of the sudden flurry of action in the
pit. The crowd voice rose excitedly; a woman somewhere close by began to chant, "Kill him, Red, kill him,
Red, kill him, Red!" I picked her out: big strawberry
blonde sitting rigidly; sweat-glazed face, hot, avid eyes,
red-gashed mouth that kept up the chant in a heavy
panting monotone. Like a woman having sex, I thought,
exhorting her lover to climax. Jesus.

In the pit the two cocks were locked together just
above the floor, spurs and beaks lashing at such an accelerated speed they were a blur. Five more seconds of
that and then they dropped and broke apart, or tried to;

one of the red's spurs had gotten hung up in the other bird's broken wing.

"Handle!" the referee shouted. "Forty-five seconds!"

The two handlers sprang forward, separated the cocks; each took his rooster to a side wall and began to work over it like a prizefighter's second. The gray chicken's handler massaged its torn breast, used his finger to wipe away the hanging eyeball, to clean out the empty socket. Then, for Christ's sake, he took the bloody, mangled head into his mouth and began to breathe heavily into the cock's nostrils in an attempt to revitalize it. I quit watching. I had no stomach for this kind of thing.

There was a place to sit at the end of the third row in the nearest tier. I climbed up there and rested my hams, scanning the crowd. Close to a hundred fanciers and spectators, all but half a dozen of them men. Mixed crowd in terms of age. And of dress: overalls and Levi's jeans, sports outfits, even one guy in a jacket and tie.

"Pit!"

The handlers were back in the center of the ring, and at the referee's cry they released the tails of their birds. The two cocks met in midair, seemed to hang suspended for three or four seconds amid a storm of feathers, blurred yellow feet slashing at each other; then they dropped, paused, lashed out, sparred, rolled against the wall and broke apart again. This time their reaction was to circle, ruffs up, heads low, exchanging fierce glances. The strawberry blonde set up her chant again, almost keening the words now.

I gave my attention to the crowd. None of the women

was Gianna Fornessi. None was under thirty except for
the big blonde, and from the look of her she was a lot
older than her years. At first I couldn't locate Chet Valconazzi, because he wasn't wearing the Stetson hat today. Then I spotted his curly black head and flushed
face in the front row on the far side; he had a fistful of
cash and appeared to be taking bets on the half-dead
gray cock.

"Five to one on my Whitehackle!" I heard him shout.
"I'll take five to one on my Whitehackle!"

Jack Bisconte? No sign of him. John Valconazzi? One
of the men seated at the weighing table, I thought, the
white-maned one in the middle—

Renewed action in the pit, sudden and furious. The
two cocks came up off the floor and seemed to explode
against each other with a tremendous whacking noise,
like two pieces of wood banged hard together. Feathers
flew, steel flashed. After a few beats they dropped
again, with not much more damage done . . . except
that the savagery of the attack had further weakened
both birds, the battered Whitehackle to a near-dazed
state. The red stag—I heard somebody label it a Roundhead—stayed above its adversary on each subsequent
clash, finally drove it to the ground and pecked relent-
lessly at its head, working on the one good eye.

"Kill him, Red, kill him, Red, *kill him!*"

The Whitehackle appeared to be completely blind
now, its entire head a welter of blood. But it kept retali-
ating by instinct, legs drawn back with the gleaming
spurs high—and the other rooster was too exhausted to
avoid every random slash. One needle point ripped

open the Roundhead's breast. And when that happened I heard Chet Valconazzi's voice lift high and frenzied above all the others, exhorting the Whitehackle as the strawberry blonde was exhorting the Roundhead.

Neither bird had strength left to get up in the air; all they could do was shuffle, their peckings and spur strikes growing slower, more sporadic. This listless sparring seemed to go on and on, until at last the red cock staggered and went down on its side, couldn't rise again and lay there quivering with its torn breast staining the sand. The gray weaved around stupidly, feeling for the other with beak and spurs. At last one blind thrust drove bloody steel into the Roundhead's neck, upward into the brain.

The Whitehackle was still staggering back and forth, pecking the air, when its handler stepped forward and scooped it up; then the bird uttered a feeble crow of victory. Chet Valconazzi's answering crow was loud, elated. The blonde had let out a moaning sigh when the red died; now she began to swear bitterly. Among the rest of the watchers the end of the hack brought about a release of tension that had an almost sizzling quality, like a sudden bleeding of steam from an overloaded boiler. I could feel the release myself—an unpleasant sensation that made me feel crawly, unclean. Sweat oiled my neck and face; I got my handkerchief out and sponged it away.

The Roundhead's handler removed the ravaged corpse from the pit. The Whitehackle's victory reward was a quick death: It was too badly hurt to survive and so its dark-skinned handler broke its neck, then tossed it into a wheelbarrow that waited near the far wall. The red cock's remains went into the barrow too.

Chickens, that was all they were—just chickens. That was one of the arguments cockers used. Another was that mortal combat was the very nature of the gamecock; that the stags always fought fair and never quit and that death in battle, with a chance to defend themselves, to survive, was a better fate than accorded the bulls in bullfights and a far better fate than having their heads whacked off with an ax so they could be served up in somebody's fricassee pot. Gallantry, raw courage—and the most exciting sport on earth. That was cockfighting, its proponents claimed, a cult and a diversion born a thousand years before Christ.

Rationalizations, every one.

What I had just witnessed was blood sacrifice, pure and simple. That blonde sitting there . . . she didn't give a hoot in hell about gallantry and raw courage and proud death. She wanted her bloodlust sated. They all did. Breeding their sacrificial birds, gathering in sweatboxes like this one, rationalizing it all so neatly in the name of sport . . . shedding their veneer of civilization, giving in to atavistic cruelty and male narcissism. The Roundhead and the Whitehackle were only chickens; but intelligent men ought to be able to rise above the level of birds and beasts. . . .

I made myself concentrate on the conversation that rose and fell around me. Listen and learn. I learned that today's main was a contest between Chet Valconazzi, who mainly bred Whitehackles and Shawlnecks, and a breeder from Fresno, Ed Levinsky, who fought Round-

heads, Dominiques, and Arkansas Travelers. Levinsky
did his own handling; Valconazzi's handler was a Mexi-
can farmhand and experienced cocker named Miguel.
The hack just completed was the second of the day, with
Valconazzi Whitehackles winning both. He had a knot
of men around him now, at the edge of the pit, and he
was strutting a little for them like one of his own roosters. As I'd guessed, the white-haired man at the table,
busy weighing birds and chalking numbers on the blackboard, was old John.

But that was all I learned. I tried to start a dialogue
with the farmer type sitting next to me, but he wasn't
having any; he gave me a blank look when I mentioned
Gianna Fornessi's name and returned his attention to
the pit, where Miguel and Ed Levinsky were working
with two fresh, sleek fighting stags. Each held his bird
under one arm, head away and legs raised in front, and
with a little saw each cut off a bit of the natural spur on
the back of the cock's leg; then they wrapped the spur
with chamois and tied on the wicked steel gaffs. The
heels were an inch-and-a-quarter in length, one of the
nearby fanciers said. He was unhappy because short
heels were being used; he preferred two-inch spurs, or
better yet, "those big knives they put on the slashers
down in Mexico."

There was a steady hum of noise in the big room—
cocking talk, bets being made, birds making throaty
challenges, benches creaking as people shifted about—
but it quickly ebbed and died when the referee moved
to the center of the pit and held up his hands. An imme-

diate settling down, then; an air of expectancy, a subtle rebuilding of the tension.

"Five-twos this time, five-twos," the referee intoned. Bird weights: five pounds, two ounces each. "Chet Valconazzi with a prize Shawlneck, Ed Levinsky with a Dominique. Standard rules—forty-minute time limit or kill."

A ripple of good-natured cheering for one bird or the other. Valconazzi's voice: "Five hundred on my Shawl—any takers? Who's brave, come on, come on, who wants some action?" Somebody else's voice: "I do. Gimme two hundred of that, Chet." Somebody else's: "I'll take a hundred. You can't stay lucky all day, by God." A woman's: "Here we go, here we go!"

The handlers moved forward. In their grasps both roosters gleamed in the brilliant light, hackles raised, wings low, combs and wattles trimmed close. The cocks' eagerness to get at each other was contagious; the renewed hunger for action, for blood, was like a living presence in there. When the Dominique waved its bottle and started to crow, I could feel the hackles rise on the back of my own neck.

"Bill your cocks!"

Levinsky and Miguel stepped closer, holding their charges forward. The hackle feathers on each rooster rose in wide-open fans; the heads darted forth and back in a series of lightninglike pecks.

"Pit!"

There was no midair collision this time when the handlers let go. The birds flapped down and stayed there, feet shifting restlessly, matching venomous stares. This went on for nearly half a minute before the first attack, a blur of steel and flying feathers . . . and I stopped watching. I'd seen enough hopeless, mindless savagery. Enough of this kind of death in the afternoon.

I watched the Valconazzis instead. Chet was wild with it, sweat streaming off his narrow face, eyes so wide they looked exophthalmic, spittle glistening on his mouth and chin as he entreated his Shawl. The old man's interest was intense but oddly passionless—the unblinking gaze of a connoisseur who sees and calculates everything that is happening in and around the pit. For him, cockfighting was more than a sport and an avocation—it was an intricate pageant enacted for his personal pleasure and careful analysis. For his son, it was the fighting itself; it was the blood.

This third pitting seemed interminable, with dozens of "Handle! Thirty seconds!" and "Handle! Forty-five seconds!" and "Pit!" When it finally ended—I didn't see or care how—the Dominique was the victor. Two hacks to one now, in Chet's favor. Nine more to go . . . ten, if the first twelve ended in a six-all standoff and a thirteenth was necessary to decide the main. There would be an intermission after the sixth hack, so the fanciers and spectators could partake of the food and refreshments, but that wouldn't be nearly enough respite for me. There was no way I could stick it through to the end. The heat and the frenzy already had my insides churning.

I got up, moved around a little. Tried again, vainly, to talk to a couple of the men about Gianna Fornessi. This was not the place for questions. The watchers' minds were so focused on the cocking, it was as if they were all subjects in an experiment in mass hypnosis.

Fourth hack. Won within the first two minutes, mercifully, by a Levinsky Roundhead to even the main at two hacks apiece. Chet Valconazzi was so upset by the outcome that he climbed into the pit and cursed the bloody remains of his Whitehackle, kicked the corpse clear over the wall toward the wheelbarrow. The crowd laughed; the strawberry blonde jeered him in a shrill voice. And I got out of there. Quick, before I puked up what was left of my Larkspur Landing lunch.

I walked slowly through the barn, taking deep breaths. Even the manure-and-hay smell was a relief. Outside, now a breeze had blown up; I leaned against one of the open doors, letting it dry my sweat.

The lanky ranchhand was still standing watch, one shoulder resting comfortably against the barn wall twenty feet away, his booted feet crossed at the ankles. He wasn't looking my way; his eyes were on the women still arranging food and drink under the oaks. When my stomach quit kicking I went over to where he was.

"Hot inside," I said conversationally. "Fresh air tastes good."

He nodded, shrugged, reached into his shirt pocket for a tin of Copenhagen. With his thumb and forefinger he withdrew a generous pinch and worked it inside his mouth until he had it seated where he wanted it between cheek and gum.

I said, "I didn't see Gianna in there."

"Who?"

"Gianna. Young Italian babe, dark hair, nice body. You know, John's friend."

"Oh," he said, "yeah."

"Not around today, I guess."

"Ain't seen her."

"She was here last week, though."

"Guess she was, Saturday."

"How about Sunday?"

"No cocking on Sunday."

"Oh? Supposed to be, wasn't there?"

"Supposed to be," he agreed.

"How come there wasn't?"

"Mr. Valconazzi called it off."

"Why was that?"

"He was away on business."

"Ranch business?"

"Horse business. Morgan breeder over in Nevada decided to sell off a couple of prize studs."

"Ah. When'd he leave for Nevada?"

"Saturday afternoon."

"Before the cocking was finished?"

"Before it started. Soon's the breeder called him."

"He go alone?"

"Seems like," the lanky guy said. His eyes, narrowed down a bit now, roamed over my face. "You a friend of Mr. Valconazzi's?"

"More a friend of a friend of Chet's."

"Who'd that be?"

"Jack. Jack Bisconte."

"Uh-huh."

"You know Jack, right?"

"Uh-huh."

"Seen him around today?"

"Nope."

"How about last Saturday? Was he here?"

"Seems like."

"Gianna leave with him, you remember?"

"Nope."

"No, she didn't or no, you don't remember?"

"Don't remember."

The sun-squinty eyes had gotten even narrower. "You say you know Chet. Whyn't you ask him?"

"Well, you know how it is."

"Can't say I do. How is it?"

I put on a sheepish grin. "That Gianna," I said. "She's got me drooling on myself. I'd like to get to know her, if you know what I mean, but I don't want to rock any boats."

"Uh-huh."

"With either John or Chet."

"Uh-huh."

"John's possessive about her—real possessive."

"Seems like."

"And Chet . . . well, I'm not sure how he feels."

No immediate response. From inside the barn annex, the cockers and their worshipers were screaming approval at another kill or near kill. Up under the oaks, the women continued to work industriously but placidly, as if they were volunteers at a church social.

Pretty soon the lanky guy said in neutral tones, "You want some friendly advice, mister?"

"Sure, why not. I've got an open mind."

"I was you, I'd back off on that Gianna woman."

"Why?"

"Just would, I was you."

"Because of John or Chet—"

I broke off because he wasn't listening; he was all through with me. He shoved off the wall, spat brownly, wiped his mouth, and walked away into the barn.

Chapter **20**

I WANDERED UP toward the house. It was cool under the oaks, the air heavily scented with food aromas. Some repast: two long tables sagged under the weight of cold cuts, cheeses, breads, salads, hot dishes. One of the hot dishes was chicken and dumplings. Made with the bodies of cocks killed in battle? It wouldn't surprise me. Pagan societies ate animals and fowl that had died for their amusement; why not these modern-day blood-worshipers?

There was nothing for me there except a mug of ice-cold beer from one of the kegs. The women all looked to be ranchers' wives and daughters; most would know about Gianna, but none of those who did would talk about her to a stranger, much less admit that she was a prostitute keeping company with their host. I stayed just long enough for the beer to ease the dryness in my throat and complete the settling process in my stomach. Then, girding myself, I walked slowly back to the barn.

The lanky ranchhand was sitting on an old milking stool just inside the entrance. He looked at me as I came in, looked away without speaking. Minding his business and letting me mind mine.

Inside the annex there was a lull between hacks. The main now stood at three-to-two in favor of Ed Levinsky, but that hadn't daunted Chet Valconazzi's fervor. He was still holding court, still arrogantly predicting victory, still taking high-stakes bets from all comers. I sat where I had earlier, well away from where he was.

Too soon to suit me the sixth hack got under way, between a Valconazzi Shawl and an Arkansas Traveler bred by Levinsky. Big stags, these, at six pounds each, and fierce in both demeanor and action; even at opposite sides of the pit, held tightly by their handlers, they beat their wings, grumbling and trash-talking each other in a treble key. Partly for that reason, and partly because this was the last hack before the mealtime intermission, the atmosphere in there seemed even more supercharged. When the referee shouted, "Bill your cocks!" and the handlers brought their birds forward, the racket surged and rolled almost painfully against my eardrums, like thunder in a vacuum.

Sweating again, I turned my attention inward—replayed and reexamined my conversation with the ranchhand. If what he'd told me was accurate, John Valconazzi would seem to have no connection with Gianna's disappearance. She'd been here when he left the ranch last Saturday, had remained for most if not all of the day's cockfighting; and by the time the main was over, old John would have been in Nevada. Or would he? Suppose he'd doubled back for some reason, say, to catch Gianna and another man together. . . . No, hell,

I couldn't buy that. He may have been possessive, as the ranchhand had indicated, but jealous to the point of violence? Over a hooker, even a young and attractive hooker?

All right, assume John did go to Nevada as advertised. By leaving as abruptly as he had, he might have been the inadvertent catalyst for whatever had happened to Gianna. One of the other men tries to take advantage of the fact that she's available . . . makes a pass, is rejected, retaliates with violent anger, and homicide is the result. That I could buy. Chet? He was into rough sex, and it was obvious that blood excited him; that kind of man is a walking powder keg. Dick Morris? He'd already had her, yes, but at what he considered too high a price. And if you dug down under that icy exterior, deep inside his prudish core, you might find something ugly. Bisconte? He was another story. The only motive I could figure for him was problematical: Gianna had decided she didn't need a pimp any longer, wanted to open shop on her own, and he'd taken exception. It could even be that Ashley Hansen had made the same decision, that that was Bisconte's motive for killing *her*. Yet it didn't ring true somehow. Didn't feel right to me.

Chet Valconazzi, John Valconazzi, Bisconte, Morris, an unknown party . . . too many possibilities. I still did not have enough information, no way to narrow down the field. Unless I confronted Chet. He had some of the answers—Bisconte's present whereabouts, for one— and what I had was just enough leverage to pry them loose. Maybe I couldn't prove he'd been harboring a fugitive at his Bolinas cottage, but I was a good enough poker player to convince him that I could. . . .

The crowd noise beat at me in waves; the strawberry blonde was shrieking again, and some of the words penetrated: "Rip his throat out, baby, kill the goddamn shuffler!" My attention shifted involuntarily to the pit, and what was happening in there had such a cruel fascination that I could not tear my eyes away for the thirty seconds it took to reach a climax.

Valconazzi's Shawl had the Arkansas Traveler down near the center, moving atop him in a series of quick strikes with beak and spurs. The Traveler was near dead, torn and bloody, but somehow it kept managing to avoid a killing thrust. It reached up, got a beakful of the other bird's hackles, pulled itself up enough to make one last shuffle. It raked the Shawl with one heel, hurt it enough to drive it back. But then the Shawl came in again, viciously, and did just what the blonde had exhorted its enemy to do: ripped a spur through the exposed throat, nearly slicing the Traveler's head off. Blood gushed; I heard the cock's death rattle even above the cries of the watchers. The blonde screamed, "Shit, shit, shit!" And the Shawl jumped on the dead rooster's chest, slashed at the corpse half a dozen more times, then let loose with a long, triumphant crow.

Part of the crowd applauded; from the rest, catcalls and curses. Chet Valconazzi stood yelling, hands clasped high above his head in the victory salute. I clambered off my seat and went outside, for clean air and to steal a march on the others to the picnic area.

I had a glass of beer I didn't really want and a place

under one of the oaks, away from the tables, when they came streaming out of the barn. Laughing, joking, moving in little packs. Chet was still toting his entourage, and they stayed with him as he heaped food onto a plate and carried it to one of the tables. Somebody brought him a beer; he drank it in one long draught, macho style, and called for another. Then he began to eat with piggish gusto. Watching him and his friends was like watching a Roman food-and-drink orgy played out in modern dress.

There was no way I could get to him yet. And I didn't see his old man: still in the cocking annex, probably. I circulated at the periphery, keeping to Chet's blind side, and managed to strike up three conversations with men eating and drinking alone—two farmers and a guy who said he was a professional gambler from Phoenix. Neither of the farmers knew or would talk about Gianna Fornessi. The gambler admitted to being at the main last Saturday, said he remembered seeing Gianna, but hadn't spoken to her. Nice piece, he said; really got turned on by the cocking. Bloodthirsty. Ed Levinsky's wife was like that too—big blonde over there, must have heard her screaming inside. Yeah, I said, I heard her. The gambler wondered what it would be like to be married to a woman like that. I didn't answer him, because I did not want to speculate on what it would be like.

Chet had finished eating by then and his pack had thinned out for one reason or another. Not much time left before the cocking would resume; if I was going to brace him, it would have to be within the next five minutes.

Four of the five minutes had passed when he finally moved away from his last two friends, started alone toward one of the kegs of beer. I went that way, too, and I would have gotten there at about the same time if a plump, middle-aged woman hadn't hurried up and stopped him halfway. She said something and I saw him frown. They exchanged a few more words and then he walked away—reluctantly, I thought—in the direction of the house.

People were beginning to file back toward the barn. I hung around next to the outdoor toilets, watching the house. Another five minutes slipped away; the picnic area was empty now of everyone except me and the women cleaning up. Valconazzi still hadn't reappeared. Fine, I thought; when he does I'll brace him alone on the way to the barn.

Some more time evaporated, and still he didn't show. What the hell was keeping him? He was going to miss the start of the next hack and that was out of character. Maybe I ought to bite the bullet, go to him instead of waiting for him to come to me. . . .

Sudden rumbling noise from that direction: car engine revving up. And a few seconds later, a pickup truck came barreling into view beyond the house. Dusty blue Ford Ranger, with Chet Valconazzi at the wheel. He swung over onto the ranch road, traveling at a good clip, raising plumes of dust.

My first impulse was to run for my car, try to catch up and then follow him. But it was a hundred and fifty yards to where I was parked, and he could drive that truck over the rutted road a lot faster than I could drive my rattletrap car. He'd be off the property before I got near the gate; and it was doubtful that I could catch him even if I were able to convince one of the guards to tell me which way he'd gone.

I stayed put, working through my surprise. What would send him away from here in such a hurry? Urgent telephone call? Have to be damned urgent to make him miss the rest of his bloodsport.

The plump, middle-aged woman wasn't in the picnic area; I went hunting and found her just coming out of the kitchen at the rear of the house. Housekeeper or cook, probably. She didn't know me and she didn't want to answer my questions; I gave her a wheedling story about needing to see Chet right away on an urgent business matter, and finally she bought it.

"Well, I don't know where he went," she said. "Must say I was surprised to see him drive off, with the main still going on. He'd rather fight those cocks of his than just about anything—"

"He had a telephone call, did he?"

She nodded. "Real important, the man said."

"What man?"

"Well, I don't know. He sounded funny."

"Funny? How do you mean?"

"Didn't talk right."

"Speech impediment?"

"No, I don't mean that. Like he was sick or hurt."

"What name did he give?"

"Just his first name. Chet knew who he was."

"Jack? Was it Jack?"

"It was," the woman said. " 'Tell Chet it's Jack and it's real important.' That's what he said."

Bisconte, all right. It was the "sick or hurt" I couldn't figure.

SEVEN-FIFTEEN BY MY WATCH when I rolled into Bolinas. The good weather had brought the weekend visitors out in droves, and most of them were still hanging around, clogging the village center, trooping in and out of the art galleries. No parking there. I crawled through onto Wharf Road. No parking there either. But I did make one discovery down toward the beach: the dusty blue Ford Ranger, empty, wedged tight against the hillside. I'd guessed right that Chet had come here from the ranch.

I got my car turned around, drove back through town and onto one of the side streets. It was a block along there before I found a place to park. Before leaving the car, and as I had last night, I unclipped the .38 from under the dash and pocketed it. I was not about to take any chances with the two of them together in the cottage.

On Wharf Road I waited at the closed gate until a van loaded with surfers clattered past. Then I eased the gate open, stepped through quickly, shut it again behind me.

The first thing I saw was that the door to the cottage stood wide open.

My scalp prickled; a bad feeling began to build in me. I took the .38 out, held it down low along my right leg, and slow-walked across to the door. The decayed mud-flat smell seemed stronger today, started me breathing through my mouth. Light showed dully inside, some-where in the big front room. Noise spilled out of there too: a radio tuned loud to a soft-rock station. I didn't like that either.

At the door I stood for a time with sweat running on my body, listening. The rhythmic beat of the radio was all I could hear. When I stepped over the threshhold I did it in a shooter's crouch. One, two, three paces—and a floorboard creaked under my weight. But that wasn't the reason I stiffened and came to a standstill.

Now I could smell cordite, faint but unmistakable.

My stomach jumped; lousy day for my insides. I eased ahead, still crouching, until I could see most of the front room. Battleground: furniture disarranged, lamp over-turned, bottle of whiskey spilled on the floor, glass door on the stereo star-cracked, CD discs scattered helter-skelter. And on the cushions of one of the chairs, streaks and spatters of still-wet blood.

Somebody dead in here, I thought.

Right. I found him just inside the kitchen, lying on his back with one leg drawn up, blood around his head like a bent and twisted halo.

Jack Bisconte was no longer a fugitive. Someone had made him another victim.

Chapter **21**

I MADE A QUICK PASS through the other rooms; parted the drapes and looked out over the deck and pier beyond. Except for the dead man, the place was deserted.

So where was Chet Valconazzi? If he'd done this to Bisconte, why was his truck still parked on Wharf Road? Same question if he hadn't done it.

I squatted beside what was left of Bisconte. Shot once just under the right ear with a small-caliber automatic, judging from the size of the exit wound and the shell casing on the floor nearby. And at point-blank range: the right side of his face was scorch-marked. Execution style, I thought. Get down on your knees, close your eyes, say your prayers . . . bang, you're dead. I put the .38 back into my jacket pocket; I didn't like the feel of it in my hand. Guns. This was what they could do. This was what they did do hundreds of times each day, nationwide; what one had almost done to me that afternoon at Eberhardt's house five years ago. Up close and personal.

Ash-taste in my mouth. I worked up some saliva,

tongued it through the dryness, swallowed it. Wet ashes then, just as bitter.

Bisconte hadn't been dead long—half an hour, forty-five minutes, by the look of the coagulating blood. A little too long for Valconazzi to have been the shooter. He hadn't had much more than a fifteen-minute jump on me; he'd have had to drive at dangerously excessive speeds to beat me here by as much as thirty minutes, and that wasn't possible with the Saturday evening traffic. Another thing: Bisconte had been badly used before he was killed. His nose looked broken, there were cuts and abrasions on his face and neck. Knocked around in the front room; that explained all the damage, why the radio was on loud. He'd been a fairly big man, and yet by all indications he'd gotten the worst of the fight. And when it was over and he was groggy, maybe unconscious, he'd been walked or carried or dragged in here and blown away.

If not by Valconazzi, then by who? And why?

I went through the other rooms again. None of them showed signs of violence, or of having been searched. Evidently the shooter hadn't been after anything other than Bisconte. Had Bisconte known him, let him in? Or had he forced his way in? I went to look at the front door. No damage to the lock. I checked the sliding glass door to the deck, the windows in the two bedrooms and the bathroom. No damage to any of those either.

The sink in the bathroom caught my attention. Used recently, by someone washing up. One of the towels had been used too. Faint stains on both the porcelain and the towel fabric. Two different stains, one reddish and the other blue-black. The reddish stain was blood. The other one . . .

Ink?

I got down on one knee so I could eyeball the small blue-black smear up close. Yeah—ink. But not pen ink; a darker, heavier variety.

Printer's ink, I thought.

Brent DeKuiper.

NONE OF THE CARS parked along Wharf Road was a dark-colored Cadillac. I stopped at Valconazzi's Ford Ranger as if I owned it and tried the driver's door. Locked. The passenger door, when I went around to that side, was also locked. I peered through the window glass. Nothing on the floorboards, nothing on the seat except issues of a couple of cocking magazines, *Grit and Steel* and *The American Gamefowl Quarterly.*

I walked back through the village, up the side street to my car. No dark-colored Caddy anywhere in the area.

Valconazzi's pickup but no Valconazzi. And no DeKuiper. Add those two facts together and you got the two of them traveling together in DeKuiper's car, headed . . . where? One guess, but no way of knowing for sure unless I went to check it out.

The probable scenario was easier to figure. DeKuiper manages to trace Bisconte to Bolinas, through Valconazzi or by some other means. Braces him, beats the crap out of him, puts the gun to his head and forces him to call the ranch; that was why Bisconte had sounded "hurt or sick" to the housekeeper. After the call, DeKuiper shoots Bisconte. And when Valconazzi shows up he throws down on him, then hustles him out of there.

Fine as far as it went. But what was DeKuiper's motive for all of this? Why shoot one man here and run the risk of taking another away alive?

What did he know that I didn't?

DARKNESS HAD SETTLED by the time I drove back into San Francisco. A velvety darkness, as much purple as black, the sky free of fog and clouds, so the bridge and city lights had a bright, diamond-hard shine. One of those rare summer nights when you could see all the way to the Farallons. The lighted outline of a ship was visible out that way, too, moving slowly southward at least twenty miles offshore.

Through the Presidio, out past the Cliff House and Ocean Beach to Balboa. Vortex Publications was the only place I could think to go. Long drive for DeKuiper and Valconazzi, just as it had been for me, but maybe DeKuiper hadn't minded it. Maybe what he was planning for Chet could best be accomplished on his home turf.

Hard choice for me, coming here. I could have stayed in Bolinas; I could have taken myself right out of it by calling the Marin sheriff's department. But I didn't want to be out of it, not yet. I had no hard evidence implicating DeKuiper in Bisconte's death, nothing but a smear of ink and a hunch; and if I reported the homicide, it would mean hours of questions and explanations—sitting around, waiting, while the authorities made up their minds to act and finally got the wheels in motion.

Valconazzi could be dead by then. The truth about Gianna Fornessi could be buried by then.

The block of neighborhood businesses was mostly deserted; the only one open at this hour was a Chinese
take-out place. The storefront housing Vortex Publications appeared dark. I drove past and through the next
block, looking for DeKuiper's Caddy; made a couple of
circuits to check the cross streets on either side. Just
one Cadillac street-parked in the vicinity, and it was
white and an older model.

On Balboa again, I parked several doors below the
print shop, on the opposite side of the street, and went
over there on foot. Peering through the dirty front window was wasted effort. He didn't have a night-light on,
so all I could make out were vague shapes. I tested the
lock on the door. Dead bolt, maybe more than one. The
only way to get in through here was to kick the door
down.

I walked to the corner, around it onto 44th Avenue.
A short ways along, a narrow dead-end alleyway cut
three-quarters of the way into the block—a service road
for the business establishments fronting Balboa. The alley was void of streetlamps, but starshine and lighted
windows in the adjacent apartment building provided
enough illumination that I could see to navigate. I
counted business back sides until I came to number five
from the corner; that was Vortex Publications. It had
two thick-curtained windows with iron grilles fastened
over them, the near one small, the far one twice its size,
both showing nothing but dark. The door set next to the

smaller window had been reinforced with metal as a safeguard against break-ins.

I went on past, walking slow. In mid-block behind the apartment building I could make out a recessed area and a row of four garages. One garage was empty; the doors to the other three were shut and locked. No way of telling, without making a lot of noise, if one of those encased DeKuiper's Cadillac.

Back to the rear door to his print shop. Test the knob: locked as securely as the door in front. Turn away, with frustration building inside—

—and there was a sudden scraping noise and the door popped outward, throwing light at me. I came around, half crouching. DeKuiper was standing in the doorway, huge and deadly with a flat black automatic in one hand.

"Figured might be you," he said. "Want in? Well, come on."

I didn't move; I was still trying to regroup.

"Pop you right there, man. Tell cops you're prowler."

Heard me out here, I thought, even though I'd been quiet. Stood inside in the dark, waiting, and made his move when I tested the door knob. Christ!

"Five seconds," DeKuiper said.

I moved, jerkily, with my hands at chest level. He backed up to let me come in; stopped and gestured for me to shut the door. Small storeroom, cluttered with cartons of paper and ink and other printing supplies. A doorway off it led to a lighted hallway, and across that, a second doorway through which I could see part of another lighted room. Lights on all the time, then. I hadn't seen even a glimmer because of the thick curtains—goddamn blackout curtains.

"Turn around, lean on wall there."

I obeyed. He found the .38 on the first pass; made a little mirthless chuckling sound and yanked it out of my pocket. Two weapons to zero now. Emotions swirled inside me, an ugly mix of fear and failure and self-disgust. Screwed up again, for fair this time. Caught and wriggling on my own smart hook.

DeKuiper prodded me with one of the guns. I pushed away from the wall, went into the hallway and across it into the room opposite. Much larger, this one—his living quarters. Rumpled daybed, four mismatched chairs, Formica-topped table, expensive TV set and stereo equipment. At the far wall, an improvised kitchenette. All of it messy, the air stale with the odors of fried food and dirty laundry and the printer's trade.

Chet Valconazzi lay on the bare floor next to the daybed, curled up on his side facing us. His hands were bound behind his back with a gaudily hand-painted necktie. He was conscious, but his eyes had gone into soft focus: the glaze on them was pain. DeKuiper had worked him over even more mercilessly than he had Bisconte. The dark, narrow face was swollen, bloody, disfigured by dozens of cuts, bruises, abrasions. Blood in his throat: his breath rattled liquidly. Internal injuries, too, possibly.

DeKuiper said, "Lookee here, Chet. Company."

Nothing from Valconazzi.

"Sit. Over there."

Those words were for me, and he punctuated them

with a hard shove toward one of the chairs. Old corduroy-covered thing, stained and dirty. I could feel my skin crawl where it came in contact with the upholstery.

DeKuiper remained standing. It was the flat automatic he held pointed at me; my .38 was tucked into his belt. Both of his massive hands, I saw then, were puffy and cut around the knuckles. I looked at his eyes. They were clear, hard—nothing wild in them or in his bearded lumberjack features. A while back I'd had to deal with a berserker holding a roomful of people hostage; DeKuiper wasn't in that category. He was in control of his faculties, knew right from wrong. Hate and rage were what seemed to be driving him, not psychosis. Point in my favor. Even a violently rational man is a hell of a lot more predictable in his actions than a homicidal crazy.

I said, "Why, DeKuiper?"

"Mean Chet there?"

"For one. Bisconte for another."

"Found that bastard? That why you're here?"

"What do you think?"

"Sure," he said. "But I found him first. Better detective than you, huh?"

"Melanie Harris," I said. "Right?"

"Right. How'd you know it was me popped Bisconte?"

"You left some ink residue on the sink. Printer's ink."

"Smart," he said, nodding.

"If I figured you for it, so will the police."

"Think so? No real connection, me and Bisconte. Or me and Chet."

"There's Melanie Harris."

"Uh-uh. Told her forget me. She will."

"Doesn't matter anyway," I said. "I called the sheriff's department before I left Bolinas. Gave them your name, told them I was coming here."

"Think I buy that, pops? No way. Called cops, wouldn't be here yourself."

I let it go. You can't run a decent bluff without leverage. "Why kill Bisconte? Wasn't roughing him up enough?"

"No. Had it comin."

"Why? What'd he do to you?"

"Nothin to me."

"To Gianna, then. Is that it?"

"Not him. Chet."

"Chet did something to her? What?"

DeKuiper's mouth changed shape, quivered—an odd, tragic expression on that Bunyanesque face. "Killed her. Didn't you, Chet?"

Faint moan from Valconazzi; no words.

DeKuiper went over and kicked him in the belly. Valconazzi grunted, moaned louder; his body spasmed into a fetal position.

"Didn't you, Chet?"

"Accident . . ."

"Accident, my ass."

"Swear to God . . . accident . . ."

"Tell him how she died, Chet."

Whimper. DeKuiper kicked him again.

"Tell him."

"Bathtub . . . accident . . ."

"He drowned her," DeKuiper said.

"In a bathtub?"

"His cottage, his tub. Sick fucker's into S&M. Likes hurt women, hold heads under water, pretend drownin 'em. Fantasy shit, gives him big thrill."

"Accident," Valconazzi said. "Swear to God . . . please . . ."

"Screwin her in tub, held head under too long. Right, Chet? What you told me? She fought him but he thought only actin, didn't let her up in time."

Jesus Christ.

DeKuiper said, "Tried revive her, him and Bisconte. Too goddamn late."

"Bisconte was there when she died?"

"Whole time. Other room, waitin his turn. Two of 'em brought her there from ranch, big night fun and games."

I said nothing. There was nothing to say.

"Got drunk afterward," DeKuiper said, "tryin figure what to do. Know what they decided?"

"I can guess."

"Yeah. Take Gianna somewhere, bury her. Pretend whole thing never happened. Figured nobody'd find out. Figured wrong."

"Is that why you shot Bisconte? Because he was there when she died, because he helped bury her body?"

"Wasn't gonna kill lousy pimp bastard, not at first. Just pound him. His fault. Had to open his goddamn mouth."

"What did he say?"

The odd, tragic expression again; and in his eyes, a kind of animal hurt. "Didn't care she's dead. Just another whore, he said. Not to *me*, by God. Special, real special. Told him that, then showed him how special."

He loved her, I thought. As deeply as any man can love any woman. Vengeance is what this is all about—blood vengeance.

"So now what?" I asked him. "Now you kill Valconazzi too? And then me?"

Shrug. "Maybe not you, pops."

That was bullshit and we both knew it. He had no intention of letting me walk away from this alive.

I said, "Why'd you bring him here? Why not just work him over at the cottage, shoot him there?"

"Too many people around, too much noise. Lucky nobody heard me do Bisconte. More private here."

"How about afterward?"

"After what?"

"After you kill him. The body."

"Got that covered."

"Sure you do. His body and mine?"

Shrug.

"So when does it happen? Now?"

"Not now. Plenty of time, hours yet."

"Hours? Why drag it out?"

"Make sure everything's quiet out there," he said. "Midnight, earliest, before we leave."

"Leave for where?"

"Ranch. Where they buried Gianna. Chet's gonna show us, aren't you, Chet?"

Valconazzi moaned again. A chill began to walk my spine.

"Chet's gonna dig her up for me," DeKuiper said. "Then he's gonna take her place."

Chapter 22

TICK.

Tick.

Tick.

Hard waiting, this—the worst kind of waiting. Nothing to relieve it; no more conversation, no sound in the room except for the faint steady drip of the kitchen faucet and the murmur of an occasional car passing out on Balboa. Twice I asked DeKuiper to turn on the TV, to have some noise in there. He wouldn't do it. He liked it quiet, he said. Shut up, he said.

In that kind of heavy-hanging quiet, time and its slowed-down passage consumes your awareness. You begin to imagine you can hear each second tick off in your mind, the spaces between them stretching out longer and longer. You keep wanting to look at your watch, keep fighting off the urge, and that makes you want even more to look . . . push-pull, push-pull, the way it must be for a newly recovering alcoholic with an open bottle of liquor within easy reach. You sweat, fidget, twitch. Your mouth and throat turn dry and your blood thickens. After a while you want to cut loose with a primal yell just to blow off some of the tension.

What made it even worse for me were the similarities between this situation and the Deer Run ordeal. Under the gun; trapped in an enclosed space; helpless, waiting to die. At first I felt stirrings of the posttraumatic stress syndrome I'd endured: claustrophobia, high anxiety, fear-goblins lurking at the edges of my mind. But enough time had passed—over two years now since the kidnapping, a year since the last severe stress symptoms had disappeared—so that I was able to fight off the demons, keep them at bay by an effort of will.

The waiting seemed to have little effect on the other two. Valconazzi was fear-dazed and in too much pain; he passed out before long and stayed out, as much in self-defense, I thought, as from his injuries. DeKuiper had pulled one of the other chairs around so that he could sit watching both Valconazzi and me; and there he sat, legs crossed, comfortable, aware of his surroundings but with a part of himself turned inward. Avenger's nerves. Insulated, cooled by icy rage and righteous hatred and thoughts of his dead love.

Tick.

Tick.

My earlier feelings of failure and disgust had faded. In their place was a simmering anger—at myself, at DeKuiper, at Valconazzi and the dead man out in Bolinas. I channeled the anger into a buffer against the effects of the waiting, by trying to devise ways to get myself out of this bind. Bleak prospects. DeKuiper had the two guns, and age, weight, and strength advantages;

jumping him would be a big risk, particularly here. The only time to try it would be if his attention was diverted. Divert it myself somehow? I couldn't think of a way that was cunning enough to fool him.

And if I couldn't do anything here? Chances were, he'd make me do the driving to Marin—his Cadillac, probably, him in front with me and Valconazzi in back, or both of them on the rear seat. Work some kind of trick with the car? Slam on the brakes, swerve, cause a minor accident . . . disarm him that way? Possible, but that sort of ploy isn't as easy as they make it look in the movies, not when the guy with the gun is wise to the possibility. Signal somebody, then—a passing cop? Also not easy to accomplish.

And if I couldn't do anything before we got to the ranch? The odds wouldn't be any better out there, maybe even worse. Dark, yes; no moon tonight. But there was starshine, and DeKuiper would have a flashlight, and I wasn't familiar with the territory—didn't have any idea of where on the property Gianna had been buried.

Dig her up for me, DeKuiper had said. Ghoul's work. What did he intend to do with her remains after he'd buried Valconazzi—and me—in her place? A week-old corpse . . . Jesus, what *could* he do with her?

Tick.

Cockfighting, kinky sex, "accidental" drowning in a bathtub, late-night burial, grave robbing . . . bizarre, all of it. I hope Pietro and Dominick never find out the full story. I hope Gianna's mama never finds out.

Tick.

John Valconazzi. Did he know about the drowning, the burial on his land? DeKuiper hadn't mentioned his name, didn't seem to think he was involved; all right, neither did I. No son would confide a crime like that to his father. Could be, though, that John had found out about Gianna leaving the ranch with Chet and Bisconte last Saturday. Pressured him about it, got him worried enough to want to consult with Bisconte on how to handle the old man. That would explain why Chet had been looking for Bisconte on Tuesday, why he'd been so worked up and ranting at Melanie Harris.

Tick.

Bisconte. I'd missed him twice at the cottage yesterday; where had he been all day? Out somewhere with Chet, probably. Making arrangements to leave the area, set himself up in some other part of the state or country. He couldn't hide out in Bolinas indefinitely; they'd both have wanted the pressure off from that.

. . . *Tick.*

Ashley Hansen. Another "accident"? Or a genuine accident? One or the other; I couldn't see it as a premeditated homicide. Accident. Yeah, accident . . .

. . . *Tick* . . .

On and on like that: random thoughts, sweating, fidgeting, while the seconds seemed to tick off more and more slowly in my mind. Until, finally, a kind of numbness began to spread through me—mental and physical both. Internal defense mechanism, like the one in Chet that had let him pass out. I welcomed it. Closed my eyes to help it along.

I was in a waking doze, my body still, when I heard

DeKuiper stirring in the other chair. Instantly I was alert again. I watched him get up on his feet, stretch his big frame; watched him watch me.

"Time, pops," he said.

I rubbed grit out of my eyes, looked at my watch—the first time I'd allowed myself to do that. Twelve minutes past midnight. Nearly three hours since I'd first come in here.

DeKuiper moved over to where Valconazzi lay inert, nudged him with the toe of his shoe. "Wake up, Chet." Valconazzi groaned, but his eyes stayed shut. "Wake up, time we see Gianna." Another groan, a curling of the battered body, the eyes still shut. This time DeKuiper kicked him, brutally, in the groin area. Valconazzi screamed, tried to roll away, and DeKuiper kicked him again, and that second kick turned *his* body and put his back to me.

I came up out of the chair without thinking about it and charged him.

But it was as if I were moving at a retarded speed, like somebody trying to run underwater; muscles stiff from tension, joints creaking. The only thing that moved fast was my brain. He heard me coming, swung around before I could get my hands on him, and cracked me alongside the head with a rigid forearm. The blow drove me sideways into the wall, off that into a sharp edge of something that bit into my rib cage and made me yell. I went down on one knee; tried to stand and couldn't seem to get any leverage. Buzzing hum in my head . . . I shook it, looked up . . . and there was DeKuiper, crowding in close with one leg raised and swinging forward. I dodged too late. The point of his shoe slammed into my chest, brought another cry out of me, knocked me over backward.

I pushed at the floor, hurting, trying again to get up. He stood looming above me and I could see his mouth moving, but I couldn't hear what he was saying until the buzzing in my ears thinned out.

". . . Stupid, pops. Old bastard like you."

Yeah. Stupid old bastard like me.

If I'd had my gun right then I would have shot him dead. In cold blood, with no compunction at all.

HIS CADILLAC WAS IN one of the garages off the alley. Valconazzi couldn't walk out there; DeKuiper made me support him, one arm around his middle; he sagged against me, so I had to half carry him. The smell of his fear and his hurt was rancid. There was nobody in the alley except a prowling cat, no lights now in any of the apartment windows opposite. DeKuiper swung the garage door up, went in and opened the Caddy's rear door. Told me to lay Chet on the backseat. I did that. When I was done I had trouble taking in enough air; my chest ached where he'd kicked me and one of my ribs hurt like hell when I breathed in—bruised or cracked from that sharp edge.

DeKuiper had opened the trunk. Along the wall nearest him was a clutter of tools, among them a long-handled shovel. With his free hand he tossed the shovel into the trunk, slammed the lid—not taking his eyes off me the entire time. Then he motioned with the automatic for me to come around to the driver's side.

But he didn't want me to drive; I'd been wrong about that. Too smart, too sly to put a potential weapon like the Cadillac in my hands. He pushed me in ahead of him, told me to slide over against the passenger door. A Cadillac is a wide car; there was a prohibitive amount of space between us when I got all the way over there and he folded his body under the wheel.

"Hands in pants pockets, far as they'll go," he said then. And when I obeyed, "Keep 'em there. One hand comes out, you're dead. Hear?"

"I hear."

The automatic was in his left hand now; he waggled it a little. "Left's good as my right. Shoot straight with both, no lie."

"I believe you."

"No more trouble, huh, pops?"

"No more trouble," I lied.

THE DRIVE TO WEST MARIN seemed as interminable as the wait at the print shop. DeKuiper was in no hurry and he was being cautious; his speed did not exceed thirty on the city streets, fifty-five on the freeway, forty-five on the back roads. I sat hurting the whole way. Propped on a car seat with your hands jammed in your pants pockets, your back wedged in the angle between door and seat, is uncomfortable at first and then painful. But I was afraid to test him by taking a hand out long enough to flex or massage it, or even by shifting position too much. He was capable of carrying out his threat to shoot me.

In the backseat, Valconazzi was in much worse shape.

He moaned every time we hit a bump and now and then when we didn't. Once he started to cough, couldn't seem to stop, and ended up vomiting on the floor.

Nobody said anything. The quiet in the car had the same strained quality as the quiet at the print shop, but with a thin current running through it. I could feel it on my skin, a tingling sensation, as if I were in contact with a live low-voltage wire.

I watched the lights of the southbound cars, the shapes of the few vehicles we passed in the slow north-bound lanes. None of them was Highway Patrol or Marin County sheriff's department, not that I could have done much about a distress signal. I watched DeKuiper too. He seemed relaxed, but he wore a fixed expression and his eyes didn't blink much. There was a hard, implacable look to his dash-lit profile that made me think of a mercenary soldier on his way to a mission behind enemy lines.

Once we got through Novato there was virtually no traffic. We passed one car between there and the turn-off to the Valconazzi ranch. The sky over west Marin was still clear, star-silvered, but the darkness had a clotted quality just the same, the shadows cast by the hills and trees ink-black and impenetrable. The Petaluma–Marshall Road, lit by the Caddy's headlights, was like a track leading nowhere through a dead landscape.

DeKuiper muttered, "Three miles on nose," and after the protracted silence the sound of his voice made me jump. Then he asked me, "Been out here before?"

"Yes, but not at night."

"Don't see turnoff . . ."

He missed the half-hidden turn; didn't spot the sign until we were on the way past. He braked sharply, bouncing us around, causing Valconazzi to cry out in back. Reversed with too much acceleration, so that we fishtailed squealing into an angle across the road. "Shit," he said, and I might have tried something then, with his attention turned briefly away from me, if my hands had been free. As it was, he didn't give me enough time to get them clear. He made a fast gear change and accelerated again, not as heavily, flicking a glance my way as he swung us down onto the ranch road. I sat still; the automatic's muzzle was steady on me again across his lap.

The Caddy's headlights picked up the closed and padlocked gate. DeKuiper stopped nose up to it, shifted to PARK. Took something out of his shirt pocket and tossed it jangling on the seat between us.

"Chet's keys," he said. "One opens gate. You do it."

I eased my left hand out of its cloth prison. Flexed the cramped fingers before I felt for the keys.

"Remember, pops—no more trouble."

"I won't do anything but open the gate," I said.

"Go," he said.

I freed my other hand, got stiffly out of the car. Rubbed the hands together, working the fingers, to restore circulation. Cold out here at this hour. The wind was up, blowing quick and chill off Tomales Bay and the ocean beyond; it seemed to transform the sweat on my body into a frosting of ice. I could hear it soughing gustily, rattling branches in the adjacent trees.

The fourth key I tried opened the padlock. I dropped

the chain, pushed the gate inward. Make a run for the trees? They were a huge shifting wall of black along this side, only a few yards away. But my chances would be slim at best. There weren't enough trees to get lost in and I didn't know the terrain and I was sure DeKuiper had a flashlight. He'd shoot me the minute he caught me.

Not here, I thought, not yet. Just one move left, and when I make it I won't be running away from him. If I'm going to die tonight, it'll be right in his face.

I walked the gate across to the far side of the road. Stood there waiting while he brought the Caddy through. The driver's window was down; the blob of him in there said, "Leave it open. Walk around front, get in."

I did that. Valconazzi was sitting up now, leaning forward shakily with both hands clutching at the seat back. In the glow of the dash lights his face had a ghastly misshapen aspect, like a Halloween monster mask.

"Where, Chet?" DeKuiper asked him.

Barely audible whisper: "Few hundred . . ."

"What? Louder, don't mumble."

"Few hundred yards . . . cow track, right side."

"Then what?"

"Half mile . . . gully, some trees . . ."

"Is that where she is?"

"Trees, yes."

"Tell me when, where."

Valconazzi whimpered, "Please . . . listen to me . . . accident, you got to believe—"

"Shut up," DeKuiper said. "Shut the fuck up. Only words from you, where to stop."

Another whimper, like a child or a hurt puppy. I felt no compassion for him. Liked to hurt women, got excited by the sight of blood and death, drowned Gianna in his bathtub during sex. . . . Chet was finally paying the price for his sins.

DeKuiper put the car in gear and we began to jounce forward through the dusty ruts. Once we turned onto the cow track, the ride got twice as rough. The surface was potholed, rutted, studded with rocks—built for a Jeep or a pickup, not for a passenger car. Even at a crawl, we bottomed out twice in deep depressions, the second time hard enough to lift me off the seat and to crack my skull against the headliner. Valconazzi made no sound that time. When I looked over the seat I saw that he'd passed out again, was lying with his head down on the floor. I didn't tell DeKuiper. Why make things any easier for him?

The track curved around the base of a low hill, along the shoulder of another, then dipped down and through a narrow, flattish meadow. The headlights illuminated dry grass, scatters of rock, a squarish blob that was probably a salt lick, the silhouettes of trees in the distance. Otherwise the darkness pressed in tight around us. As near as I could judge we were moving away from where the ranch buildings were situated, in a southeasterly direction.

We drew closer to the gather of trees. Then the track dipped downward again and the lights picked out a long, ragged tear in the earth that took shape as a shallow gully. There was water in it, but not much more than a trickle; we splashed through it, up through a cut in the bank opposite. The gully, I saw then, doubled back on itself ahead and that was where the trees were clustered—along it on both banks. Some sort of natural spring there, I thought, to support that much vegetation.

"Half mile," DeKuiper announced. "Those trees, Chet?"

"He's out again," I said.

"What?"

"Passed out again."

"Shit." He braked, angling the car so that the lights splashed over the thicket; the trees seemed to be waving at us like waiting mourners in the windy dark. "Wake him up," he said to me.

I leaned over the seat, took a handful of Valconazzi's shirt, lifted him into a sitting position. Slapped his face —forehand and backhand, steadily, until he made aware noises and his eyes came open. At first the eyes were unfocused. Then he said, "Oh Jesus no," and I knew he was seeing the trees and the gully—what lay ahead of him over there.

"This it, Chet?" DeKuiper said.

". . . Yeah."

"All right, out."

"I can't . . ."

"Help him, pops."

I got out, got Valconazzi out. His legs didn't want to support him, but I held him upright and the cold air and the movement seemed to give him strength. As I'd expected DeKuiper had a flashlight, a big six-cell that he switched on even before he keyed open the trunk and removed the shovel. The shovel went under the arm that was holding the torch.

"Chet, you lead."

Over toward the gully, in among some scrub oak—me again supporting Valconazzi, DeKuiper crowding close behind but to one side, shining the flash beam ahead of us. The trees were buckeye and pepper, mostly, their combined smells giving the night a spice-closet scent. The ground under them was grassy, some of it dried out, some of it still spongy with life. No recently turned earth that I could see . . . and then there was, at the base of a flowering buckeye.

"There," Valconazzi said weakly.

DeKuiper said to me, "Untie him."

The knots in the necktie binding Valconazzi's wrists were tight, slick with sweat and blood. It took me a while to work them loose, because I had to hold up his sagging body at the same time.

"Let him go," DeKuiper said when I was finished.

"He'll fall down . . ."

"Let him go."

I let go, stepped away, and Valconazzi fell down. Lay on his side shivering, hands pressed to his breastbone area. Ruptured spleen, maybe; there was blood on his mouth from his earlier vomiting.

DeKuiper threw the shovel down next to him, told him to stand up. Valconazzi didn't move.

"Get up. Dig."

"I can't . . . hurt too bad . . ."

"Want me really hurt you?"

"No . . ."

"Get up, then. Dig."

Somehow Valconazzi found the strength to obey. He grasped the shovel, used it to lift himself upright. And by the light of DeKuiper's flash, he began opening up Gianna Fornessi's grave.

THERE WAS A TERRIBLE, hellish quality to it, like a scene out of a Poe story. The black night, the gibbering wind, the flash beam, Valconazzi's slow, painful movements, the sound of the shovel chunking into the dry earth, even the deceptively fresh spice-closet smell. And all the while, DeKuiper kept talking, urging him to hurry, while I stood off at the edge of the light, where DeKuiper had positioned me—too far away to do anything except watch and wait and try to keep the lid screwed down tight on my emotions.

Valconazzi kept falling down. Two or three shovelfuls of dirt, fall down, get up slowly, two or three more shovelfuls of dirt. After the first couple of times I'd tried to go help him—not because I cared to ease his suffering but because I wanted a chance to use that shovel as a weapon. DeKuiper must have guessed what was in my mind; he wouldn't let me move. The second time he said he'd shoot me if I tried, and I knew he meant it.

On and on it went, the three of us enacting our little nightmare. And the hole under the buckeye got deeper . . . wider . . . and now the spice-closet smell wasn't the only one in the air . . . and then the shovel bit into something that wasn't earth or rock.

Valconazzi pulled the blade back, sank to one knee. DeKuiper stepped forward at an angle, changing the trajectory of the flash to give himself a better look at what lay revealed. When the light shifted, something gleamed on the ground to my right—a chunk of rock, softball-sized, partially imbedded in the earth. Eighteen or twenty inches from where I stood, in line with my right foot.

"Goddamn sheet, huh?" DeKuiper said. "That all you bastards buried her in?"

Nothing from Valconazzi. I eased my right foot closer to the rock, eased my left after it. DeKuiper didn't notice; his eyes were on Valconazzi and the grave.

"Get up, finish diggin."

"Can't . . . legs . . . no feeling . . ."

"Stay there, then. Use hands. Dig!"

Valconazzi pawed at the dirt with hooked fingers, exposed more of the white-shrouded body. While they were talking I'd made progress toward the rock; I kept on moving, slow inch by slow inch. The rock was near my right heel when DeKuiper's voice lashed out again.

"Enough. Unwrap her, Chet."

"No . . ."

"Unwrap her!"

Valconazzi caught hold of the filthy sheet, tugged and tore at it, his breath coming in sobbing pants, until it opened up in his hands. What he saw inside made him gag, turn his head away.

"Gianna," DeKuiper said.

One more step and I would be close enough to get at the rock with my fingers by dropping to one knee. If it was loose in the ground, not buried too deeply so that it required prying, I might be able to pick it up and throw it in one continuous motion. Lousy odds, even so, but time was running out and I was not going to just stand here and let him shoot me. . . .

DeKuiper said Gianna's name again, and this time his voice trembled and broke on the last syllable. He seemed to go rigid, to solidify like a substance hardening into stone.

"Sick bugger," he said to Valconazzi. "*Not* just another whore, damn you, not Gianna."

On the last two words his arm, the one holding the automatic, locked out straight. Valconazzi knew what the motion meant, just as I did, and he reacted to it by trying to throw the shovel at DeKuiper. Only he did it in such a frenzy of fear that his fingers slipped off the handle before he completed the motion. The shovel clattered harmlessly at DeKuiper's feet.

In that same instant DeKuiper shot him, the automatic making a noise like a thunderclap in the light-spackled dark.

I was already moving by then. Not after the rock; there was no time for that. Straight-on rush at DeKuiper.

He saw me, heard me, pivoted my way. The automatic swung up in line with my face so that I was looking right down the bore, and he fired again, and if his foot hadn't slid in the grave dirt and thrown off his aim he would probably have blown my damn-fool head off. As it was, the explosion deafened me and I was nearly blinded by the muzzle flash; I felt the sting of burnt powder against one cheek. The bullet went by close on the right side of my head. How close I'll never know.

In the next instant I hit him, first with my upthrust hands, then with my shoulder—a solid lick, jarring us both. But I had all the momentum: he spun off his feet and I stayed upright, bounced back a step. I saw the gun come loose but he hung on to the flashlight, its beam making crazy yellow-white swirls as he fell. I staggered after him. He was down on all fours at the edge of the grave, still clinging to the torch, trying to pull his legs under him. The collision had dazed him; he was having trouble with his motor responses.

I locked my hands together, brought them down hard on the back of his neck. The blow flattened him but he was such a big bastard that it wasn't enough to take him all the way out. He tried to roll over, punch at me with the hand holding the flashlight. I caught a grip on the flash, yanked it out of his grasp, then hammered him across the side of the head with it. Had to do it twice more before he quit fighting me and went limp.

I rolled him onto his back, ready to clout him again if he was playing games. He wasn't. Out all the way this time.

Reaction set in immediately, left me shaking and incapable of movement for a little time. *Right in his face, yeah . . . and almost right in mine. Sweet Jesus.*

Another thought crawled into my head and seemed

to lodge there, like a voice talking to me. A sly voice, with a hint of mad laughter in it.

Not your night to die after all.

IT WASN'T CHET VALCONAZZI's night to die either. The bullet had bitten through the fleshy part of his right shoulder; the wound wasn't half as serious as the probable internal injuries DeKuiper had inflicted on him with hands and feet.

The shock had made him lose consciousness again, so I left him lying half in and half out of the grave and went back to DeKuiper. I already had both guns; I looked for the necktie I'd stripped from Valconazzi's hands. Found it, used it to bind DeKuiper's in the same way. Then I took a two-handed grip on his collar and dragged him through the scrub oak to his Cadillac. The trunk lid was still raised. I hoisted him up, draped his body over the edge, then lifted his feet and flopped the rest of him inside and banged the lid.

Valconazzi was not much easier to deal with. I virtually had to carry him to the car. By the time I had him arranged on the backseat, my rib was giving me fits. I sat on the driver's side, with the door open and my feet on the ground and my head braced in my palms, until I could breathe more or less normally again.

I did not go back to the grave. I wanted nothing to do with what had been buried there; I hadn't looked at it once, not once, while I was taking care of DeKuiper and Valconazzi.

I wanted nothing to do with Chet's old man, either,

but I had little choice there. The nearest phone was at the ranchhouse, and I was in no shape to drive far anyway.

I started the car and went to get the rest of it done.

Chapter **23**

John Valconazzi gave me a little trouble, but nothing I couldn't handle. I would not have stood for much from him. In the beginning he was mostly concerned with his son's health. With the help of one of the ranch-hands and the housekeeper, he got Chet into a bedroom and undressed and into bed. I let him make the first two calls—county emergency services, for paramedics and an ambulance, and then his family doctor. Then I put in my call to the sheriff's department.

Old John refused to believe his son was a murderer. I offered to escort him out to his south forty and show him the grave and Gianna Fornessi's remains; that shut him up for a while. But pretty soon he started in again, and this time he twisted things around so that I was partly to blame for sticking my nose in, almost getting Chet killed. Some old man. In his way he was as fierce and proud and tenacious as one of his fighting cocks.

The paramedics and the sheriff's deputies arrived simultaneously, along with a county meat wagon. By then DeKuiper was conscious and raising hell in the Caddy's

trunk—yelling, kicking at the lid with both feet. He
stayed wild when he was finally let out. Even with his
hands tied behind his back, it took three deputies to
subdue him, replace the necktie with handcuffs, and
stuff him into the back of one of the cruisers.

Chet was still unconscious; the paramedics loaded
him into the ambulance and took him away. Not long
after that, the sheriff himself showed up, along with a
Highway Patrol investigator, and we all went out to
where the grave was. I didn't venture near it, but old
John took a long look at what was wrapped in the sheet.
It shut him up for good. And hurt him bad; I could see
the agony in his face when he came back to the cluster
of cars. Some other time, some other place, I might
have felt pity for him. Not here, not tonight.

Back at the house the questions started in earnest.
None of the authorities treated me badly, or accused
me of anything; as far as they were concerned, I was
both a peer and a victim. It might have been different if
I'd told them the truth about finding Jack Bisconte's
body in Bolinas and not reporting it, but I didn't. I said
DeKuiper had told me he'd shot Bisconte at the cottage
—beat him up first, then killed him, then kidnapped
Chet at gunpoint. I admitted to having been at the
ranch on Saturday afternoon, looking for information
about Gianna, and to having questioned the housekeeper about the call Chet had received; but I said I'd
had no idea where Chet had arranged to meet Bisconte.
I'd gone to Vortex Publications on a hunch, I said, and
been careless and DeKuiper had nabbed me. I didn't
admit to ever having been inside the Bolinas cottage.

DeKuiper might contradict that story later on, but it was his word against mine.

Cover your ass—that was the name of the game these days, wasn't it?

The endless night eventually ended. Just as dawn was bleaching darkness out of the sky and a new day was borning.

But this one wouldn't be a good day for me, either.

ONE OF THE DEPUTIES drove me back to the city and dropped me at my car. I managed to stay alert long enough to drive home, where I tumbled straight into bed. I slept until quarter of one; that was when the phone hammered me awake. I was oily with sweat, stiff and sore, and I couldn't seem to get my eyes unstuck. I fumbled blindly for the receiver, whacked myself hard with it on the cheekbone before I got the thing to my ear.

Kerry. I told her what had happened, omitting the grimmer details. She wanted to come right over, and I wanted to say yes; I needed her, as I always do in the bleaker moments of my life. But I said no, I had some things to do this afternoon; how about tonight? Anytime, she said. Come to her place, she'd fix me dinner, how did that sound? It sounded fine. What I didn't say was that I would surely need her then even more than I did now.

I lay there for a time, testing my breathing. Not too bad; the ache in my rib was dull even when I drew a deep breath. Just a bruise, to go with the one on my chest where DeKuiper had kicked me. Before long I got out of bed, took a hot shower. Strong black coffee, three cups, and some toast, and I was ready to face the afternoon. As ready as I would ever be.

THE OLD MEN WERE playing bocce, of course. Every Saturday, every Sunday—a ritual that could only be ended by disaster or death. As long as there were two healthy players left to compete, as long as the city kept the Aquatic Park courts open to the public, the games would go on. Maybe they always would, here and on other courts like these in other cities; maybe I'd been wrong about bocce being moribund. Seven thousand years of history . . . it was not just a sport, it was a kind of Italian olympiad, a measure of the race itself. It only takes a few torch bearers to keep the flame from ever going out.

Neither Pietro Lombardi nor Dominick Marra was among the players today. I waited until one of the contestants made a difficult carom shot to finish a game, then talked to two of the men whose names I knew. Pietro and Dominick hadn't been around all day, they said. Neither knew where I could find them.

I left the players to their match and drove to North Beach.

THEY WEREN'T AT Pietro's apartment, they weren't at Dominick's apartment, they weren't at Spiaggia's saloon. One of their drinking cronies said he thought he'd seen them in Washington Square Park after church, and that was where I found them. Sitting side by side on a bench across from the Saints Peter and Paul Catholic

Church—Pietro in the sun, Dominick in the shade of a big leafy tree. Not talking, not looking at each other, not doing anything except sitting there in the slumped, bowed-head posture of *la miseria*.

I sat in the sun next to Pietro. He didn't look at me, but Dominick raised his head and laid his sad eyes on my face. He did not seem surprised to see me.

Pretty soon he said, "You got something to tell us."

"Yes."

"About Gianna."

"Yes."

"You find her?"

"Last night. In Marin County."

"Dead," Pietro said to his hands. It wasn't a question.

"More than a week now. Since last Saturday night."

Dominick crossed himself. Pietro closed his eyes; that was his only reaction.

She's been dead to him ever since he found out about her, I thought. Dead in spirit. Dead in the flesh doesn't mean much after the spirit is gone.

Dominick said, "How she die?"

"How doesn't matter," I said. "What matters is that one of the men responsible is dead and the other one is in police custody. It's finished."

"Two men?"

"Two men were involved, yes."

"Bisconte, he's one?"

"An accessory. You don't know the man who did it."

He didn't ask the man's name; he didn't want to hear it.

I said, "Bisconte didn't kill anybody. The police still

think he caused Ashley Hansen's death but they're wrong."

More silence. Dominick asked the question with his eyes: You know who, then?

"It was Pietro," I said.

Pietro looked at me for the first time. And nodded; there was no denial in him. "But I don't mean to. I don't want to hurt her."

"I know that."

"Ah, *Dio*," Dominick said, and crossed himself again.

I said to him, "You've known the truth for days. Pietro told you. The same night it happened, after you and I talked at Spiaggia's."

"*Sì*. He's got to tell somebody."

"You both should have told me."

"We talk about it. But you say the police, they think it's Bisconte. All right. Maybe they catch him, maybe they don't, and maybe nobody he ever finds out it's Pietro. But you . . . ah, I should know you find out, good detective like you."

"I don't want to hear that," I said.

"Hear what?"

"Good detective. I don't feel much like one today."

Pietro said, "Everybody, he's gonna know pretty soon." He sighed heavily, looked past me at the looming Romanesque pile of the church. "This morning I make confession to priest. Now I make confession to you. Then you take me to police and I make confession to them."

"Maybe he's already tell police," Dominick said.

"No." I touched Pietro's arm, gently. "What happened that day, *'paesan?'*"

He wasn't ready just yet to talk about it. Reliving that time was something he had done once with Dominick and once this morning with his priest and probably many more times in his own mind, but each replay would be as painful as the original experience. He took out one of his twisted black cigars, lit it with a kitchen match. Its odor was acrid, sulfurous on the warm afternoon air—the same odor that had been in his granddaughter's apartment on Wednesday, that I'd pretended to myself I was imagining as phantom brimstone. The truth was, nothing smells like a Toscana; nothing. And only old men like Pietro smoke Toscanas these days. They don't even have to smoke one in a closed room for the smell to linger after them. It gets into and comes off of the heavy user's clothing.

That was one of three things that pointed to Pietro. The other two were words spoken at Giacomo's restaurant on Friday night. Dominick's claim that he'd confessed the truth about Gianna was one; it had rung false to me. In almost the same breath he'd said he would rip his tongue out before he'd hurt his friend—*that* had been truth. Pietro had already known about Gianna when Dominick went to see him on Wednesday; he'd found out by confronting Ashley Hansen. The other thing was Pietro calling Ashley "that *bionda tintura.*" *Bionda tintura:* dyed blonde. Last Sunday he'd told me he had never been to Gianna's apartment, never met Ashley Hansen, so how had he known she had dyed blond hair? The newspaper report of her death wouldn't have mentioned it. His granddaughter might have, except that they hadn't spent much time together in the past eight months and it wasn't a likely comment in any case. She might say "I have a blond roommate" but not "a dyed blond roommate."

So I'd known Friday night that Pietro was responsible for Hansen's death. Or I would have if I'd let myself think about it. But I hadn't wanted him to be guilty; the "good detective" had wanted it to somehow turn out to be Bisconte. Today there was no denial left in me either.

Pietro was still silent. To ease him into talking about it, I asked, "Why did you go to Gianna's apartment? To see her or to see Ashley Hansen?"

He continued to sit rigidly, smoking his Toscana. Kids ran past us, chasing each other, yelling. Over near the statue of Benjamin Franklin, a Chinese girl squealed as her boyfriend tickled her. On one side of the path not far away, a middle-aged man in a business suit and a younger man in street clothes exchanged an envelope for a small packet, both of them trying so hard to be nonchalant that they achieved the opposite effect. On the grass across from them, a homeless black man in rags lay sleeping or passed out in the sun, his belongings heaped around him like a half-destroyed bunker. Summer Sunday in Washington Square.

"Not the *bionda*," Pietro said abruptly. "I don't go to see that one."

"Gianna then?"

"*Sì.* Last Sunday, after you tell us about Bisconte, I call up there. I want to ask her about this man." By "her" he meant Gianna; he couldn't seem to bring himself to say her name. "Only she's not home. So I talk to the *bionda tintura*. She's polite but she don't tell me nothing. Next day I call back, I talk to her again. This time she's no polite, she's tell me mind my own goddamn business and she's hang up on me."

"So you decided not to wait for me to find out about Bisconte. You decided to ask around the neighborhood yourself."

"Bisconte." He spat the name this time, as if ridding his mouth of something foul.

"And Wednesday somebody told you he wasn't just a florist."

"I don't believe she's know him that way . . . she's sell her body for man like that. But I got to know. I go to her apartment. She's not there, only the *bionda tintura*. She don't want to let me in, that one. I go in anyway. I ask if she and . . . if they sell themselves for money. She laughs. In my face she laughs, this girl what have no respect, this whore. She says what difference it make? She says I am old man—dinosaur, she says. But she pat my cheek like I am little boy or maybe big joke. Then she . . . ah, *Cristo,* she come up close and she say, 'You want some, old man, I give you some.' To me she says this. Me."

Pietro shook his head; there were tears in his eyes now. "I push her away. I feel . . . *feroce,* like when I am young man and somebody, he make trouble with me. I push her too hard and she's fall, hit her head on the table and I see blood and she don't move . . . *mio Dio!* She was wicked, that one, but I don't want her to die. . . ."

"Accident," Dominick said, nodding at me. "You see?"

"I think, call doctor quick. But she's dead. And I hurt here, inside"—he tapped his chest with a gnarled forefinger—"and I think, what if my . . . what if the other one, she come home? I don't want to see her no more. She's dead too. For me, in here"—again he tapped his chest—"she's dead too."

Grim irony: Gianna really *was* dead then, four days dead. Two young women, roommates, hookers, dead by violence in separate and unrelated incidents four days apart. Coincidence, quirk of fate, divine punishment . . . call it what you wanted. High-risk professions breed bizarre happenings; and these days prostitution is a damned high-risk profession.

Pietro finished his cigar. Then he straightened on the bench, seemed to compose himself. His eyes were clear and sad now, the tears dried to thin cakes at their corners. "We go now, hah?" he asked me.

"Go where?"

"Police."

"No," I said. "We're not going to the police."

No reaction from Pietro, but Dominick brightened a little. "How come we don't go?"

"As far as they're concerned it's a closed case. As far as I'm concerned too. Pietro's made his confession to God. Nobody else is important; nobody else ever has to know."

We sat there, three men who had lived a lot of years and seen too many things, cut off for the moment from the ebb and flow of park and city life around us—as if all the activity were happening behind a thick pane of glass. After a time I glanced at Pietro, and on his face was an expression of the deepest pain. He might have been thinking of Ashley Hansen, or of his granddaughter, but I doubted it. I had the idea that he was thinking of the old days, the days when families were tightly knit and there was respect for elders and the teachings of his church, the days when bocce was king of his world and that world was a simpler and better place. The bitterest of woes is to remember old happy days. . . .

In a voice so low I barely heard the words, he said, *"La bellezza delle bellezze."* The beauty of beauties. He had used that phrase in my presence, and whenever he did he had been referring to Gianna Fornessi. Not this time.

"Sì, 'paesan," I said. *"La bellezza delle bellezze."*

Chapter **24**

MONDAY MORNING, as usual, I went down to the office at nine o'clock—and half of it was missing.

Eberhardt's half.

Eberhardt was gone.

He had made his decision sometime after I'd left him on Saturday . . . if he hadn't already made it before I showed up at his house. And on Sunday he'd acted on it. Come in here with one or two people to help him, like a pack of thieves in the night, and moved out his desk, computer, creaky old swivel chair, ugly mustard-yellow file cabinets, even the frigging porcelain water cooler that he'd bought at a garage sale and never used. Everything that belonged to him, down to the chipped coffee mug with his name on it. And when they were done he'd locked the door from out in the hallway and shoved his key through the crack underneath. I almost stepped on it when I walked in.

On my desk was a single sheet of paper with a hurriedly written check clipped to it. One of his personal checks, not a joint agency check; an unused stack of those was sitting there on my blotter too. His check was made out in my name, in the amount of $750, with a notation on the bottom that read, "One half June rent." On the sheet of paper itself was a message, likewise hurriedly scrawled in his sloppy hand. A one-word message.

"Quits."

So this was how it ended—not with warmth but with cold, not with a bang but with the finger. Afraid or unwilling to face me again; no more dialogue, no more conflict. Just one word on a piece of paper and gone. Neat, clean . . . from his point of view. But not from mine.

I still didn't know why.

I still didn't know what he imagined I'd done to him.

For a long while I stared at the check and the note, not moving, not letting myself feel anything. Then, slowly, I tore both in half and kept on tearing the pieces until I had confetti. I let the confetti fall like dirty snow —like ashes—into my wastebasket.

Qual' rincoglionito di mio nonno, I thought.

And: *Good-bye, Ashley Hansen.*

And: *Not just another whore.*

And: *La bellezza delle bellezze.*

And now: *Quits.*

Epitaphs. All of them, epitaphs.